THE STRANGER AT NO. 6

GEMMA ROGERS

B

Boldwood

First published in Great Britain in 2025 by Boldwood Books Ltd.

Copyright © Gemma Rogers, 2025

Cover Design by Judge By My Covers

Cover Images: iStock

A CIP catalogue record for this book is available from the British Library.

Paperback ISBN 978-1-80549-522-2

Large Print ISBN 978-1-80549-521-5

Hardback ISBN 978-1-80549-520-8

Trade Paperback ISBN 978-1-80635-233-3

Ebook ISBN 978-1-80549-523-9

Kindle ISBN 978-1-80549-524-6

Audio CD ISBN 978-1-80549-515-4

MP3 CD ISBN 978-1-80549-516-1

Digital audio download ISBN 978-1-80549-518-5

This book is printed on certified sustainable paper. Boldwood Books is dedicated to putting sustainability at the heart of our business. For more information please visit https://www.boldwoodbooks.com/about-us/sustainability/

Boldwood Books Ltd, 23 Bowerdean Street, London, SW6 3TN

www.boldwoodbooks.com

For Mullers

Phrogging
[frog-ing]

Phrogging is the act of secretly living in another person's home without their knowledge or permission.

A person who engages in phrogging is sometimes called a phrog or, less commonly, a phrogger. The verb form phrog is sometimes used.

Phrogging is similar to squatting, except that phrogging involves living in an occupied property.

PROLOGUE

If I could go back, I wouldn't have stepped a foot inside the house. Just remember that whenever you next cross a threshold, you don't know what could be waiting for you. What you see on the outside, the beautiful structure and the picturesque setting, can appear like a dream, but it doesn't always represent what's inside. The house contained secrets; ones it took me too long to discover. By the time I did, I was too caught up in it to leave. People got hurt, someone died and lives were changed forever, mine included.

* * *

Blog Post #1

www.phrogging.com

After two successful phrogging experiences so far, I wanted to share my tips and tricks with you and record my third attempt from start to finish. I'll be posting daily so you can follow my journey, but before we begin, below are the rules I live by.

- Property must be watched for two weeks minimum before attempting access.
- No home workers or those on night shifts in residence. They must have regular, contractual office hours. Travelling on business is permitted.
- Large house, enough space to cohabit without owners suspecting.
- No internal or external cameras covering rear of property or point of access.
- No pets.
- No children under five.
- Three months maximum before moving on. Use only enough food/toiletries/supplies from owners to remain unnoticed.
- If caught… run.

The rules are to keep me safe. The main purpose of phrogging is to cohabit peacefully without being detected. Free room and board with minimal interference with homeowners' lives.

1

The house was huge, undergoing a renovation despite it only being thirteen years old. Modern in design but still managing to keep a certain Sussex charm, the first floor was russet brick, the lower rendered and painted an elegant cream. As you faced the picturesque building, the welcoming covered entrance was in the centre. Maintaining the country style, a large panelled oak front door with an adjacent patterned glass insert matched the double garage. A sweeping resin driveway led to waist-height sage wooden entry gates. The only stain on the canvas was a giant yellow skip filled with the remnants of kitchen cabinets and a bathroom suite. My initial thoughts were that although it was a great size, it would likely be chaotic inside with workmen coming and going, but during the course of the two-week reconnaissance they had almost finished.

The owners were new, having only lived there for about a month, which meant plenty of hiding spots may lay undiscovered, noises which could be deemed 'just the house' and, best of all, no cameras at the rear. From what I could gather, they had a camera doorbell like most properties now, but that was it. The burglar alarm was old and rusted, with no flashing light to indicate it was working, and I guessed the buyers thought it was pretty secure, as adjacent to the house was a disused railway line with a steep embankment. At the rear, although overgrown and thorny, it was relatively easy to climb through the jungle and over the fence into their landscaped back garden which wasn't overlooked by the neighbouring house.

I'd made a couple of visits, which meant walking almost around the block to get to the woodland, breaking off branches and clearing a path each time. I got as far as the garden, nestling beneath the overgrown shrubs to watch, more inconspicuous than doing it from the quiet road at the front. Dressed in black, armed with binoculars and my dad's old thermos filled with tea, I sat under the cover of dusk and watched the couple and their young son through the bifold doors of their open-plan kitchen/diner in the late February afternoon. On both occasions, the wife arrived halfway through her husband cooking dinner. Sharply dressed in a fitted suit, lips slicked in pillar-box red and wearing patent heeled boots, her son rushed across the parquet floor into her arms the moment she entered the room.

For all intents and purposes, it looked like a happy home and one which would be perfect for phrogging. I'd seen no dogs being walked, no cats, no cameras or alarms and, from what I could tell by the lights glowing through the windows when it got dark, all of them slept on the first floor, leaving the loft conversion empty.

Spotting the house had come at the right time. I needed to move on from my best friend Megan's sofa, picking up the vibes from her flatmates that I was slowly outstaying my welcome. To be fair, it was cramped. Megan lived in a flat above a betting shop in Crawley high street and there were already three of them sharing before I'd turned up a few weeks ago.

I'd lived at home until last winter when my parents had decided they were selling up to move to

Spain as retiring expats and had a secured a long-term visa that would be renewed if they decided to stay. Most of my things went into storage and Megan kept some of my clothes for me, but I preferred to travel light anyway. I'd considered going with them, but my life was here and so were my dreams and aspirations. Strangely, they didn't involve sandy beaches and weekend trips to Benidorm. I wanted to be on the editorial desk of a tabloid newspaper. For now, I'd have to take the snippets I was given at the *Crawley News*, a local rag where my job as Junior Reporter mainly involved reviewing the latest cinema releases and covering the odd school fayre.

I was Molly Hudson the aspiring journalist – that being a misnomer – who didn't even have a proper desk, the one who was outsourced to do all the shit the others deemed not worthy and it paid peanuts. Being the youngest at twenty-two and the least experienced, I understood. It would do for now, but I'd work my way up, and because it was all done remotely, I didn't have to put up with the nine-to-five life.

That's how the phrogging started, I could barely afford a bedsit, the money Mum wired occasionally didn't stretch far and I was running out of friends with sofas. Fed up with working out of the local library every day using their free Wi-Fi, I had looked first at getting a live-in job, like a nanny, but my heart wasn't in it. I wanted to write and even though I was at the bottom of the ladder, a change of career wasn't an option. I dreamt of owning my own camper van, being free to roam wherever I wanted, but I couldn't even afford a car. Things would change, they always did, and when someone at the *Crawley News* Christmas bash mentioned phrogging occurrences were steadily growing in the UK, I was intrigued and did my research.

More common in the States than here, cohabiting secretly with an unwitting family fascinated and terrified me in equal measure. It was against the law as far as breaking and entering was concerned, perhaps even stealing as you'd use their electric, water and internet during your short-term stay, but the main appeal was living for free.

A journalist to my bones, was I even committed to my job if I wasn't going to blog about doing it? Anonymously, of course, no YouTube videos or Tik-Toks but good old-fashioned articles people had to read. I'd phrogged twice so far, since my parents left, in between sofa-surfing at Megan's. Using those as trial runs to build my confidence and learn how to live undetected. This time, I wanted to record the whole thing from day one, so I had to make sure I picked the right house and the right family to ensure I wasn't discovered. It had slipped my mind with the upcoming festivities until Megan and I had gone for a long walk on Christmas Day after stuffing ourselves at her parents' house. Our intention was to walk the length of the Worth Way – a seven-mile expedition which started in Three Bridges, Crawley, and ended in East Grinstead. We made it halfway before blisters from our inappropriate footwear crippled us and we hobbled back the way we came.

It was along Church Road, before the small stone bridge over the disused railway line, we passed the beautiful house with its sold board outside, standing out amongst the glowing houses surrounding it because there were no twinkling Christmas lights to be seen.

'They must be moving soon,' Megan had said as we blew warm air into our frozen hands.

'They must be, not having any decorations up. Unless they belong to a religion which doesn't celebrate Christmas,' I'd pondered aloud.

'I don't think so, Mol, my dad knows the owners. They're downsizing as their children are grown up. Wonder who the new occupants will be.'

'Lucky, that's who'll they'll be! Lucky to live in such a gorgeous house.'

We had carried on limping in our Converse trainers, but the idea had blossomed again in my mind.

I always overdid the research, but better safe than sorry. I knew the floor plans and had photos of the inside of the house thanks to the particulars still being available on the internet when it was up for sale for a whopping eight hundred and seventy-five thousand pounds. I didn't know specifics of what the new couple did yet, but the wife left early and the husband took the son to school at eight o'clock before heading off for his day, returning with him around four. He wore a suit to work, although it was lived in; his appearance relaxed in contrast to her sharp yet glamorous attire. If I had to guess, I'd say she was the breadwinner. The couple looked to be in their mid- to late-thirties and I estimated the son, a blond boy with freckles, was around six or seven. It seemed a perfect fit.

Now all I had to do was get in.

I climbed over the fence, my large rucksack which contained all my worldly possessions snagging on a rusted nail that had come away from the post.

It was a grey, miserable day, the sky full of drizzle and through the bifold doors number six Church Road looked gloomy and uninviting. I checked my watch; it was just after two o'clock, but I waited in the shrubs for a while to ensure the place was empty. When I eventually approached the house, I tried the door, knowing it would be locked but worth a go. Moving down the side to the utility-room window, I saw that too was closed and locked.

Gaining entry was usually the most difficult part of phrogging, people were more security-conscious these days and never left the house without making sure their property was secure. Perhaps it would be like the last house, where I'd had to slip inside the garage as the owners were leaving, the door slowly lowering as they drove away. I shivered, partly from the memory, but also, despite the many layers I was wearing, the air temperature was only a few degrees above freezing. I didn't want to wait around outside for too long, but at the same time I had packed all my things and was reluctant to come back another day.

As I was debating, a shadow passed by the window and I ducked down beside the water butt, my heart jumping into my throat. No one was supposed to be home. Muffled voices carried from behind the double glazing, followed by the noise of the bifold door sliding open. I shrank back against the rendered wall, exposed. If they came down the side of the house, I'd have nowhere to hide. The side gate leading onto the driveway was locked and my only option of escape would be to scale the six-foot fence and tumble down the steep bank to the disused railway line.

I tried to steady my increasing heart rate. *Calm down, Mol.*

'I wanted to show you this.' A man's gruff voice intertwined with the slap of heavy boots on the patio. I held my breath, praying I wasn't about to be caught trespassing by these strangers – a man, maybe two, who weren't the owners. Had they broken in? Were they here to burgle the property? Could I have stumbled across a crime being committed, and if so, what would they do when they discovered me hiding?

2

I was finally able to exhale when the sound of footsteps led away from the house and towards the end of the garden. If I'd still been tucked in the shrubbery, they would have seen me for sure. I stole a look over the water butt and watched the two men with their backs to me, pointing out various sections at the end of the garden.

I had to act fast and while I had the chance, I crept out from behind the water butt and towards the rear of the house, my eyes never leaving the men talking. In my haste, I kicked a trowel, the metal scraping the patio jarring the stillness. My entire body froze, the sound seemed to ring in my ears, but neither of them turned around. They were too far away, the pair deep in conversation discussing improvements to be made, new fence panels to be put in, potentially a rockery and vegetable patch. They weren't burglars, they were workmen. With my heart almost exploding out of my chest, I darted around the edge of the house and through the open bifold door while they were distracted.

The warmth from the central heating smacked me in the face as soon as I crossed the threshold, turning my cheeks pink. There was no time to appreciate how neat everything was as I struggled out of my muddy boots, not wanting to be seen by the men in the garden when they turned around. Keeping low, I carried them through the kitchen with its midnight-blue cabinets and into the bright magnolia hallway, where a grand oak staircase awaited me. Taking the stairs two at a time, the heady mix of fabric softener and pine-scented toilet cleaner hit me as I climbed to the first floor. The carpet was seagrass and rough beneath my socks, flowing into each room off the landing, all of them painted the same magnolia.

I stepped into the boy's room first, where the name Nathan was spelt out in large green wooden letters on the wall above a single bed. The duvet was a pattern of racing cars and tucked tightly beneath the mattress like my mum used to do to my bed when I was little. Through the window overlooking the back garden, the two men were finishing their cigarettes and I struggled to tell the difference between the plumes of smoke and their hot breath wafting into the air around them. Now that I could take a better look at them, I recognised the shorter man as someone I'd seen at the property before when I'd been staking the place out. He had to be managing the refurbishment and looked relatively smartly dressed in chinos and a shirt. The other one, tall and thin with close-cropped hair, was more dishevelled in grubby faded combats and a sweatshirt. I guessed he was a landscape gardener.

More people coming and going in Church Road could potentially be a problem for my stay. I'd thought the work on the house was finished, the kitchen downstairs and the bathroom across from Nathan's room were both brand new, but perhaps next on the list were plans to sculpt the garden.

With my pulse slowly returning to its usual steady rate, I peeked into the other bedrooms, committing to memory where the squeaks in the floorboards were. I'd been right about the sleeping arrangements, the largest bedroom on this floor was clearly being used by the couple. Their bedside tables contained books, sleeping medication called Heminevrin that my mum used to take, a water bottle each and framed photos. They had a small en suite which seemed to be Helena's domain when I looked inside, by all the bottles of body wash, scrub and shampoo. Back in the bedroom the smell of expensive perfume lingered in the air and I picked up a book on what had to be the wife's side, a Lisa Jewell thriller she was halfway through. The king-size bed had been hastily made, a bright mustard rumpled duvet cover was the only pop of colour in what otherwise was a bland room.

In the third bedroom, there was no bed, just a beige sofa and a desk beneath the window where a monitor and keyboard had been placed. The hard drive was stored underneath, with box files stacked beside it. I spotted the Wi-Fi router and took a photo of the sticker on the back where the password was printed. It would come in handy later if they hadn't changed it. I guessed the room was going to be used as an office, although I'd not seen either of them work from home while I'd been watching the house. They usually came and went like clockwork.

I climbed the second set of stairs to the master suite, nerves pulsing with adrenaline. It was all open plan, there was no door, the stairs entered straight into the bedroom. I presumed the couple's intention was to eventually move up to the loft conversion with another en suite. It would make sense for them to be up here, but perhaps Nathan's parents didn't want to be a floor away from their young son. For all I knew, he could suffer from night terrors or separation anxiety.

Either way, it worked out better for me as that's where I'd planned to hide out. It might be tricky being in such close proximity, but if I was as quiet as a mouse it could work. Knowing their schedules meant I'd be able to shower and get in and out as long as they weren't home, so it wouldn't impact on my job, not with my irregular hours. Using the toilet may be a different story, though.

The loft conversion had a huge skylight which flooded the room with natural light and I watched the grey clouds swirl ominously above. The space was being used for storage; empty boxes and black bags were dumped in the middle of the carpet, but at least this one was plush beneath my socked feet.

The only furniture was a dusky pink chaise longue positioned under the window which looked out over the driveway below. I sat, hoping to calm my nerves, surprised by its plumpness, but I wasn't intending to sleep on it. I couldn't allow myself to be so exposed if anyone came up to this floor. What if I was out for the count and the wife came up to rummage through one of the boxes; we'd both get the shock of our lives. My eyes fell on the wall to my left, which housed a row of white built-in wardrobes, perfectly fitted to slant down with the roof at the front of the house. I slowly drew one open, acutely aware of the slight squeak on the track.

It was perfect. The wardrobe was empty, one side had space on the floor of around five feet that would suit me and my sleeping bag if I was able to make the floor softer. As long as I didn't bang my head on the rail above for hanging clothes. In the middle wardrobe was a built-in vanity table and mirror with a small stool pushed beneath and the last one was smaller with some drawers taking up half the floor space and another rail for clothes above.

Buoyed by my new digs, I moved on to the en suite, where a small but perfectly adequate white suite was encased in cream floor-to-ceiling tiles. I had no idea what their plans were for the space or how long it would take them to fill it but with phrogging there were opportunities to listen. If I got wind they were planning to move upstairs or relocate some belongings, I could make sure I was gone.

I was jolted from my thoughts by the slam of

something outside and I crept over to the window overlooking the drive to see the two men from the garden climb into a liveried van with JE Property Renovations on the side. The wooden gate swung open as if by magic when the van edged towards it. At waist-height, I was sure they were electric more for convenience than security, but unless you knew the code, you couldn't drive your vehicle onto the property. I watched until they chugged out of sight, my shoulders loosening as the sensation of an empty house consumed me. It was just before three, which gave me approximately an hour to have a quick look around and get to know the owners before retiring for the evening. In preparation, I laid my sleeping bag and rucksack on the floor inside the wardrobe, leaving the door open wide enough for me to squeeze through.

Now it was time to explore, scanning for clues about the family I was living with, because the more I knew, the easier it was to hide. It was amazing how much you could discover from letters left on the dining table, photos attached to pinboards, but unlike the last house I'd stayed in, there was barely anything on display. That one was permanently messy and I couldn't do more than a week before I was back at Megan's. Perhaps these homeowners were neat freaks who didn't like anything cluttering up their space or maybe they were still unpacking and making the house a home. There was a grey plaque above the door from the hallway into the kitchen/diner I hadn't noticed before. The Reilly Family in white carved-out letters with three names beneath: Jack, Helena and Nathan.

'Hello, Reilly family,' I whispered, looking back to the front door, where I found a shot of the three of them on a white console table beneath a large round mirror. The table had a dish for keys, a Jo Malone reed diffuser and a vase of fake white roses. The photo in a silver frame was taken on a fairground ride, the family's eyes squinting because they were laughing so much.

Helena was beautiful, a sharp brunette bob tucked behind delicate ears, with a small nose and thin lips. She had high cheekbones and chocolate eyes that drew you in, lined with long thick lashes. Jack was punching for sure, although he did have a kind face. His hair was short, strawberry blond and slightly receding at the temples, but there was a depth to his eyes, which were almost a sea green in colour. Nathan, who sat between them, was grinning from ear to ear, missing one of his front teeth, his knuckles white on the bar of the carriage. It was a great shot; they looked so joyful and full of life, I felt a pang of guilt intruding on their happy home.

I continued my search, hoping to find something that would tell me a bit more about the Reilly family, where they worked maybe or a calendar or diary with information, but without rummaging through drawers, there was little on show. On the kitchen island, I found a pad with the beginnings of a shopping list on it in a neat cursive: apple juice, butter, kitchen roll, but it wasn't the contents which caught my eye, it was the branding on the top. St Wilfrid's School was a local secondary school – in fact, the same one I'd left six years ago before going to college to study media. It seemed like yesterday I was roaming the corridors, dragging my feet to get to class. Nathan was too young to be a pupil there, so where had they got the pad from?

Just as I was contemplating, an engine spluttered outside, sending my spine rigid. I strained to listen, vaguely making out the squeak of the gate closing. Dashing out of the kitchen and up the stairs, I heard voices out front, then the click of a key turning in a lock. Whoever it was, they were home early.

3

'Daddy, can I go on the iPad please?' Nathan's chirpy voice coincided with the sound of keys clanking against the dish in the hallway.

I'd made it to the second set of stairs up to the master suite, listening to the activity below, my heart still going ten to the dozen. Why were they back so soon?

'Sure, bud. Mummy will be home soon though, so let's get out of your uniform, wash your hands and I'll get you a snack, okay?'

'I like the school club snacks,' Nathan griped.

'I know, but it's parents' evening, no after-school club today. When Mummy comes home we'll be going back to school to see Mrs Milton.'

Their voices got quieter as they moved into the kitchen and I slowly climbed up to the second floor. Thank God I hadn't left it any later to gain access to the house today as I might have been caught red-handed. As much as you planned or knew someone's schedule, there were always little deviations or movements to a routine, that was life. The important thing was to have a plan, but I didn't, bar making a run for it if I was discovered. I needed some time alone in the house to find alternative hiding places, spaces where I could store my stuff in case I couldn't get back to the top floor. At least it was Tuesday, which gave me three more days where I'd have the place to myself, if only between the hours of eight and four.

My stomach rumbled, reminding me I hadn't had any lunch, then clenched as footsteps thundered up the stairs, thankfully stopping on the first floor. It was Nathan rushing to his room to get changed or grab his iPad. I lowered myself down onto the floor of the wardrobe, sliding the door almost fully closed, and dug around in my rucksack for some biscuits to curb the ache in my belly. I checked the Wi-Fi on my phone after ensuring it was set to silent, all devices had to be whilst phrogging, and tried to log in with the password on the back of the router. It worked straight away. I imagined it was a new broadband installation as they'd recently moved in and perhaps Jack hadn't changed the password yet, or maybe he wasn't intending to at all. Some people weren't overly conscious about online security or au fait with technology. If that was the case, it would make life easier for me. If you knew where to look, it would be easy to spot an unidentified log in to your Wi-Fi, but I had the feeling Jack wasn't that clued up. I logged off anyway, just in case.

Around ten minutes later, I heard the front door again, this time high heels clicked on the parquet floor which ran from the hallway into the kitchen.

'Mummy!' Nathan trilled, followed by thundering footsteps down the stairs. I imagined him leaping into her arms and being scooped up into a hug the same as I'd witnessed before. Voices were muffled and I couldn't make out what was being said, but it was too soon to leave my safe space to eavesdrop. Eventually I'd be able to move around a little once used to the noises, ensuring the impact I was having on the family was insignificant. I wasn't here to spook them, play tricks or be a voyeur, phrogging was about cohabiting. I guessed it was thrill-seeking in a way. I couldn't deny it was exciting knowing you were somewhere you weren't supposed to be, but your life had to mould around theirs, I'd learned from my research and two previous phrogging experiences. Sometimes it worked, sometimes it didn't.

Thankfully I was able to focus on settling in because I'd submitted my latest article by email to Des, the editor in chief of the *Crawley News*, earlier today in Starbucks, buying myself a chai latte and a pastry as a treat. He'd wanted a piece on the new layout of the roundabout in the centre of town which had already caused multiple car accidents and I was pleased I'd managed to get a quote out of the local councillor. That was the typical kind of dull news I was asked to cover and why no one took me seriously as a journalist. I kept pitching new ideas to Des, relentless in my efforts to build my portfolio further than traffic violations. Most of the time, he humoured me, he was an all-right boss, and occasionally if he was in an exceptional mood he let me go off on one of my tangents with the understanding there was no guarantee of my article being published. I considered myself lucky; the wage wasn't great, but I had no rigid hours, just assignments to complete.

I knew I was a good writer, however, and should be working on bigger things. A local magazine had picked up two articles I'd submitted last month, but unfortunately they didn't pay well. I wouldn't be able to survive being freelance, not until I was established. For now, the *Crawley News* would have to do.

My phone flashed and I saw I had a message from Megan.

> Where are you? I just got home
> and all your stuff is gone!

Phrogging, I hastily replied.
Within seconds, three dots popped up on screen to indicate Megan was replying.

> Again? Where? I wish you
> wouldn't, it's not safe! Be careful!!!!

Megan always went overboard on exclamation marks, but despite her looking out for me, I knew deep down she'd be relieved to not get it in the neck from her flatmates tonight, unimpressed there was a freeloader bedding down on the sofa for the third week in a row.

'Honestly, Jack, you need to have a word with Marcus, they trod mud in everywhere. It's the last thing I need when I've been at work all day. And you need to get that burglar alarm reconnected too or at least make the light on it flash.' Helena's plummy voice travelled from the floor below; she was somewhere upstairs.

'Okay, I will. Can we just get going as it'll be a nightmare to park and Nathan's appointment is at four thirty.' Jack sighed audibly, sounding every bit the nagged husband.

'Yes, yes, I'm just going to use the toilet and put a bit of lipstick on,' she quickly dismissed him. I tried to visualise her strutting around her bedroom, she looked like the type of woman who might. High-powered job and a control freak at home maybe, with Jack the downtrodden husband who followed her around like a lost puppy. I shouldn't jump to conclusions, I knew nothing about them yet, but first impressions were everything.

I listened to muffled movements below me, making sure I didn't move a muscle. The last thing I wanted was to shift my weight and creak the floorboards.

'Ready,' Helena called, padding down the stairs. Moments later, the front door shut, and I crept out to watch the Mercedes SUV leave through the window as the sun started its descent.

Back downstairs, I made tea to fill my thermos,

perusing their kitchen cupboards to see what they had. Thankfully, Helena had left the under-cabinet lights on. There wasn't much in the way of snacks, other than fruit strings and Fibre One bars in a clear box with Nathan's name on. No sugary cereals, instead there was home-made granola and sourdough bread. I rolled my eyes, continuing the search until I found a box of crackers shoved at the back of one cupboard that looked like they were from a Christmas hamper. Tucking them under my arm, I nosed around a bit more but found nothing out of the ordinary. The fridge was filled with salad and vegetables, beef mince and lamb chops, plus a few yoghurt pouches, all either brand names or from Waitrose.

Perhaps they had a weekly delivery to stock up on fresh food. Helena or maybe Jack obviously liked their meals cooked from scratch, but I felt sorry for Nathan, there wasn't a chocolate bar or a packet of crisps to be seen. At least the fruit bowl was well stocked with bananas, pears, clementines and apples, and I took the shiniest red one and added it to my haul. It was freeing being out of the wardrobe and having so much space to move around in. The radiators rumbled to life at four and the house was already warming up.

Off the kitchen was a utility room in the same midnight blue. It was spotless, with a Sheila Maid fixed to the ceiling for drying clothes in the colder months, something I'd only seen on television. How the other half lived. Cabinets containing cleaning and laundry products were fitted either side of a butler sink, with a washing machine on the end. I took the opportunity to swipe a roll of toilet paper from one of them to use upstairs.

In between the kitchen and the lounge was a small study with another desk and wall-to-wall shelves housing books and ornaments. This room looked more lived in, the desk with its iMac was messy compared to the one upstairs. Perhaps this was Helena's domain?

Moving on to the lounge, the space was dominated by an enormous dark grey L-shaped sofa with patterned cushions and folded throws at either end. A solid wood coffee table had been perfectly positioned in front of the sofa on a cream rug. On it was a stack of arranged books which looked more decorative than anything else, titles such as *Tom Ford*; *Made for Living*; *Eat, Drink, Nap*; *Plantopedia*, their spines intact without a crease in sight. I rolled my eyes again, moving on to sniff the candles which had never been lit. Everything looked like it was for show and although from the outside number six Church Road appeared to be a beautiful family home, it didn't seem much like that on the inside. Nathan had no toys lying around and there was no hint of his presence downstairs except for the odd photo. I was miffed on his behalf; was he chastised for being messy?

The Reillys also had a log burner stove and a large flat-screen television mounted on the wall of the lounge. Orange curtains hung from the ceiling all the way to the floor by the window, which looked out to the front of the house, and a spiky retro light fitting hung centre stage in the middle. It was a nice room, more personality than upstairs, but everything was too perfect.

My gaze drifted back to the coffee table and I noticed a business card sticking out between the pages of Tom Ford's fashion book. Sliding it out, I saw it was Helena's. She was the marketing manager for Oxalis with a London address and telephone number, although I had no idea what they did. I slipped it in into the pocket of my jeans and continued looking around.

Off the hallway on the left as you came through the front door was access to the garage and further along a downstairs toilet with a shower, but there was nothing more to see down here.

Juggling the crackers, apple, thermos and roll of toilet paper, I climbed the stairs when a loud knock at the door made me jump. Whipping my head around, the crackers slipped out of my hand and bounced to the bottom as I froze like a child playing Grandmother's Footsteps. The security light outside illuminated an animated figure looking through the frosted panes in the decorative side panel.

'Open the door!' an angry female voice shouted as I stared wide-eyed through the glass. My insides squirmed as I watched the shadow peer in, hands cupped to the pane, disjointed because of the pattern. 'I can see you!' she hollered, hammering again, and I slowly backed up the stairs until I was sure I was out of view. Terror swept through me. Who was she?

4

'Helena, I need to talk to you.'

The blood drained from my face as I waited for her to leave. I'd been seen; the game was up, but she thought I was Helena. Leaving the crackers where they lay, I climbed to the top floor to look out of the window, wanting to watch her go. When the woman finally gave up and stalked back down the driveway, I saw she was blonde and wearing a green coat, but that was about it. I half expected her to turn around and glare back up at the house, surely knowing she was being watched, but she didn't. Instead, she turned right at the end of the driveway and disappeared out of sight over the bridge. How did she know the code to get in via the gates? I didn't think they opened without one.

Going back downstairs to retrieve the crackers, I no longer felt comfortable and debated whether to pack my things and leave. Whoever she was, she was angry and assumed I was Helena refusing to answer the door. Perhaps they were friends and had a falling out? Maybe she was an unsatisfied client of Oxalis? My main concern was whether I going to be exposed by a stranger when the woman finally caught up with Helena.

I chose to stay, knowing it might make life difficult for Megan if I turned up at hers again and the mystery played on my mind while I munched through the box of crackers. Taking advantage of having the house to myself, I found a pillow and blanket stored in the spare room under the sofa and took those along with a towel from the back of the airing cupboard. An attempt to make the floor I would be sleeping on a little softer.

At half past five, the Reillys returned and soon after the smell of spaghetti bolognaise wafted up to my floor, making me salivate. I half expected another knock on the door, for the angry woman to come back demanding to speak to Helena, but she didn't and unless they looked at their app for the camera doorbell, I guessed she would be none the wiser. However, there was no robotic voice announcing her arrival, so I assumed it wasn't connected.

I struggled to relax, which wasn't unusual. The first night phrogging at a new property always gave me the willies. It was the unexpected. I didn't know if Helena or Jack would get restless in the night, if they wandered the house or if Nathan sleepwalked. For all I knew, they could be into devil worship and this room was used to sacrifice virgins. That's why research was key. But the snippets of time spent watching the family only gave me a glimpse of what their life was like and you never really knew what went on behind closed doors until you were trapped inside with them.

The first time was terrifying and I barely slept at all. I only managed a week in a three-storey town-house, hiding out in the basement where I couldn't hear anything except for footfalls overhead. If my parents found out, they'd go mad; it was hardly safe and not at all ethical. I'd be horrified to find someone living in my home without my knowledge, but it wouldn't be for long and I wasn't causing the homeowners any harm. It was more of a social experiment, but I doubted other phroggers were as harmless as I was. I logged on to the Wi-Fi again and busied myself checking my email, enjoying the light. It was dark in the master suite, but I couldn't put a light on, working by the small torch I always carried with me in my backpack, along with plenty of batteries. I responded to Mum's weekly check-in, read on my ancient Kindle and watched the moon rise in the sky through the window.

When I needed to use the toilet, I crept to the en suite as quietly as I could, aware they were all downstairs on the ground floor watching television and unlikely to hear me. Around seven o'clock, I listened to Helena bring Nathan up for a bath and put him to bed after he read her a chapter of *Captain Underpants*. A short time later, I heard the distant pop of a wine cork from the kitchen and muffled laughter. When they came upstairs at around ten, I shut my ears to the soft groans of pleasure and creaks of the bed below.

I drifted off at some point after midnight satisfied the family were asleep and I wouldn't be disturbed. The house had grown cold and I snuggled deep into the sleeping bag. The only light was what came through the windows and a small plug-in for Jack outside his bedroom. Six hours later, I woke with a start to footsteps climbing the stairs. My stairs.

Unable to breathe, I watched Jack come into the

master suite through the tiny gap of the sliding door before disappearing into the en suite. My stomach rolled, my entire body tensing. Did he come up here to relieve his bowels in the morning? Was this a regular thing? He was dressed in shorts and a T-shirt, like he was going to the gym. I heard a clank of porcelain, my view blocked by the half-open door to the en suite.

Would he see my urine and paper in the bottom of the pan and know someone had been here? I'd only ever flush the toilet if I knew the house was empty, never at night. I gritted my teeth as my calf cramped, wiggling my toes to get some blood flowing but reluctant to move any more than that. Rustling came from the bathroom, then Jack emerged, slipping something small and black into his sock before heading back downstairs, not even glancing my way.

I let out a sigh and flexed my leg, pulling myself upright in the wardrobe and banging my head on the rail when I heard the front door close. Rushing to the window I saw Jack make his way down the driveway, put in headphones and start to jog when the gates swung open. I hobbled around the room, waiting for the cramp in my leg to pass, groggy at being pulled from sleep so abruptly.

Well, that was new, Jack liked to run in the mornings, something I didn't foresee, nor observe in my reconnaissance, although I was never here that early. But why the hell did he come up here?

In the en suite, a damp sandwich bag lay discarded in the sink, but otherwise nothing was different. He hadn't flushed the toilet, although I couldn't tell if he'd used it. Whatever he'd retrieved from the bathroom, I was well aware he'd likely be putting it back on his return and I had to make sure I was out of sight.

Downstairs, all remained quiet, but fifteen minutes later I heard a faint alarm and Helena got up. Glad I'd had a chance to stretch my legs, I crept back to the wardrobe and listened to the Reillys get ready for their day. Coffee was first on the menu and the smell made me crave a cup. Soon after Helena got Nathan up for school, Jack came back from his run and showered. Toast was burnt somewhere in the house, setting off the smoke alarm, and like a whirlwind they rushed around until Helena left.

A car waited, blocking the gates, to pick her up at half past seven, a woman waving from the driving seat. I guessed if Helena worked in London, then she got a lift to the train station every morning. She yelled a goodbye and a reminder for Jack not to forget Nathan's lunchbox and off she went. Thirty minutes later, Jack hurried Nathan out the door and into the Mercedes to take him to school. Finally, after what was a frantic morning all was quiet again. Jack hadn't come back up to the top floor at all, so whatever he'd retrieved, he still had it on him.

Could it be cigarettes? Was he a secret smoker, hiding his packets from Helena? I had no idea, but I was dying to find out. With the Reillys gone, the priority today was getting a key to the back door cut, so I could come and go with ease. Also I wanted to see if I could get onto their doorbell camera feed. If it was working, then usually there would be a tinkling or a voice signifying a person approaching the door, but I hadn't heard anything yesterday. Was it connected or broken?

I had a quick shower in the en suite, being sure to wipe it down after me, and flushed the toilet. I was glad to wash off the sweat after being sautéed in the sleeping bag. Once dressed in the same jeans but a new top, I ventured downstairs and made myself a slice of toast and peanut butter, washing my plate and knife and putting them back where I found them. Seeing the notepad again, with more items added to the shopping list, reminded me I hadn't checked the website for St Wilfrid's School.

Googling on my phone, I looked at the list of teaching staff and found Jack halfway down the page, his green eyes jumping out at me immediately. He was Head of Pastoral Care.

It had been a relatively new concept when I was there, the addition of pastoral staff employed to ensure the well-being of the students. Someone you could go to if you were being bullied or had a problem at home. I admired the concept and Jack, I suspected, with his friendly face, would be good in the role.

While downstairs, I checked which key unlocked the bifold doors, removed it from the ring and slipped it into my pocket. Back in the master suite, I cleaned my teeth, rolled up the sleeping bag and hid it in one of the wardrobe drawers, making sure I'd left no trace behind. Taking my rucksack, I left via the bifold door. I always took my bag with me, in case there was a chance I wouldn't be able to get back in. While in the garden during daylight hours, this time I noticed the fence had come away from the post at the corner, one of the slats was loose and with a bit of force I made enough of a gap for me to squeeze through. Much easier and cleaner than scaling the fence.

The bus stop was empty and I waited for the

number three to take me into town, where I got the key cut and popped into the *Crawley News* office.

'Hey, Molly, any traffic cones blocking the road today?'

'Piss off, Jeff.' I sighed as he chuckled, ducking down behind his PC. I knew I was the office joke, but it only made me want to try harder, especially to prove myself to idiots like Jeff.

'Now, now, Jeff, wind your neck in.' Des came out from his office. 'I've got something juicy for you to-day, Mol.'

My spirits lifted and I followed him inside his office, turning to give Jeff the finger.

'Ignore them, they're only jealous that you have the thirst for it, theirs dried up a long time ago. I know *Crawley* isn't exactly the hive of news stories, but as I said—'

'Everyone's got to start somewhere,' I inter-rupted. 'I know, Des.' I dropped my rucksack and slumped into the seat in front of his desk.

'St Wilfrid's School,' he said, and my ears pricked up. 'They've got a big event planned for World Book Day on the sixth of March and they've asked us to help promote.'

I groaned audibly. 'I thought you said it was juicy.'

'It is, as far as word count goes. We'll be running a feature next week and one after the event. I've got you an appointment with the librarian and pastoral – they're organising it. Tomorrow at eleven, okay?'

I sat straighter in my chair, a fluttering in my stomach. Would I be meeting Jack?

'Okay, sure.'

'Great stuff, I knew I could count on you. I'll email you the details.' Des grinned at me, revealing his coffee-stained teeth.

I smiled to reassure him and rose from the chair. It would be one way to get to know Jack Reilly better and find out exactly whom I was living with.

5

With my investigative nose on the scent, I walked around the corner to the library and booted up my laptop, proceeding to read everything I could find online about Jack Reilly, but there wasn't much available. Other than the limited information on St Wilfrid's School's webpage and an inactive Facebook account, I couldn't find anything of interest.

When I tried Helena, it was the opposite. She had a dynamic Instagram account, mainly posting photos of food, shoes and the occasional one of her and Jack. She mentioned Nathan, but there were few photos of him and the ones that did include him obscured his face. That didn't surprise me, many people didn't like to post pictures of their children.

Instead, fashion and a healthy diet was her thing, she followed lots of influencers and designer brands but clearly had her favourites.

Jack had bought her a Hermès tote bag for her thirty-fifth birthday in November that she'd gushed about online, there were photos of it from every angle. Scrolling back, I saw she'd posted a photo of a two-tier birthday cake for Jack in the August when he'd turned thirty-seven. Their eighth wedding anniversary was on the fourth of May last year, and Helena had posted a photo from their nuptials, Jack gazing adoringly at his wife in a simple yet beautiful ice-white column dress. The inscription below the photo a summary of how they met.

On a rainy October in 2015 we happened to be queuing at the bar, waiting to get served. You let me go before you, then insisted on buying the round for me and my friends, asking for ten minutes of my evening. We spent the rest of that night huddled together in a corner, talking and laughing. Seven months later we were married! Everyone thought we were mad, but two years passed and Nathan arrived, completing our family.

Happy anniversary, Jack Reilly, I'll be by your side always.

So it appeared they'd had a whirlwind romance, the perfect picture of family bliss.

All of the Reillys' life events, the house move, the birth of Nathan and Christmas spent in a cabin in the Cotswolds were documented between photos of high heels, jewellery and artisan dishes of delicious looking meals.

When I clicked on Oxalis, whom Helena had tagged in one of her fancy dishes, I saw it was a small chain of vegan restaurants in London and the food photos made sense. When I googled them, the restaurants were extravagant, all with the same black and gold décor. They looked high-end, which was confirmed when I saw the à la carte menu and the prices that went with it. So Helena was the marketing manager for their chain and I guessed as she travelled up to London every day, it was why Jack did the school run.

Closing down my laptop, I popped to the nearest shop to get some snacks and chocolate before waiting for the bus back to Church Road, messaging Megan en route to let her know I was perfectly fine and we'd grab a coffee or dinner when she was next free. The downside of phrogging was that it was safer to already be inside the house when the family came home; you couldn't come and go freely without fear of exposure. Especially not when your way into the house was through the living quarters and I wasn't brave enough, even with a key, to come in the back while they were sleeping, not yet anyway.

When I reached Church Road, I double-checked the driveway was empty before fighting through the brambles at the back and into the garden, thankful it wasn't overlooked. It was one of the things I'd considered when choosing number six.

The key for the back door worked perfectly and I reattached the one I'd borrowed so it wouldn't be missed. Inside, the house was cold and I guessed the heating was on a timer and would come on later. Stomach rumbling, I looked through the freezer first, hungry for something more substantial than crackers. Leftovers in Tupperware boxes were labelled with what they were and dates to be eaten by, but then I saw last night's spaghetti bolognaise in the fridge. Whoever had made it appeared to be feeding the five thousand and wouldn't notice if I took a small portion.

Although cold and not particularly appetising, it would do to stifle my hunger pains. Sacrifices com-

mitted phroggers had to make to stay hidden because reheating it would mean the smell would
linger.

I took it upstairs, barely reaching the master
suite before I heard the front door open. *Shit!*

'It smells nice in here,' I heard a female voice,
which I didn't believe was Helena's, travel from
below.

'Probably last night's dinner,' Jack explained before footsteps climbed the stairs.

Not wanting to risk dashing across the room to
the wardrobe, I stepped inside the en suite still
clutching the Tupperware box, praying they
wouldn't come up to the top floor.

'Not up here, Grace, come on.' Jack sighed, followed by slurping noises and the tinkle of a belt
buckle.

I gasped, my brain connecting the dots. Who the
hell was Grace?

'I want you to fuck me on your bed; the bed that
will soon be mine.' She'd gone for sultry, but it came
off weak with barely any conviction. Jack didn't put
up a fight, though, because I didn't hear him speak
again, only the sound of kissing, then the squeak of
bed springs below, followed by Grace's exaggerated
moans of pleasure. I couldn't believe my ears. Jack

was having an affair and here they were, in broad daylight, coming into the marital home for a lunchtime shag. So much for Jack and Helena's perfect love story.

The camera doorbell couldn't be working unless Jack was so brazen he didn't care. I couldn't imagine that was the case, and anyway, wasn't he supposed to be at work? I checked the time and it was half past one, surely he'd have to be back soon. With them in full flow, I tiptoed to the wardrobe and hid inside, looking around for my rucksack. Fuck! I'd left it downstairs in the kitchen by the breakfast bar.

Idiot! I berated myself; my laptop was in there and my wallet with my driving licence in. What was I thinking! I shouldn't really carry identification for that exact reason, but I needed it in the pubs sometimes otherwise I wouldn't be served. If the rucksack was found, he'd know someone was here and he'd know who too. When he called the police, I could hardly deny it. Even if I hid, they might search the house and would find me easily. I'd have to come clean.

My chest constricted. Inside the wardrobe, I was suffocating, there was no air and either my brain was tricking me or the smell of bolognaise was leaking from the box. I had to risk it, creep downstairs and get my rucksack, but as I pulled open the wardrobe door, Jack's voice sounded close.

'Hang on, I just need to do something.' Jack padded up the stairs, his footsteps getting louder.

I shrank back against the wall. The wardrobe door was open about six inches. Would he notice?

More footsteps followed, the creak of the top stair I'd learnt to avoid.

'You need to tell her, Jack,' the person I now knew as Grace called up from the hallway below.

'I will. It's complicated,' he shouted back.

If I hadn't been so terrified of being discovered, I might have rolled my eyes. Complicated. It always was for the married husband having an affair. What about the poor woman who was being strung along, let alone the wife who had no idea what her treacherous husband was doing?

I heard the familiar chink of porcelain, the same as this morning, then she climbed the stairs and they met at the top. I watched her sidle up to him in the reflection of the window, wrapping her arms around his waist. God, she was young, around my age. Such a cliché.

'Don't you want to be with me, Jack?' Grace's voice was like syrup and my jaw dropped as she took his hand and placed it inside her unbuttoned blouse.

He cupped her breast and she moaned, throwing her head back and exposing her neck. Jack kissed it, as she'd intended, and as if that was her green light to continue, she unzipped his fly and pushed her hand inside.

'Grace, stop,' he mumbled, eyelids fluttering as my cheeks flamed. 'I have to get back to work.'

I didn't want to watch the private moment, but I couldn't tear my eyes away. Grace giggled, moving her hand until he grabbed her wrist.

'Stop,' Jack said, breathless.

'You're hurting me.' Grace tried to pull her hand away, but he held her tight.

'Don't play games.' His voice was low, the words hissed, but he let her go and she took a step back, pouting.

'Tell her. Soon. I won't wait forever.' Grace descended the stairs and Jack ran a hand through his hair, raising his eyes to the heavens before doing up his trousers and going after her. He didn't seem like a man in love, more one who was sick of her juvenile demands.

I blew air out through my cheeks, my stomach squirming at witnessing something I clearly wasn't supposed to.

Minutes later, the front door slammed and it was

then I remembered the rucksack. Waiting until I was sure the coast was clear, I ran downstairs and found it untouched, exactly where I'd left it. The tension I'd been holding fled my body in a rush and I took the rucksack back upstairs where my lunch was waiting, although food was now the last thing on my mind.

Holy shit, that wasn't what I'd been expecting, not after Helena's Instagram feed. So Jack was screwing someone called Grace. She wasn't much older than me, of similar size and blonde too. Could she be the woman who'd been hammering at the door shouting for Helena, ready to tell her about their affair. Poor Helena, who clearly had no idea her husband was straying, if their lovemaking last night was anything to go by. Not only that, but they also had a son in the midst of all this. Whatever happened, it wasn't going to end well. Did Jack intend to leave his marriage or was he telling Grace what she wanted to hear?

I had so many more questions than I knew the answers to, but this house had got interesting and potentially dangerous if Jack was coming and going in secret. I'd have to be a lot more careful. Maybe I should cut and run, go back to Megan's and look for another property, but now I had to know more.

The bolognaise filled the hole in my stomach and I went back downstairs to wash up and refill my thermos. I lingered in Nathan's room, sad for the boy who clearly adored his daddy. Without thinking too much about it, I slipped a small chocolate bar under his pillow beside some dinosaur pyjamas. It was breaking a major rule, but the situation pulled on my heartstrings and every kid needed a little chocolate in their lives.

Back upstairs, I hunted for what Jack had been hiding in the en suite, but the room was bare. The memory of the sound of porcelain led me to wrestle the top off the toilet cistern – and there it was, a small black Android phone wrapped in a sandwich bag. It had to be their phone, how they communicated without raising any suspicion, but now I was invested, I needed to know how long it had been going on. Unfortunately it was protected by pin code and my first try of four zeros wouldn't let me in, but I wasn't about to give up that easily.

* * *

Blog Post #2
www.phrogging.com

One thing I've learned about my third phrogging experience already is, I cannot emphasise enough the need for research! The first time I wasn't prepared and the location I chose – a basement in a townhouse – gave me little opportunity to watch the family. I had no idea what was going on upstairs and venturing into the upper levels of the house was terrifying. I only managed a week. After that, I investigated online, having to rely on information mainly from the States where phrogging is more common. Of course, their houses are very different to ours, and they have a lot more space!

The second time, I found an unused granny annexe at the bottom of someone's garden, but it was cold and damp and I didn't last long there either. The living conditions were not great for winter. However, for my third go, I've made sure to do some reconnaissance before going in and I cannot stress enough how important it is.

Yesterday I got in through the back garden, which conveniently runs alongside a disused railway line: the same way I'd managed to watch covertly for a couple of weeks and, so far, no suspicions have been raised. I gained access to the house while workmen were in the garden so the property was un-locked, no breaking and entering committed. The owners have recently moved in and a lot of work has been done already. I hoped it would be finished by now, but at least they're no longer inside.

Currently I'm taking shelter in an unused bedroom on the top floor of the property, a loft conversion, which luckily for me has a bathroom attached. I still need to look for al-ternative spots to hide, in case I'm not in the bedroom when the family arrive home.

Unfortunately, since my arrival yesterday I have already had two near misses. The first was an unexpected caller on the afternoon of my arrival who may have seen me on the stairs through the glass panel by the front door. The second was a rookie error which I've made so you don't have to. I left my bag downstairs today when one of the owners came home unexpectedly for lunch. Take your belongings with you at all times, phroggers! I nearly got caught out, but thankfully it wasn't noticed in the short time he was at the property.

I had some of their food, but nothing they'd notice was missing, making sure to leave no trace. I washed the dishes and put everything back where I found it, so it was like I was never there. Same with the shower, which was amazing by the way. I've secured a good spot to sleep out of sight and it's pretty comfortable. The first night I was anxious, but it ended up being fine with no late-night wanderers and no unexpected guests.

All was going well, but there's been a major bombshell today. You know I mentioned he came home for lunch; well, he had a guest with him and it was for something other than food, if you catch my drift. So the husband of the family I'm cohabiting with is having an affair. Not sure what to do with that information, but it kind of throws all the routines I thought they had out of the window if he's sneaking home to diddle his mistress.

Will keep you posted as I've decided to stay on for now.

6

Back in the wardrobe, I ensured my laptop was set to silent and checked my blog on the phrogging website. It had a few hundred likes which wasn't bad and I'd promised to write daily. Despite multiple attempts to crack the passcode of Jack's burner phone, I couldn't get in. Eventually, it locked me out, so I stuck it back in the cistern. I'd tried Nathan's date of birth and Jack's wedding anniversary, which I'd saved from Helena's Instagram account, but I imagined it had to be something she wouldn't guess if she found the phone.

Writing the second instalment of the blog was tricky, I wanted to provide enough details to keep it interesting, but not so many the property or the

Reilly family could be identified, especially as there was an infidelity in the mix. Plus the last thing I wanted was anyone to guess my location, but I hadn't even mentioned what county I was in. I could include photos, but it would be too risky. Anyway, it was all writing experience, reporting to a certain extent.

Back at the day job, I checked my emails to find Des had sent me details of my meeting scheduled with Jack Reilly and Claire Gilbert tomorrow at eleven as promised. The thought of coming face to face with Jack under normal circumstances made my stomach churn. Even though he wouldn't have a clue who I was, I'd seen his underwear drying on the airer and listened to him have sex... twice. It was more than a little inappropriate.

Now the house was empty, I went for a wander, taking advantage of the peace, this time keeping away from the front door, but there were no visitors. I searched for a hub for the camera doorbell but found nothing; perhaps the previous owner had a subscription which had since been cancelled. I'd been meaning to check for places to hide if I was stuck downstairs. The toilet and shower room off the hallway had a large towel cupboard which I could squeeze into if necessary and I found a recess in the utility room behind the washing basket. The cupboard beneath the staircase was large enough, containing lots of coats and wellingtons, as well as the hoover. It ran beneath the stairs and if I crouched down out of sight I wouldn't be spotted even if someone came in to retrieve their outdoor wear. It was handy to have spaces around the house I knew I could dart into at a moment's notice if anyone arrived home unexpectedly. It would be stupid to assume I'd be able to get back to the top floor every time.

Back upstairs, I checked beneath the beds. Nathan's was a divan with drawers so that was a no-go, but the Reillys' was wrought iron with storage boxes beneath containing all of Helena's shoes. She had an addiction. It was there, as I pulled out a box, that I found a lacy pink thong, hooking it out with one finger and holding it away from my body. Who knew what I could catch from that thing? I wrinkled my nose at the thought. Was it Helena's or Grace's? I flicked it back where I'd found it and had a quick peek in Helena's underwear drawer. The vibrant pink lace didn't look like the type of underwear she wore. Hers were black lace and silk or muted tones and designer labels, but it was a cheap shot if Grace had left it there for Helena to find.

As I debated about what to do, noticing Jack hadn't even bothered to smooth out the bed sheets after his and Grace's quickie earlier, I heard the Mercedes pull onto the drive. Jack and Nathan came into the house a few minutes later, but by then I was back upstairs in the wardrobe on my phone.

Jack's Facebook account was pretty much inactive, the same as Helena's. He had a few friends but no one by the name of Grace. However, Helena's Instagram had a few thousand followers, way too many to go through, but I had an inkling I wouldn't find Grace there.

Like yesterday, Nathan dashed upstairs to retrieve his iPad and change out of his school uniform. He was like a bulldozer in his room, crashing about, then for a second it went quiet.

'Dad! Dad!' Nathan screamed and my breath caught in my throat. Had he hurt himself?

Footsteps thundered up the stairs and I strained to listen.

'What is it?' Jack wheezed.

'The chocolate fairy has been!'

I couldn't help it, a grin bloomed across my face at the joy in Nathan's squeal and the rustle of the wrapper.

'Where did you get that, bud?' Jack said, a note of surprised amusement in his voice.

'I told you, the chocolate fairy!'

'Well, she must know your birthday is coming up. I can't believe you're going to be seven!' Jack must have tickled Nathan as he melted into a fit of giggles.

Warmth spread through me at the interaction between father and son, until Grace popped into my mind ruining the picture.

'Let's not tell Mum about this, okay, otherwise the fairy might not come back.'

'Okay, Dad.'

The sound of a phone ringing broke through the moment of calm as I imagined Jack giving Nathan a cuddle.

'Hey, honey,' Jack said, followed by a pause. 'You know I have that thing tonight... Well what time will you be back?'

I heard Jack pacing in the hallway below and I slid the door to the wardrobe open a little, straining my ears to eavesdrop. Picking up on the tone of his voice, he sounded irritated and I guessed as the black phone was still hidden in the cistern, it was Helena and not Grace he was talking to.

'For fuck's sake... Yes, I know... Yep, but I have

commitments too... Okay, you know what, I'll call Sam.'

Jack or Helena must have hung up because I heard him mutter something, then his voice became more upbeat when he told Nathan Sam was coming over to watch him. Who was Sam, a babysitter?

I barely had time to draw the wardrobe closed when Jack climbed the stairs to retrieve his phone from the cistern. He seemed harassed as he punched at the keys. Was he texting Grace? Was she 'that thing' he had to do tonight?

He made another phone call downstairs, but it was muffled so I couldn't hear what was being said and a short while later the smell of cooked food drifted upwards as the room grew dark. It was a whole month until the clocks went forward, but I couldn't wait for the lighter evenings. I crept out of the wardrobe to use the bathroom, figuring Jack had come up to get the phone so wouldn't be back for a while. Megan messaged, asking if I wanted to meet up for dinner, and after they'd eaten, Jack shouted at Nathan that he was getting in the shower. By then it was almost six and I wasn't sure if he was going out or if Sam was coming, but I wanted to see Megan and reassure her I was fine.

Once I heard the water running and the pipes

rumbling, I sneaked down the stairs to the first floor. From the hallway, I could see Nathan's legs on his bed. He was laying on his front, I assumed playing on his iPad. Jack was humming from the shower, easily heard through the open bathroom door. Treading carefully and keeping to the edge, I snuck past Nathan's room and down the second set of stairs. As I got to the bottom, someone knocked loudly on the front door, their silhouette moving across the glass.

'Nathan, was that the door? It's Sam, can you get it?' Jack's voice shouted from the bathroom.

Little feet padded down the hallway and I ran into the kitchen and out the bifold door as fast as I could. The cold air smacked me in the face and I got out of the garden via the broken slat in the fence in record time.

* * *

'Oh my God, so he's having an affair?' Megan said as the waitress brought us two small glasses of wine. I'd met Megan at the Italian restaurant down the road from her flat, messaging her when I was on the bus going towards the centre of town.

'Yep, brazen too. Can't believe he brought her to the house.' I munched on a breadstick.

'Wow, nice guy! Do you think he's meeting her tonight?'

'I think so, I don't know where though. I don't even know who she is or how he knows her.'

'Looks like you've got some investigating to do.' Megan lifted a laminated eyebrow, her smile growing. She knew with secrets I was like a dog with a bone.

When the waitress returned, I ordered pasta carbonara, my favourite, despite having eaten earlier in the day, always happy to stock up on the carbs as sometimes with phrogging you didn't know where your next meal was coming from, or what it would be. Dried crackers, cereal and toast were staples, anything the family wouldn't know was missing, unless you were going to bring in your own food, but I found the less I travelled with, the easier it was to up and run at a moment's notice.

Megan informed me dinner was her treat before she ordered a spinach risotto. She worked in recruitment and had a bumper month on commission in February for all the contractors she'd placed in December and January. Always generous as she knew I earned so little. I couldn't wait for the day I'd get to pay her back, treat her to a meal on me for a change.

'Do you think this new place will work out?' she asked.

'It's too early to say. I'm not sure as they've been a bit unpredictable so far.'

'I really don't like it, Mol, what happens when you eventually get caught, because you will one day. What happens when someone catches you in the shower. You haven't even told me where the place is!' Megan screwed her face up but quickly reverted to normal when the waitress arrived with our food.

'It's better if you don't know.'

'Hey, it's not that place in Church Road, is it?'

It was my turn to pull my expression into one of innocence. Megan was too smart for her own good and we'd been friends for so long it was impossible to hide anything from her.

I reached out to touch her hand as she picked up her fork. 'It'll be fine.'

She fixed me with a steely gaze, fully aware I'd avoided her question. 'It better! I don't want to find out you've been buried under the floorboards.'

7

Dinner with Megan was the tonic I needed and when I left the restaurant to make my way back to Church Road, it was after eight, but I was full and happy. Talking about the Reillys without naming any names made the load I carried a little lighter. It didn't sit right with me; Jack was cheating on Helena right under her nose, but who was I to judge? My parents had a happy marriage without infidelity, to my knowledge, but I knew plenty of couples cheated. It was the fact I was a witness of sorts, one of my own making, which made me uneasy. I didn't want to watch the Reillys fall apart while I was under their roof.

Megan said her sofa was always available, but I didn't want to put her in that position again. I needed to sort my life out, earn enough money to rent somewhere or to buy the dream camper van which would ultimately solve the problem of having nowhere to sleep. That way, I'd be as free as a bird and ready to travel for the nearest story at a moment's notice. I just needed a break.

While waiting for the bus, I checked the traffic of my blog post on phrogging.com. It had over a thousand likes and multiple comments from people following my journey and I kicked myself at not doing it before now. Tomorrow's excerpt would have to be interesting to keep up the momentum, but that didn't mean I was hoping for any excitement back at the house. A nice calm night would be welcome, but I was already apprehensive about getting in. Should I have gone back to Megan's for a couple of hours and waited until the Reillys were all asleep? Perhaps that would have been the safest option, but I was tired and wanted to be well rested for tomorrow's meeting with Jack. Something I also needed to prepare for.

It was after nine by the time I got back so Nathan should be in bed, but was Helena back yet and had

Jack gone out or was Sam still babysitting? I couldn't see much from the front of the house, only that there was light coming from the lounge. I found my usual spot at the back of the garden and waited, trying to build up the courage to go in. I had no idea who was in the house or where they were and my anxiety had me trapped in a vice-like grip. Going out for dinner had been a bad idea and now I was stuck, damp and cold, being dripped on by the overhanging trees. I picked at my nails, waiting for a sign; a light to go on upstairs or even in the kitchen, but from the back, the house was cloaked in darkness.

'This is stupid, I could be sitting here all night,' I muttered to myself, rising up from the undergrowth.

As I stepped out from amongst the shrubbery and was halfway across the lawn, the kitchen light turned on, blinding me momentarily. I gasped, like a spotlight was shining down on me, and dashed towards the side of the house, taking refuge behind the water butt. I heard the swish of the bifold door open and light footsteps come out onto the patio. I chewed on my lip, sure it was Helena; I could smell her perfume, albeit faint. Was she putting the rubbish out or something? The click of a lighter came next and smoke drifted into the air, followed by a groan.

'Long day?' Jack asked, and I imagined him following his wife, stepping onto the patio and handing her a glass of red wine, rubbing her shoulders, but his voice had an edge to it.

'I told you I'd *try* to make it back earlier, I didn't promise. Anyway, I got back before you did and sent Sam home,' she replied stiffly.

'I just want you to recognise you're not the only one with commitments.'

'I do, but you have to recognise that I'm the one bringing in the lion's share here. If I have to work late, then I have to work late.'

'How could I forget.' Jack's voice dripped with sarcasm.

'Look, I'm tired, let's not do this now.' Helena sighed.

'Maybe take one of your sleeping pills,' Jack said.

'I wouldn't need them if you didn't stress me out so much,' Helena bit back.

Silence followed and Jack must have gone back inside because all I could hear was Helena sucking on her cigarette like her life depended on it. I hadn't even known she smoked. Maybe it was something she leaned on when she was stressed.

A few minutes later, the door rolled shut and the smell of smoke dissipated. Things obviously weren't all rosy between the pair of them and clearly Jack felt emasculated by Helena's role as the breadwinner. Was that why he was having an affair, to feel more like a man? I scoffed at the thought, but it wouldn't surprise me.

When the coast was clear, I crept back to my spot at the end of the garden, the cold seeping into my bones and threatening to spread. What if Helena had left the key in the bifold door? Why hadn't I considered that? If she had, then I'd be stuck out here all night. Perhaps it was safer to make sure I was inside before they all came home from now on.

Twenty minutes later, the upstairs light went on in their bedroom and Helena's silhouette could be seen moving around the room. When I saw Jack close the curtains, I couldn't wait any longer, the rock in my stomach growing. I had to know if I could get in.

Thankfully, my key slid into the lock and turned with ease, allowing me to inch the door open wide enough to squeeze through. I could hear them talking in their bedroom as I removed my shoes, their muffled voices coming from upstairs, and knew it wouldn't be safe to go up yet, so I waited in the dark hallway, my bladder wanting to expel the wine I'd had earlier.

Eventually, when I heard their bedroom door close and the squeak of the bed as they got in, I waited another ten minutes to ensure no sex was on the cards, then slowly took the stairs. Nathan's night-light glowed outside his door, which was left slightly ajar, his iPad on the carpet in the hallway. I didn't see it until I stubbed my toe on the corner, holding in a yelp, as it banged against the skirting board. My jaw clenched, but the sound of a bed creaking made me dash into the spare bedroom as Jack's bedroom door opened.

He seemed to loiter in the hallway, confused about what he'd heard, as my heart pounded so fast it made me dizzy. I hid behind the door, not daring to move, barely able to make Jack out through the sliver. He looked in on Nathan before going back to his room.

'What was it?' Helena asked, her voice already sounding on the edge of sleep.

'I thought Nathan might be trying to get his iPad thinking we were asleep, but he's flat out, or he looks to be.'

The door closed on their conversation and I knew there was no way I could leave for a while, despite my bladder protesting. I ignored it and sat on the sofa, yawning silently, glad to be back in the warmth. With the house toasty, dark and quiet, I struggled not to fall asleep.

While I waited for the Reillys to settle, I prepared for my meeting with Jack tomorrow at St Wilfrid's and wrote some questions on my notes app, contemplating how I was going to turn World Book Day into an exciting article.

When the muffled sounds of Jack's snoring floated through the wall, I made my way upstairs to the en suite to relieve myself. In the wardrobe, I laid out the sleeping bag, feeling like Harry Potter in his cupboard under the stairs, and snuggled into it. It didn't take long to nod off, content with a full belly, thoughts drifting to what the following day would bring.

* * *

Despite the hard floor, I slept a little too well, jerking awake as the front door slammed and scrambling up to watch Nathan and Jack climb into the Mercedes. I'd slept through the entire morning routine and had no idea if Jack had come up to collect the phone in the cistern. It was still there when I checked before taking a shower.

I put more effort into my appearance, knowing I

had a meeting. My clothes were a little rumpled from being folded in the rucksack, but I hoped the creases of my blouse would fall out. I'd washed my hair, letting it dry in tousled waves as I applied make-up in the mirror, taking the time to assess my slim face, slightly upturned nose and eyes which seemed too far apart. It was like painting a canvas, creating cheekbones and defining wayward brows, with a slick of pink lip gloss finishing the look.

Before going downstairs for breakfast, I checked the bedroom and en suite for any sign I'd been there. I fancied a hot cross bun, but as there were only two left, I didn't take the chance, opting instead for some of Helena's granola and a scoop of Greek yogurt from the fridge. If the Reillys realised food was going missing, I had a problem and the workman weren't even around to take the blame for it.

I left the house at ten, circling back past the front and narrowing my eyes when I saw Marcus had returned with the landscape gardener. It looked like work on the garden was imminent, which meant I might find it difficult to get in later. He had a key to the side gate and was helping the younger lad carry materials through.

Convinced the camera doorbell either didn't work or wasn't connected, potentially it would be easier to get a key for the front door, but what if a neighbour saw me go in? At least with the workmen, there were plenty of comings and goings, but it only needed one nosy neighbour peeking through their curtains to put a spanner in the works and there was too much at stake to get caught.

8

I arrived at St Wilfrid's early and waited in reception, watching kids roll in late, or come from class to ask for paracetamol, trying to persuade the receptionist to let them go home sick. One of the teachers came down to ask her if she could get on to the agency as a teaching assistant hadn't shown up for work. It was the same as I remembered and anticipating I might bump into one of my old teachers made my stomach fizz. I observed the typically busy school reception area, and my attention was caught by an exchange in the playground that looked like it might escalate, so I didn't see Jack approach.

'Molly?' I turned, my head snapping up as he

loomed over me, no hint of recognition in his green eyes.

'Umm, yes. Jack?' I ventured.

'Yes, Jack Reilly, pleased to meet you.' He held out a hand to shake and I stood up on wobbly legs, taking his hand.

Up close, I could see the attraction, the shine in his eyes, the warmth and openness of his body language.

'Apologies, I'm a bit late, it's been a hectic morning already.' He smiled, charismatic without coming across as smarmy, and he smelt so good.

I couldn't help but get tongue-tied as I shook his hand, the heat from his grip making my fingers tingle. The flash of physical attraction was unexpected, but I pushed it away. He was married, with a mistress, and far too old for me anyway, but at least now I understood the appeal.

He stood back and stared at my face for a second. I blushed and averted my eyes.

'Sorry, you look like someone I know,' he said, a smile creeping onto his face.

Was that a line?

'Please, come this way?' He outstretched his arm, the cuffs rolled up on a green shirt which matched his eyes perfectly.

'Sure,' I swallowed, hoping I wasn't about to make a fool of myself.

Claire Gilbert was the exact tonic I needed as we entered the library and I saw her waiting for us. She was in her fifties and wore vivid colours with long dangly earrings. If I had to guess, I would have said she was an art teacher and not the school librarian, but her enthusiasm was infectious and she soon put me at ease. I vaguely remembered her from my time at school; she had joined a few months before I left.

Claire did most of the talking, but instead of Jack's attention wandering, he took notes as she explained the school's plan for a readathon, a used-book sale and the two local children's authors she'd managed to get on board. Surprisingly I found myself interested in the topic, Claire's passion for encouraging children to read was obvious.

'They're going to do a reading and a book signing; one has offered to run a creative writing lesson to encourage those aspiring future writers we might have amongst the student population.'

'You've really gone for it this year,' I said, my smile almost as wide as hers, looking around. 'The library looks bigger than I remember.'

'Yes, we've recently extended it. I wanted it to be the hub of the school and create something special for World Book Day, which is why we've asked *Crawley News* to cover it.' She paused to tug on one of her earrings before continuing. 'We need the book sale promoted and I think the readathon and author visits would be great to feature with photographs.'

'Of course,' I agreed, scribbling the details down on my notepad and asking the questions I'd pre-pared last night, general ones about the numbers of students, their typically preferred genres and how the school promoted reading at home. I planned to pull in some statistics about the importance of get-ting children interested in books, how reading can lead to higher exam grades and a better command of the English language.

'I think I've taken up enough of your time,' I said when we reached a natural lull in conversation. 'When I return on World Book Day, will I be allowed to stay for the day and capture as much as I can?'

'Of course,' Jack smiled, 'you're more than wel-come. It will be great to have another enthusiastic body on site.'

His words sent a ripple through me and I men-tally gave myself a shake as I stood up and shook Claire's hand.

'It's been lovely to meet you, I'll see you on World Book Day,' I said.

'Looking forward to it.'

Jack gestured for me to lead the way out of the impressive library, holding the door open for me. We walked side by side down the corridor towards reception, our arms almost touching.

'I'm kind of surprised, to be honest, I thought the English department would be running the event, not pastoral,' I asked, genuinely interested.

'I like to get involved in the extracurricular events if I can. Helping students find their tribe is my vocation and we have some avid readers that might not have the best... social skills, shall we say; they can be quite introverted.'

'The teenage years are tough, I remember it well,' I said, realising we'd reached reception all too soon.

'It's been a pleasure, Molly, and I look forward to seeing you next week. Des has got my contact details. If you need anything, don't hesitate to get in touch.' Jack shook my hand again and pressed the button to open the automatic door. Cold air rushed in, cooling my inflamed cheeks.

'Thanks for your time,' I replied.

I decided to walk back to Church Road, which took me half an hour, but it was good to clear my head. I hadn't expected to be so relaxed in Jack's company, believing I'd be like a cat on a hot tin roof, but there was something about his manner which put me at ease. While I walked, I called Des to tell him the meeting went well and I'd have something for him tomorrow morning. I hadn't taken any photos, but he said he was going to pull some from the internet on this year's World Book Day along with the current logo. Surprisingly, he agreed that Michael, the freelance photographer, could come with me next week to get some shots of the events as they happened. I assumed I'd have to take them myself. On top of that, there was a new movie out he wanted a review of and I couldn't deny I loved those jobs.

Scrolling through Facebook on the local Crawley group was something I did daily as a town reporter. Titbits of information often came through there, the start of a story or a lead on something exciting, although it wasn't always reliable. However, looking through as I walked, I froze mid-step on the pavement, causing someone approaching from behind to almost bump into me.

MISSING

My daughter Grace Stewart has not been seen since yesterday afternoon. Her phone is switched off and I cannot get hold of her. It's unusual behaviour, but the police won't do anything because it's not yet twenty-four hours and she's an adult. Grace is twenty-three years old, blonde, 5'3" and of slim build. Last seen wearing jeans, trainers and a green Joules coat. If you've seen her, please contact me.

It wasn't the words or Grace's name in black and white that made my heart jump into my throat, it was the photo of her, smiling into the camera wearing the green Joules coat. The exact same coat I'd seen the woman who'd knocked on the Reilly's door wearing as she'd walked away. I didn't need to put two and two together to work out Grace Stewart was Jack's mistress, the one who had come to the house and whom I'd seen in the reflection of the window fondling Jack whilst I hid.

I stared at the picture; Grace was beautiful, with piercing blue eyes that seemed to leap out of the photo, and she was only a year older than me. Had Jack met her last night?

A chill descended my spine as I took a screenshot of the post and forwarded it to Des with the message, *'Know anything about this?'* I carried on walking, not paying attention to my surroundings, and nearly stepped out in front of an oncoming car when I crossed the road. The driver honked his horn, jolting me back to the present, and I raised my hand in an apology, only one question bouncing around my mind: Had Jack Reilly had anything to do with Grace Stewart's disappearance?

It didn't take long for Des to respond. He hadn't seen the post but dismissed it almost immediately; she was holed up somewhere with a hangover, it was nothing more than an overprotective mother who'd jumped the gun. Grace would turn up later today with her tail between her legs, he'd seen it a thousand times before. I hoped he was right, but deep down something in my gut told me that wasn't the case. Of course Des didn't know the context and I wasn't about to tell him how I knew who Grace was and definitely not about the phrogging, even if I could palm it off as immersing myself as part of a feature I was writing. He wouldn't touch it with a barge pole, too many blurred lines with legality for *Crawley News* to run it. So I was on my own, but I couldn't ignore it.

I slipped into a nearby café for a coffee and a

sandwich, reluctant to return to Church Road straight away. I had to find out if Jack had met Grace last night and if so, where, which meant I had to get into the burner phone, but how? I had no idea what the passcode was, but I pulled out my notepad regardless and trawled through Helena's social media for more possible dates or number configurations I hadn't thought of.

Half an hour later, I had nothing. Wrapping my half-eaten sandwich to take with me, I hurried back to Church Road, hoping I might be able to find some more clues there. I wanted to ring Megan and tell her what I'd found out, but she didn't know I'd been to see Jack today. I deliberately didn't mention it last night in case she thought it was too close for comfort, and I didn't want her to worry about me. She'd have a fit if she knew Jack's mistress had gone missing. Instead, I sent her a text thanking her for dinner and asking if she wanted to catch the movie Des requested I review, knowing he'd cover her ticket on expenses. I was sure I could stretch to a bucket of popcorn, even though funds were already tight this month.

As I walked, I checked the missing post on Facebook, where the comments were piling up. Mostly, people were saying they'd shared it, but one caught my attention. It was by Dawn Cottrill; she'd shared the post but added she was worried as Grace had not turned up for work today and no one had been able to get hold of her. I took a screenshot, then typed Dawn's name into Facebook's search bar, bringing up her profile. Dawn hadn't listed a profession, but her account wasn't locked, allowing me to scroll through her feed, pausing at a photo of a Christmas party. A group of girls sat around a table in a restaurant, holding crackers and wearing party hats. The caption beneath made my legs weak: 'Watch out Crawley the TA Girls are out for our Christmas Do'.

TA Girls – TA short for teaching assistant. And the receptionist at St Wilfrid's had been told to contact the agency as one hadn't turned up today.

9

At least now I knew the connection. Putting it all together, it was fair to assume Grace worked as a teaching assistant at St Wilfrid's School, no doubt where she'd met Jack and how their affair began. When I zoomed into Dawn's photo, I recognised Grace raising a glass of Prosecco in an off-the-shoulder top, her collarbones sparkling with glitter. Should I message Dawn to find out what she knew? I couldn't do it in an official capacity, not when Des had dismissed Grace's disappearance off the bat. If Grace and Dawn were friends, would she know about the affair? It was a rabbit hole I was being pulled down and I had to tread carefully.

Maybe Grace would turn up safe and sound and

all my angst would be for nothing, but after what I knew about her affair with Jack, I feared for her safety. She'd wanted Jack to tell Helena about their affair, what if she'd backed him into a corner? I shuddered at the thought, trying to relate the man I'd met properly today with someone who could hurt another person. It didn't feel right; if anything, from what I'd witnessed, Grace had been more forceful than he had when they'd been together, but who knew what he'd do if she'd threatened to expose their affair. If Jack was intent on protecting his marriage, would he shut her up and how far would he go to do that?

The idea sent shivers through me. Could I be living with a man who was violent towards women?

You don't know anything yet, Molly, stop jumping to conclusions. I worked on cold, hard facts and that wasn't about to change because I was personally involved in this story.

Back at Church Road, the landscape gardener's truck was still on the driveway, the open-topped container empty of materials. Sighing, I moved around to the disused railway line and up the steep bank to their fence, which, to my surprise, had a panel missing entirely now. I stayed back, snagging my blouse on a thorn. Workwear was not meant for wading through overgrown thickets and I gritted my teeth, moving carefully.

'Yeah, I'm leaving to go and pick it up... Yeah, I've got the key, I'll lock up.' The young lad held the phone away from his ear as he rummaged in his pockets.

It seemed my luck was in; the gardener was just about to leave the house, which meant I had some time to myself for a thorough search and another crack at the phone. When I watched him leave, closing and locking the side gate, I entered the garden. The lawn was full of pieces of wood, laid out like they were a puzzle to solve. Bags of soil and potted plants still in their orange containers were scattered haphazardly too. The opposite corner from where I'd gained access had been dug up and raked over. It wouldn't be long before the fence would be repaired and it spurred me on to sort a front door key.

Inside, the house was a little chilly, the radiators cold. I took my time, going through each room again but found nothing else which would link Jack to Grace, although I didn't expect to. I was sure Jack would have covered his tracks well, knowing what was at stake.

The phone was still in the cistern and I tried

some more number combinations, but nothing worked. How else could I find out if he saw Grace last night? I should have followed him, but I wasn't to know she was about to go missing. Deflated, I put the phone back where I'd found it and got to work on the World Book Day piece for Des.

At first I found it difficult to drag my mind away from Grace, routinely hopping back to Facebook to check the missing post and reading the comments which were increasing by the hour. Eventually, I focused on the task at hand and completed the thousand words Des had asked for, sending them over as Jack and Nathan arrived home. I used the bathroom and was tucked inside the wardrobe before the front door opened and Nathan's familiar footsteps raced up the stairs.

'Ah, she's not been!' he shouted down to his dad.

'Who?'

'The chocolate fairy.' He sounded so disappointed.

I chuckled to myself, had Nathan been more excited to race upstairs to find out if he had a mini bar of chocolate under his pillow than for his iPad today?

'Never mind, bud. I've got a quick call to make and you know the drill. Wash your hands, get out of your uniform and grab a snack, okay.' Jack's voice got louder as he climbed the stairs, coming all the way to the top and immediately retrieving the phone.

I watched through the crack as he rubbed his five o'clock shadow, tapping away at the screen, then putting the phone to his ear. He paced the room, at one point coming so close to the wardrobe I could hear his nose whistling and thought I might combust with nerves. I'd taken it for granted how vulnerable I was, with only a thin piece of wood between us. At any moment, he could slide open the door and there I'd be, exposed with no explanation as to why I was hiding in his wardrobe. Heat streaked my face as I imagined how embarrassing such a confrontation would be, especially now we'd met in a professional capacity.

Eventually, he moved over to the window and I could tell by the deep trivets in his forehead and the way his top teeth pulled at his lip, he was worried about something.

Was it the fact Grace was missing which troubled him or that it was now public knowledge? He was impossible to read on that front, but the tension in his shoulders was obvious. Jack glared at the phone as though he was waiting for a reply or maybe he was thinking about his options, I couldn't tell.

'Dad, can you come help me,' Nathan shouted.

'Hang on a minute,' Jack called back, irritation in his voice.

'I spilt the juice.'

'For fuck's sake,' he hissed, jaw clenching, chucking the phone onto the chaise longue and jogging down the stairs.

I eyed the phone, stomach churning. I had a minute at least, longer depending on how long the clean-up would take, but had to act quickly before the screen locked. Sliding open the wardrobe door, I scurried on my hands and knees the few feet to the chaise longue, snatching up the phone and opening the messages. There was only one string of conversation from a contact called Ian. It had to be Grace, the phone had no other contacts saved, but the male name made me smirk nonetheless. Scrolling back they'd started contacting each other months ago, around the end of October. Had the affair been going on for over four months?

There was nothing overtly sexual in the messages or anything to give away what the pair of them were doing. In fact if I didn't know Ian was female, I wouldn't necessarily have guessed. The messages were all about logistics. When they were meeting and what time, but the location was vague, no address, but in one message Jack mentioned 'on the corner'. I listened out for Jack's voice, he was berating Nathan, not aggressively, more frustrated.

Knowing I didn't have long left, I scrolled to the most recent messages, starting with yesterday.

IAN

I have something to tell you.

JACK

Usual place 6:45pm.

The call log told me he'd just tried to ring 'Ian', something which didn't happen often; they usually communicated by text.

'I'll be back in a minute,' I heard Jack say as the footsteps began to climb. I quickly returned the phone to the exact spot where he'd left it, rushing back to the wardrobe and praying the door wasn't still wobbling where I'd rapidly slid it shut. Jack didn't notice, bounding straight into the room and scooping up the phone, checking for calls or messages. I chewed my lip as panic struck me. Would he think it strange his phone was unlocked and hadn't automatically locked in his absence? Thankfully he didn't seem to notice and his whole body sagged when he discovered there was no reply from Ian.

Was he trying to cover his tracks or genuinely attempting to get in touch with Grace? If it was the latter, he must have no idea what had happened to her either. I fidgeted in the wardrobe, my head full of questions. Maybe they'd had an argument and she'd stormed off. Gone off radar to teach him a lesson or something; I didn't know. Perhaps she'd changed her mind and wanted to call the whole thing off; she'd said she had something to tell him in her message, it could have been that. An ultimatum, it was her or Helena. There was nothing to do but wait.

The afternoon drifted into the evening, Helena returned home and Jack cooked a chicken dish which smelt delicious. Salivating, I ate the other half of my sandwich, which was now curling at the edges, wishing I could go down and join them for a bowl. Phrogging could be quite antisocial with strict curfews – no going out having fun with friends, no chance of a love life. It was like you were living vicariously through the householders, as well as being a parasite.

Nathan came up for a bath as per his usual routine and it was lovely to hear him singing and splashing around. He seemed like a good kid, well behaved and funny too. Once he'd gone to bed, Helena and Jack argued in hushed whispers from the lounge. Ignoring my safety rules, I sat on the stairs, trying to eavesdrop.

'If you want this marriage to work, Jack, you're going to have to commit.'

'I am committed, what are you talking about? I'm here, I look after Nathan.'

'You think I don't see the way you look at other women; am I not enough for you?'

It all went silent and I heard Helena sniff.

'Come on, don't cry, you and Nathan are my world, you know that.'

He was so sincere even I would have been convinced if I hadn't listened to him having sex with Grace on their bed.

* * *

Blog Post #3
www.phrogging.com

So my second night was interesting. I had to sneak in after they went to bed, which was a bit of a challenge, and keep quiet until I was sure they were asleep. It was going well until I stubbed my toe creeping around and they jumped out of bed to see what the noise was.

I was terrified I was about to be discovered, barely concealed behind an open door, but I got to my hiding place in the end. Despite that and breaking the cardinal rule of slipping a chocolate bar under the kid's pillow so he now thinks there's a chocolate fairy, I don't think they suspect anything. I'm psyched that I'm managing to coexist with another family who have no idea I'm here, but I do need to be more careful.

Unfortunately, the house I thought was going to be perfect hasn't lived up to expectations. Not only is the husband having an affair, which throws off the routine of when everyone is out of the house, but workmen are visiting the property to make improvements. Thankfully they are mostly outside, but it looks as though I'll need to find an alternative means of entry. Will keep you posted on that.

The room where I'm hiding out also happens to be the place where the husband is concealing the burner phone he uses to contact his mistress. That was a morning wake-up experience I don't want to repeat as I'm not sure my heart can take it.

To say life has become weird since I've

been here is an understatement. I met the husband today in a professional capacity, which was bizarre, knowing exactly who he was when he didn't have a clue we'd woken up under the same roof this morning. What I am worried about is that the mistress has gone missing and it's all over social media. I'm hoping she'll turn up, but if she doesn't, am I sitting on evidence which could help find her? Does anyone else know about their affair other than me?

I'm conflicted between protecting myself and doing the right thing. Maybe it's nothing and all a misunderstanding, but what if it's not? I'm right in the middle of a real-life situation which is evolving and, I have to say, if I was watching this as a television drama, I'd be telling my character to pack up and go. Hopefully tomorrow the mistress will resurface. Until then, phroggers, stay safe and out of sight.

10

I'd decided to get it out in the open, knowing it's what the readers would want. I read it three times before I posted, sure there was nothing which would lead anyone to work out who I was or where I was phrogging. I fell asleep with my stomach rumbling, waking on Friday morning utterly ravenous. Nathan was screaming that he couldn't find his PE kit and downstairs it sounded like there was a riot going on. Everyone had woken later than planned and they were running around like headless chickens to get out of the door. Helena had missed her colleague Emily's lift to the train station and Jack was going to have to take her before dropping Nathan at school.

I couldn't wait for them to leave, so I could go

downstairs and eat whatever I wanted for breakfast. I could always replace it. Des had sent me an email late yesterday; he'd loved the article, which had made it to page three, and the paper was going to print tonight. World Book Day was next Thursday and tomorrow marked the first of March, the arrival of spring, although it was still cold outside.

While I waited for the Reillys to vacate the premises, I checked Facebook for Grace's missing post. There were now over seventy comments and I scrolled through the ones I hadn't read. The last one posted twenty minutes ago made my mouth go dry.

Grace is still not home and an official missing person report has been made. If you have seen her, please get in touch.

So Grace still hadn't turned up. I swallowed, a lump forming in my throat, and unzipped my sleeping bag, kicking my legs out. The wardrobe was suddenly claustrophobic. Should I tell the police I knew she was having an affair with Jack Reilly, which would be lighting a match to his and Helena's marriage? What if Jack had nothing to do with it, what if he'd gone out for work or a meeting that night; he had said it was a 'commitment'. For all I knew, it could be a badminton tournament or something just as mundane. He seemed nice enough when I met him, he genuinely cared about his students and it looked as though he'd been trying to call Grace, worried even that he couldn't get in touch with her.

But what if he had something to do with her unexplained disappearance, the voice in my head piped up, electrifying the hairs on the back of my neck.

Perhaps I'd give it a few days, a week maybe. What if they arrested him and searched the house, the image of a police officer drawing back the wardrobe and finding me fast asleep in the early hours of the morning freaked me out. I had to speak to Dawn Cottrill, Grace's friend and fellow TA at the school. See what information I could glean from her without it looking like an interrogation or an interview for that matter. If Des found out I'd gone rogue, he'd fire me.

I tapped out a quick message to him.

That girl is still missing. Can I do some digging... pretty please. I have nothing else other than the film review. Might come in useful if she doesn't turn up, we'll be ahead of the game.

I added the last sentence on purpose. *Crawley News* was hardly a tabloid newspaper getting the scoop, but it would give him a thrill to be ahead of the *Brighton Argus*. He didn't take long to respond.

> Okay kiddo, I don't think it's going to turn into anything, but fill your boots.

Excited I had the green light to move, I waited five minutes to be sure the Reillys weren't going to return and ventured downstairs, filling my face with toast and some of Helena's granola, making sure to wash and dry everything I'd used. Whenever I left any room in the house, I checked whether there was any evidence I'd been there. Like with the bag, it was so easy to unconsciously put something down and leave it. It might be something innocuous but easily spotted as out of place by the homeowners. The whole point was to cohabit without raising suspicion, which wasn't proving easy in this house. The last thing I wanted to do was to freak anyone out and, ethically, I knew phrogging wasn't right. If I was Helena and Jack, with a young son at home, I'd be livid to know another adult was living parasitically in my house. They didn't know my intentions, that I wasn't there to harm him, like some kind of weirdo or pervert. I'd read enough cases about those.

I'd fallen down a wormhole of American cases during research, namely Daniel LaPlante, a teenage boy who had been residing in a family's crawl space for weeks, harassing them during that time. It was a phrogging that ended in murder. Also, the homeless woman who'd infiltrated Pamela Anderson's home, eating her food and trying on her clothes, stalking her. So I understood the fear someone in my position might cause and wanted to do everything to avoid it.

Clearing up after a second round of toast, I was finally sated and knowing I had little time before the gardener arrived, I went through the keys hanging up on the hook by the front door, checking which one worked. I kept the door pulled as closed as I could, not wanting to advertise what I was doing to any of the neighbours across the road. The camera doorbell was as dead as a dodo, no lights flashed and no sound was made when I opened the door. When I found the spare key, I took it off the key ring with the intention of getting another cut today. If the fence was replaced, at least I'd have another way in, even if I didn't want to use it. I couldn't imagine creeping in the front door while they slept.

Back upstairs, I got ready and messaged Dawn via Facebook to see if she'd be free to meet today for a quick chat about Grace. I got a response quickly. Her reply stated she'd happily help if it meant Grace was found and told me she had half an hour free at midday for her lunch break. I arranged to meet her outside the school and thanked her for agreeing to see me. Before I left, I slipped another chocolate bar, the last of my stash, beneath Nathan's pillow, knowing I was walking a fine line but unable to resist.

The landscape gardener had still not arrived so I was able to slip out of the back to catch the bus into town, heading straight for the newsagents to pick up a copy of the *Crawley News* and grab another stash of chocolate bars. It still gave me goosebumps seeing my name in print and, as promised, Des had put the feature on page three with a small photo of me above my name. There were larger photos beneath, of the school, the World Book Day logo and two of the authors who were attending the event, but I was finally getting somewhere. I took a photo of the piece and forwarded it to Mum, who I knew would get as much of a kick out of it as I did.

Megan rang while I was waiting for the key to be cut and I stepped outside to take the call.

'Did you see the post on Facebook of that missing girl?'

'Grace?' I frowned; did Megan know her?

'Yes, don't you remember, she was the year above us at school, the one who was caught making out with her boyfriend behind the bike sheds, like literally behind the bike sheds – what a cliché!'

My brow furrowed as I remembered my time at school, I had no memory of her, but Megan barely paused to inhale.

'My friend Sandra knows her, she does her nails on the side for a bit of extra cash as she's a qualified technician, and said it's weird. Grace had an appointment booked yesterday, but didn't turn up, phone was switched off.'

'Does she think something's happened to her?' I wasn't ready to share what little I already knew and definitely not the connection to Jack; Megan would go crazy that I was still at Church Road.

'She's convinced, so yeah. Apparently she was seeing some bloke, but it was all hush-hush, no idea why, but I guess he was married. Sandra said there must have been a reason she was so coy about it.'

'Well, at least a missing report is going to be taken seriously now,' I said, feeling awkward holding information back from my best friend.

'I'm free for the cinema whenever you want by the way. What are we going to see?'

'Something called *The Last Breath*, about deep-sea divers. I don't know much about it, if I'm honest.'

'A night out is a night out,' Megan chuckled, 'just let me know when.'

'Does tomorrow sound okay? We could see if there's an afternoon showing?' I suggested. The thought of being shut in the wardrobe all weekend if the Reillys stayed home didn't fill me with enthusiasm.

Megan said that sounded good, wishing me a good day before she hung up and I collected the freshly cut key to Church Road.

Perusing the surrounding shops, I bought some more supplies, wincing at my bank account, which was closer to zero than it had been for months. As good fortune would have it, shortly after I'd checked, Mum sent me an email gushing about my feature in the *Crawley News* and letting me know she'd deposited a couple of hundred pounds into my account. It was guilt that did it; we both knew I should be earning enough to support myself.

My monthly pay would stretch to rent a room in a shared flat, but I refused to touch my savings for the camper van. Megan paid over seven hundred pounds on her tiny place, with another hundred on food and god knows what on utility bills, it was such a lot of money. It was another reason I wanted to try phrogging, free living being the ultimate draw, but only until I saved enough for the van.

I treated myself to a coffee, getting ready to make my way to St Wilfrid's, which was a bit of a walk from the centre of town. As I was noting down questions I intended to ask Dawn, my phone flashed and I saw Des was calling.

'Hey, Des, everything okay?'

'Yeah, just giving you the heads-up. I've heard from Neil's contact at the station, a body has been found, it's female, so I've put Neil on it, in case it crosses over.'

'What if it's Grace? It's my story, Des, you said I could investigate.'

'Mol, you know I've got to put Neil on it. A missing person, sure, fine, go ahead, but a body. I've got no choice. Carry on with this Grace woman in case it's not her, but anything you get, you need to share with Neil, okay.'

I bit my lip so hard I might have drawn blood, balling my free hand into a fist, but I couldn't tell him I'd seen Grace and the circumstances, that I could have a massive story on my hands.

'Okay, Molly?' Des repeated firmly, waiting for my agreement. He knew I was pissed.

'Sure,' I replied, unable to keep the bitterness out of my voice.

Des hung up and I shoved my phone back into my pocket.

Bollocks to that. I was going to talk to Dawn and there was no way I was going to share any intel. I was living in a house with someone who could potentially be the chief suspect in the police investigation. I was in it up to my neck and I couldn't walk away now.

11

As my initial rage subsided, guilt about Grace gnawed my insides. I'd been so focused on getting the story, I'd not stopped to think about the poor woman the police had found deceased. What sort of monster was I? Was it ambition which had clouded my mind and made me think of the story first, neglecting there was a human involved. It wasn't the person I wanted to be.

I was going to find out the truth. I had a head start over Neil, although he was in a league above me, more experienced and with better connections. I did have one advantage though, I had insider information, and living with Jack, I could watch and listen. If he was going to slip up or hide evidence, I'd make sure I was around to be a witness.

Nausea made my stomach swirl as I carried on to the school to meet Dawn, knowing full well we would be talking about Grace Stewart, who may no longer be missing, but dead. Could Dawn have heard the news already? Gossip spread like wildfire, but I doubted it had reached social media yet.

I needed to find out Grace's movements on Wednesday night. It was what the police would do, work backwards. Who was the last person to see her alive and what would her phone tell us, if it was found? I had no idea how close Dawn was to Grace, but I hoped she knew some of her secrets.

When I reached the school gates minutes before twelve, Dawn was already there waiting and she eyed me curiously as I approached. I recognised her from the Christmas party photo, although she looked a lot less glamorous today. Heavy bags sat beneath her eyes and her unwashed hair was scraped back into a ponytail.

'Dawn?'

She nodded, pulling a vape out of her pocket and raising it to her lips with a shaky hand. 'I need to go to the shop to get some milk, fancy a walk?'

'Sure,' I replied, on the back foot as she turned

and walked up the road. I hurried after her, trying to keep her pace.

I should introduce myself.

'Like I said in my message, I'm Molly Hudson, journalist for the *Crawley News*. I'm looking for a bit of background on Grace. Are you two friends as well as colleagues?'

'She's my best mate. I can't believe she's disappeared out of nowhere.' Dawn sniffed, wiping her nose on a tissue taken from the sleeve of her long puffa coat.

Inside, I had a spark of hope, I had access to one of Grace's closest friends, but I had to play it just right, gain her trust so she would open up.

'I'm not going to print anything you tell me off the record, okay?'

'Don't they all say that?' She had a slight sneer in her tone.

'I guess they do, but I'm a local journalist, I live in this community. I attended this school and I care about it deeply. We need to find Grace and I want your help to do that. Have the police been to see you yet?'

'No, they haven't been to the school or anything. It's bloody ridiculous; she's missing, but because she's not a kid or vulnerable, she's not a priority.'

I let her rant, drawing deeply on the vape. It was obvious how much Grace's disappearance was affecting her.

'Do you know where she went on Wednesday evening, was she at work that day?'

'We both were, we had lunch, had a laugh, but no, as far as I was aware, she was having a quiet night in.'

'Does Grace live alone?'

'Her parents are pretty well off and she lives in this annexe thing at the end of their garden, proper nice. Has its own kitchen, bathroom and that. Her dad has stage three cancer and he's undergoing treatment, so she's home as much as possible.'

My heart sank, as if Grace's parents didn't already have enough to deal with without their daughter going missing. Especially if she was being carted off to the morgue as Dawn and I spoke.

'That's awful, how are they holding up?'

'They're in bits, obviously, because it's so out of character.'

'Was she seeing anyone?' I held my breath, keeping everything crossed Dawn was going to give me that golden nugget of information I'd been waiting for.

'Not that she told me.'

I visibly deflated, even my pace slowed until Dawn stopped and looked back at me.

'But she had been cagey about men recently. Normally she was a right flirt when we were out and she got lots of attention. Lately she's been knocking back anyone that approaches. There was a really fit bloke in the pub last weekend who asked for her number, but she wasn't interested.'

'Was she holding out for someone, do you think?'

Dawn pondered for a second. 'Nah, she would have told me.'

The rest of the walk to the shops didn't give me much to go on and I suspected Dawn wasn't as close to Grace as she made out, or maybe it wasn't reciprocated. There was a chance Grace was a secretive person by nature and she was having an affair with a married man, perhaps she didn't want anyone from school to know. Maybe Jack had insisted. The thought of him made the acid burn in my stomach.

Dawn told me how much Grace loved her job at the school, that she worked with some of the children who had additional learning needs but planned to do her teacher training degree.

When we returned to the school, I had an idea. It

would likely get me in trouble with Des, but I was now in a race against Neil and potentially the police.

'Where does Grace live; do you think her parents will talk to me?'

'She lives near Worth Church, they've got a bungalow up there, can't remember the number, but it's got a red front door.'

I tried to stifle my gasp. Church Road was named due to the church being set back off it, where the Worth way began.

'Do you know which road?'

'Mayfield, I think. Her mum's name is Sally.'

My mind was buzzing. Grace lived practically around the corner from the Reillys.

'Thanks, Dawn, you've been a great help.'

'Don't you write any crap about Grace, you hear,' she called after me as I walked away from the school.

'I promise I won't, I just want to help.'

I sped up, widening my stride. Probably an overreaction; things moved fast in television shows but not in real life. The body of the unidentified female would be in the morgue. If she had no signs of identification on her, they would check DNA and look for matching missing female descriptions. If it was Grace, it wouldn't take them long to determine it, but surely it would be at least a day.

By the time I got to Mayfield, I was panting, all the carbs I'd eaten that morning lodged in my stomach like a rock. I wandered up and down the street, looking for a bungalow with a red door, finding two possibles. I tried to look around the back of both properties to see if they had an annexe, but I couldn't tell.

The first door I knocked on had no response and I guessed the owners were at work or out because there was no car in the driveway.

The second bungalow had a white Fiat 500 on the driveway and the front door whipped open barely seconds after my knuckles left the wood.

'Hello?' The resemblance to Grace was uncanny and took me aback. The woman wedged in the doorway was in her mid-forties, silvery blond with lipstick bleeding into the lines around her mouth. Her polite expression couldn't mask the desperation behind her grey eyes. 'Is this about Grace? Have they found her?'

I'd been so thrown off by Sally's similarities to Grace I'd forgotten to speak and hurried to engage my mouth with my brain.

'Hi, Mrs Stewart, my name is Molly Hudson, I'm a journalist at the *Crawley News*.'

The look of disgust on her face was as though I was something to be cleaned from her shoe.

'Vultures,' she muttered, already closing the door.

'Please, Mrs Stewart, I want to help find Grace. We have a website, not only the weekly newspaper. We need to get her name out there, get her found.' My plea made her pause and she slowly drew the door back again.

'Do you know Grace?' she asked.

'No, but we're a similar age. I live in this community; it's times like this we need to help each other.' Rehashing what I said to Dawn. It wasn't that I didn't believe what I'd said, this was personal to me, but I was already lying to her.

'You better come in. My husband is upstairs having a nap, he's not well. I'll put the kettle on.'

12

Sally led me into the kitchen, where I could see Grace's annexe out of the window, its sky-blue PVC cladding making it look like a small summer cottage that would be perfect looking out onto the beaches at Camber Sands.

'She's been missing for almost forty-eight hours now and no news from the police. Something's wrong, I know it is.' Her hands shook as she made the tea and I wished I had the words to comfort her.

'Tell me about your daughter, Mrs Stewart.'

'Call me Sally, please.'

She brought the cups to the table, taking a moment to retrieve a tissue from the side and dab at her eyes.

'Grace is kind, she's beautiful, always putting others first. She works with special kids, you know, absolutely adores them. At home, she's like a busy bee, fussing around her father who is currently having chemotherapy. A real daddy's girl.'

'I'm sorry,' I interject, and Sally gave me a weak smile.

'She's everything we could ask for in a daughter.'

'Is Grace an only child?'

'Yes, we had trouble conceiving, so she was our little miracle.'

My chest tightened and I pinched my lips together. Imagining the Stewarts' loss and how devastated they'd be if the body was confirmed as Grace, their miracle child, tore me up.

'Tell me about her friends, is she dating anyone?'

'Grace has lots of friends, she's really bubbly, but no, I don't think she's seeing anyone, not seriously anyway.' So Grace's mother was kept in the dark like Dawn. Did anyone know she was sleeping with Jack? Had he ensured it, giving him the perfect alibi and the ability to walk away without any consequences?

Sally told me Grace went to work as normal on Wednesday morning, came home at four and went to the gym. She returned for dinner, around six for shepherd's pie, then left.

I knew what Sally meant, but I frowned. 'Left?'

'Oh, she lives in the annexe.' Sally pointed over her shoulder and I nodded enthusiastically at the purpose-built building.

'Wow, that's lovely.'

'We built it for her, to give her a little bit of independence. She kept saying she should move out; she was too old to be living at home with her parents, but then her dad was diagnosed.'

Sally talked a little more while I made notes. When I asked Sally for a photo of Grace, she took one from the fridge and handed it to me. Grace was beautiful in this shot, her golden hair was being gently taken by the wind and she grinned at the camera, a sparkle in her eyes. Not the dead, milky eye of her corpse, if it was her they'd found. I hoped for Sally's sake it was someone else.

'Would you like me to take you down there?' she offered, and I had to stop myself jumping up from the table and racing down the garden path.

I nodded. 'I think that would be helpful, to give me a sense of who she is.' I made sure I used the present tense as Sally had throughout our conversation. In her eyes, her daughter was still alive, and although I hoped she was right, my gut told me otherwise.

The annexe was girly inside, pretty pale pinks and soft pastel yellows coated the walls, with gingham accents. I took my shoes off at the door, the carpet beige and still with the new smell that took months to wear off. There were three small rooms, a bedroom with a double bed, a lounge area which led into a kitchenette and a bathroom. Each space was immaculate, as though a cleaner had been in, or maybe Sally had tidied up. I could be doing Grace a disservice, she might be a neat freak like Helena. Perhaps Jack's taste lent to women who tidied up after themselves.

Sally moved around, rearranging items, smoothing down Grace's bed cover and plumping the cushions on the sofa, as if she was getting ready for her imminent arrival. It hurt to watch, so I turned away, scanning every surface for something that looked like it didn't belong. I didn't know if Jack had ever been here. Had he crept in late at night when the Stewarts were fast asleep, a little like I'd been doing in his home? It seemed like the perfect place to carry out an illicit affair.

'It's beautiful,' I admitted. 'Grace must absolutely love it.'

'Yes, she did all the decorating herself, has quite an eye.'

On Grace's white bedside table was a book of love poems with a faded cover. I wasn't sure if it was for decoration or she was reading it.

'Grace was into poems?' I gestured towards the book.

Sally looked up from where she'd been staring at a small stain on the carpet. 'No, it was a gift I think.'

I opened the book and a handwritten note on the title page caught my eye.

I am like a fish in love with a bird wishing I could fly away.

Was that Jack's handwriting? I surreptitiously took a photo and placed the book back where it was.

I needed to get the feature written and sent to Des, it had to be up on the website before the body was identified and I had an idea.

'Do you have another photo of Grace I can borrow?'

'Of course, there's more in the house.' Sally hovered by the door and I sensed my time was up.

'Did you know Grace went out on Wednesday night?' I asked as we made our way up the path.

'No, there's a side gate for her to come and go, she doesn't need to come through the house. She wanted to have her own entrance, so she didn't disturb us.'

'When did you first realise she was missing?'

'I popped down to collect some washing from her on Thursday morning, expecting to find her getting ready, but it looked like she'd not returned home. Her bed hadn't been slept in and her car is on the driveway. I called her mobile, which was switched off, and later I called the school, who said she'd not come in. I knew straight away something was wrong, but the police weren't interested.'

'Have you seen the police since you made the official missing report?'

'Not a dickie bird.' Tears sprouted at the corners of Sally's eyes and I rested a hand on her arm.

'I'll make sure her photo is on the website today; it'll go on all of our social media pages too.' I shouldn't be making promises I wasn't sure I'd be able to keep, but Sally's world had crumbled around her and I wanted to help.

'Thank you. Here's another photo.' She retrieved another from the fridge. It was covered in them, some family shots but mainly of Grace, their angel. My heart broke and I thanked Sally for her time, telling her I'd be in touch, although it would likely be Neil or the police who knocked at her door next.

It took five minutes to walk back to Church Road, so Jack didn't have far to go if he was sneaking out to visit Grace. The weather had taken a turn and rain fell diagonally, soaking my hair and face. My feet were like lead, each step an effort as if I'd consumed Sally's turmoil since being in her presence. I stood underneath a tree for shelter, across the road from the Reillys' house. Today there was a liveried car with Merry Maids on the side, which explained why the house was always so clean. While I weighed up my options of entry to the house, I called Des.

'Any news on the body?' I asked, without bothering to say hello.

'Not yet. Have you got anything for me?'

'I have a piece on Grace to send over, with photos and quotes from her mum and friend.'

'You have been busy.' I could hear the wisp of a smile in Des's voice.

'Can you get it on the website and socials as soon as I send it?'

'Sure and I'll let Neil know you'll be in touch – if it's her, of course.'

'I'd like to know as soon as you do.'

'Of course, kiddo.' His constant use of the nickname irked me, but I let it go.

'Thanks, Des,' I said, hanging up, knowing I had

to get inside and write the feature as soon as possible.

The Merry Maids car drove past me and I made my way around the back, trying to avoid the puddles of mud forming in the garden. Taking my shoes off immediately once inside, the smell of a citrus cleaning fluid emanated from every surface.

It was after three and Jack would be home soon with Nathan. I hadn't eaten since breakfast and quickly made myself a sandwich to take upstairs, coming back down when I remembered I had to return the spare front door key to its rightful place.

The phone was still in the cistern and I'd left the photo of Grace propped up on the sink. It was a cruel trick, but I wanted to see how Jack would react, hoping it would tell me what I was desperate to know.

Jack and Nathan didn't return home until after six and Helena was already with them. I guessed they'd met and gone for dinner because I heard no rattling of pans or the smell of dinner cooking. Nathan came upstairs to change, dancing around and singing to himself when he found the chocolate fairy had been. This time he didn't alert his parents to his discovery and for that I was grateful. It would be our secret.

Before they got back, I'd written the feature on Grace and scanned the photos Sally had given me with an app on my phone. A short time later, it was up on the website and social media pages. Her name was out there and if anyone had any information about Grace and Jack's affair, hopefully it would prompt them to come forward. If not, I could call in anonymously with a tip-off, but if they investigated him, selfishly I knew my time at Church Road would be up.

'Nathan, come on, buddy, it's movie night. We've got popcorn,' Jack called from the hallway below, and I heard the familiar creak on the stairs leading up to the master suite.

He went straight into the en suite, freezing at the threshold, noticing Grace's photo straight away.

'What the fuck!'

13

I knew immediately I'd made a mistake. Jack stalked around the room, the photo gripped tightly in his hand, muttering under his breath. He rushed over to the window and looked out onto the driveway below. What had I been thinking? I might as well have advertised I was there because he knew someone had been inside the house. Unless he suspected Helena – or Grace, if he knew nothing about her whereabouts.

I shrank back against the wall when his footsteps came close, watched as his hand reached out to tug the wardrobe open. My throat closed, mouth turned to ash, heart stopping in its tracks. My time was up, it was game over; I'd been such a fool. What would he do when he discovered me here, living in his house, a plate at my feet and a sleeping bag on the floor?

He'd recognise me for sure and how would I explain myself? That I was doing a feature on phrogging and decided his house would be perfect for the exercise? Was he violent? Would he drag me out by the scruff of the neck? I had no idea what he was capable of, whether he'd been the one to make Grace disappear. I'd have to run. I'd push past him with my laptop and flee, everything else could be left behind.

The door wobbled and I bit down on my lip, Nathan's angelic voice filled the oppressive silence.

'Daddy, come on. Mummy's waiting for us. We're watching *The Lion King*.'

I heard the scrunch of the photo and bit my lip.

'I'm coming, mate, was just having a wee.' Jack's voice was strained, but thankfully footsteps descended the stairs and I was finally able to exhale.

Would he come back and search this room? Why had I done something so reckless. I shoved my things into my rucksack, needing to find somewhere else to sleep, but where? Did I attempt to sneak out and go to Megan's? As I was debating, footsteps came up the stairs again. Jack was back, but this time he went straight into the en suite and locked the door.

I heard him remove the phone, the tinkle it made

when it was switched on, then he spoke. His words were hushed, but I could still make them out.

'Have you been here? Inside my fucking house? That's not acceptable, we're done. Stay the fuck away from me and my family.'

Had it been a call or a voicemail? Had he just spoken to Grace, was she alive and well? My mind whirled, but I had no time to gather my thoughts. The toilet flushed and he unlocked the door, trotting back down the stairs.

'Sorry, dodgy stomach,' he called as he went, 'I'm ready now.'

All the research I'd done clearly hadn't been enough. I'd only been here for three nights and already so much had happened I hadn't been expecting. I spent the time they were watching the movie working on my blog post, although I didn't report a body had been found. I switched between the blog post and monitoring the comments on Grace's updated missing Facebook post and any coming through to the *Crawley News*. Plenty of well-wishers but nothing of any substance. No word from Des either.

When Jack and Helena came upstairs while Nathan was in the bath, I heard them discuss plans to visit Hever Castle in Kent tomorrow, the place where Anne Boleyn grew up. It seemed they'd got over their row, or rather he'd convinced her there wasn't anyone else. At least she had some sense of what was going on but maybe was prepared to over-look his indiscretions to ensure the future of their family. My heart went out to her, trying to hold all the pieces together.

When they went to bed, I listened to them talking in whispers, unable to make out what they were saying. Eventually, the hallway light went out and Jack began to snore. I set my blog to post overnight and shut my laptop down. Megan mes-saged to find out when we were going to the cinema because I hadn't confirmed and I hurriedly booked tickets for the Saturday afternoon two o'clock show-ing. With Mum's charitable donation, at least I'd be able to buy her lunch for a change.

I got comfortable, as much as anyone could in a wardrobe, with Grace on my mind, visualising Sally sitting by the phone and waiting for news that might never come. No one in the community had reported a body had been found, but it wouldn't be long; to-morrow I was sure the news would be everywhere. The police could only keep it out of the media for a day or so. In fact, I was surprised no one locally had posted about police vans and yellow tape. Even if they didn't know what the situation was, people were usually so nosy they'd put a post up to try to find out what was going on. It had to mean the body they'd found was somewhere inconspicuous or off the beaten track.

Eventually, I fell asleep, soothed by the repetitive snores coming from Jack and Helena's room below and the rain tapping on the skylight. In the morning, Nathan's shouting woke me up. He was excited about his trip, especially as Jack had promised to buy him a sword and told him he could get knighted at the castle. From that point on, he would only be addressed as Sir Nathan and Helena was exasperated trying to get him ready, wanting to make a start on their journey before the traffic got busy.

Once they'd left, I slipped downstairs to eat, having a nose around in the fridge, when I heard the key in the front door.

'Fuck!' I hissed, shutting the fridge and darting into the utility room to hide behind the washing basket. Was the landscape gardener working the weekend? Did he have a key to the front door? I was partially dressed, freezing on the tiled floor as adrenaline coursed around my system.

'Bloody hell, Jack, you left it on the side,' Helena shouted, grabbing whatever it was Jack had left behind and marching out the front door, slamming it behind her.

'That was too close.' I let air out through my cheeks, hoisting myself up on the empty basket, making it wobble precariously, my gaze drawn to the washing machine opposite. It was off, but something sat at the bottom of the drum, something green. My skin prickled as I opened the door and pulled out a freshly washed but still damp green Joules coat.

'Oh my God.'

I held it up, hands trembling as I searched for signs of stains or anything to confirm it was Grace's. What did I expect, her name sewn into the lining? She wasn't twelve, for goodness' sake! Maybe Helena had the same coat, it was possible.

You know that's bullshit, the voice in my head interjected, breaking the chain of thought before I could convince myself.

What was the likelihood of Helena and Grace having the exact same coat? It had to be Grace's, but now it had been washed, was there any of her left on it? I put it back in the machine, not sure what else to do. There was only one reason he'd have her coat and that didn't bear thinking about. How brazen of Jack not only to wash it, but to leave it damp in the machine. Wouldn't Helena see it or did he take care of the laundry in the house? I knew Helena was a high-flyer with a top London job and Jack did most of the cooking, but did he do the other chores too? It was evidence, cold hard evidence, right before my eyes and I couldn't ignore it. I had to tell the police.

As if the planets had aligned, my phone flashed where I'd put it down on the tiles. It was a message from Des tearing me away from my discovery.

> Body has been identified, no name released yet, but family has been informed.

My empty stomach rolled, bile rising in my throat as my mind turned to Sally and the knock on the door she could have received last night or early this morning. The world of pain her and her husband would be in right now. As soon as it was confirmed as being Grace, I'd tell the police everything, not about the phrogging, but about the affair, the coat, the phone and the handwritten note in the book of poems.

The latter had slipped my mind and I left the utility room to look for the shopping list on the kitchen side. A few more items had been added, but

I wasn't interested in the food the Reillys were going to buy. Pulling up the photos on my phone, I checked the one I'd taken of the inscription inside the book of poems. My legs turned to liquid and I reached out to grasp onto a chair at the breakfast bar. The handwriting was a match. Jack had written that for Grace in a book of love poems he'd gifted her.

Had he been in love with her, so infatuated he'd killed her when things went wrong? Either she'd wanted to end things or had gone too far in her threat to tell Helena about their affair? It made sense, but what I didn't understand was who Jack had called on his burner phone once he'd discovered the photo of Grace I'd left for him. If he'd hurt her, why would he be calling her? The only possibility was he was being smart, trying to contact her after the event, so when the police found her phone, it would show he'd rung her. If that was the case, it meant he was even more calculating than I'd realised.

* * *

Blog Post #4
www.phrogging.com

Things are seriously weird. I'm not sure how much longer I'll be able to stay. None of the family suspect I'm here. I've not been seen or left anything lying around that could cause them to question a presence in the house.

There are workmen in the garden, which is like a mud bath due to the rain we've had, but I've managed to get in and out safely, clearing up after myself. They have a cleaner too, I saw her yesterday as she was leaving, but I'm not sure if it's more than a weekly visit yet, but it's another unexpected arrival I might have to take into consideration when I think I have the place to myself. I mainly use their food for breakfast and no one appears to have missed anything. I'm taking the minimal amount to stay under the radar, eating cold or dry food so as not to leave any odours.

But here's the thing, the mistress is still missing and I don't know whether the husband has anything to do with it. I think I need to go to the police with what I know because it seems no one knew they were having an affair. I've found underwear and a burner phone which I believe might be connected to her.

I'm still hoping she'll eventually turn up safe and sound, but as the hours pass, it's looking unlikely. If the police investigate him, they might search the house and I'll have to be out of here by then.

Thank you for all your comments. I'm glad you're enjoying the blog. What started out as a way to document my experience has turned into something much more. I can't emphasise research enough, phroggers, maybe if I'd watched the house for longer, I might have realised not all was as it seemed.

As always, I'll keep you updated. Stay safe out there.

14

There were so many notifications popping up from my blog, my phone would not stop buzzing. I reread it, but considering what I now knew it sounded stupid and immature. A woman's body had been found, but I couldn't include that information without knowing more, I wasn't so desperate for likes. Knowing she had been identified and the family informed, the gravity of the situation was sinking in. It could be Grace and I was bloody blogging like a teenage influencer trying to make herself heard in a wall of noise. Yet people needed to know what was happening, that had always been the reason I wanted to be a journalist. Spreading news and keeping the public informed, but my words now felt like clickbait. Dirty and sordid.

Still reeling from the coat, which was pretty much a smoking gun in my eyes, I retreated back upstairs for a shower, no longer hungry for breakfast. Once washed and dressed, I scoured social media for any mention of a body being found, but it wasn't in the public domain yet. I messaged Des, asking when we'd get a name, but he didn't respond. A local murder, if that's what it was, was rare and *Crawley News* or rather Neil, would be all over it, trying to get ahead of the game.

I attempted again to get into the burner phone Jack had switched off but couldn't get past the code. I picked at my nails in frustration, tearing at the cuticles. What more could I do. Nothing except wait until the body was confirmed as Grace's. I debated whether to contact Dawn again, ask how well she knew Jack from St Wilfrid's School and whether she thought he might be having an affair, but in reality it wasn't likely she'd be partial to that information. If Grace had kept him a secret, the only one who had answers was him and he was enjoying a day out at Hever Castle, playing the perfect family man. It was bullshit and I hammered the wall with my fist, a ball of rage which had nowhere to go.

My phone buzzed impatiently.

Phrogger365: Oh my god, what if he's murdered her?

Phrogster79: Is there a basement, I bet she's down there?

MasterofPhrog: Dude wanted to have his cake and eat it too.

Yourplaceismine: Geez, you need to get out of there, doesn't sound safe.

The comments kept coming, springing up before my eyes with each refresh. No valid suggestions, just people sat at their laptops watching my journey unfold and waiting with bated breath for the next instalment. Voyeurs wanting horror and scandal, starving for it. They repulsed and fascinated me in equal measure, like rubberneckers at the scene of an accident.

The walls of the bedroom were closing in and I was eager to get out into the fresh air. After yesterday's downpour, today it was dry, the sky a pale grey with the sun trying to break through. I wanted to be outside, to try to lift my mood and get rid of the dark clouds consuming my mind. Tidying my things and stacking them at the top of the far wardrobe, as out of sight as possible, I took my rucksack with me and left Church Road via the garden.

With no clear destination in mind and the cinema not until the afternoon, I didn't go straight for the path I'd created through the bracken. Instead I headed down the bank at its flattest point to walk along the disused railway line. I knew I'd made a mistake almost as soon as I reached the old line and my trainers squelched in the mud. Cursing and about to turn back, a voice in the distance made me press on through the sludge to where the track curved. Around fifty feet ahead of the bend, two police officers in uniform guarded a gazebo erected behind a string of yellow tape. It flapped in the breeze, secured to each side of the bank so I couldn't go any further even if I'd wanted to.

Retreating behind a tree, I watched as scenes of crime officers in white suits gathered beneath the flimsy structure that looked as though it might take off. I'd stumbled upon the location of the body. Who had come down here to slog through the mud and found it? I guessed a dog walker, it always seemed to be, but the body had since been moved. The police had to believe it wasn't an accident or misadventure if SOCO had been called out. Was it a coincidence being so close to Jack's house and not far from Grace's either? I wasn't sure there were such things any more, not where he was concerned. It all added up and the reality hit me. If it was Grace, I could be living with a killer.

I stumbled backwards, falling on an exposed tree root and hitting the ground with a thud. Scrambling up the bank, not wanting to be seen, I headed straight back into Jack and Helena's garden, covered in mud. My plan for fresh air forgotten, I let myself into the house, struggling for breath, my entire body shaking. What if I'd been seen? How would I explain I was just out having a Saturday morning ramble, surely the police would want to know who I was. The proximity of the body being dumped to the house freaked me out.

I waited by the back door, letting the comforting silence envelop me. Everything was filthy, my jeans and trainers, even the sleeves of my coat. I stripped where I stood and put everything in the washing machine, taking the Joules coat out with the bare tips of my fingers and leaving it on the floor. I might as well wash all my clothes while I was at it. Running upstairs in my underwear, I put on Helena's bathrobe, the smell of her perfume cloying, and collected the rest of my clothes, throwing them on a quick wash and dry cycle.

I wandered the house like a ghost in the white robe, looking in cupboards and drawers. Now I'd found the coat, I was sure there must be other clues, more evidence linking Jack to Grace. I checked whether the pink lacy thong was still under their bed and it was. There was bound to be plenty of DNA evidence on it, perhaps both of theirs. It was gross. What else could I find?

Nathan's room looked like it had been hit by a tornado. The wrappers from the chocolate bars I'd left him had been stuffed behind the headboard and I slipped them into Helena's robe to get rid of the evidence. It occurred to me to check Jack's coat pockets and I padded down to look through the cupboard under the stairs.

Inside was a multitude of coats and jackets for all of the family and I painstakingly pulled out tissues, coins, sweet wrappers, checking all the receipts until I found one in a tweed jacket with leather patches on the elbows.

'A real country gent, eh, Jack.' I sniggered as I unfolded it, checking the date.

A thud came from behind me and I dropped the

receipt, jumping out of my skin. The front door rattled and I practically climbed inside the cupboard until I gathered it was the postman. He'd put a parcel through the door, followed by multiple letters, and I had to resist the urge to scoop them up once my heart rate returned to normal.

You don't live here, remember, Molly; this isn't your house.

Once the postman had gone, I dropped to my knees, rummaging through the shoes and looking for the receipt, finding it in one of Helena's mud-crusted trainers.

The Golden Lotus was a small Chinese restaurant on the edge of town. A family-run place which had been going for years and was somewhere my dad loved to take my mum for crispy duck. They often took me too; we were regulars there for about a decade. Looking at the date, Jack had been dining out on the same night I'd had dinner with Megan. On the receipt was a set banquet for two and a bottle of red wine. So while Helena had been working late, Jack had called in Sam to babysit and gone out to enjoy dinner. Conveniently on the same night Grace didn't come home.

If he'd done something to her, harmed her in any way, he hadn't been an expert in covering his tracks.

Although if that was never his plan and an argument had escalated, he had to be in damage-limitation mode now. Was he so confident he wouldn't get caught he'd left the Joules jacket lying around for anyone to find? Helena already suspected his dalliances with other women, she'd said as much to his face. Did he have some kind of hold on her or was she so driven to keep the family together she'd put up with his indiscretions? That didn't tally with the impression I had of Helena, but perhaps like many women, she was strong and powerful in the corporate world but at home her husband was the one in charge.

15

I closed the cupboard, pocketing the receipt, and went back upstairs, killing time until the washing machine finished my clothes. Sun blasted through the skylight, heating the master suite, and I lazed on the chaise longue in Helena's robe like I was lady of the manor. These were the moments I liked best, when the house was empty and would be for hours. I could make noise, use appliances and exist without creeping around, pretending the place was mine.

I took the opportunity to give Mum a call and thank her for transferring me money. As far as she was aware, I was still lodging with Megan and she nagged at me to sort out a place of my own, but my heart lay in the camper van I was saving for, not for four concrete walls and a roof.

My mind found its way back to the receipt once I'd finished listening to Mum tell me how her and Dad had ended up at a foam party last night. Who even were my parents anymore? Were they regressing? Some of what they did made me cringe, but at least they were happy. I didn't tell them a local woman had gone missing and a body had been found, I didn't want them to worry Crawley was no longer a safe place to live. If they found out I was potentially living with a killer, they'd both have a coronary.

I guessed it was impossible to find out whether Grace had dinner with Jack on Wednesday night. The police would have access to any local CCTV and phone records, whereas I was on my own with limited resources. CCTV didn't have to be only accessed by the police though; there might be a way around it. With an idea popping into my head, I dashed downstairs and waited impatiently for my clothes to finish. They still had another fifteen minutes, so I made myself a sandwich and a cup of tea. I ate and washed the dishes, having a quick look around the house to make sure there was no evidence I'd been there.

Eventually, the cycle ended. My clothes were

rumpled, but at least they were clean and dry. I quickly got dressed, returning Helena's bathrobe to its rightful place and putting the Joules coat back in the washing machine before heading out. Knowing the tumble dryer would cool before the Reillys returned. I guessed they'd be back around mid- to late-afternoon. It was lunchtime, but I didn't have to meet Megan until quarter to two at the cinema, I'd have plenty of time to get to the Golden Lotus and back.

The Chinese restaurant wasn't close enough to walk, so I waited for the bus after having a good look over the bridge as I passed to see if the tent was still up. I couldn't make anything out through the trees, so perhaps they'd taken it down, having found all the evidence there was to find. I shuddered in my jacket despite the sun. The air was crisp and I couldn't get the image of Grace lying on a mortuary slab out of my head.

I told myself it wasn't confirmed yet, but who else was it going to be? I needed to tell the police what I knew: Jack had the coat and he was having an affair with her, those two things I knew for certain. However, I couldn't say for definite Grace was who he'd called from the burner phone or had seen the night she disappeared. Hopefully, if it was Grace, they'd find DNA evidence on her body and once Jack's name had been anonymously given to the police, they'd have their man. My gut instinct told me he was involved and a renewed sense of worry clung to me. Who was I living with?

The bus finally arrived and I sat next to an Indian woman in a colourful orange and blue sari who had a bag of shopping nestled between her feet. Hot air pumped out of the vent and the journey was uncomfortably warm. Crawley was made up of small pockets of residential areas which surrounded the town centre, each having their own parades of shops and I was making my way to Tilgate. The bus was going the longest, most scenic route and by the time I got off, I was sweating.

Glad to be back out in the fresh air, I walked past the local Co-op, the estate agents, hairdressers and betting shop, where people milled about outside, heading for the Chinese restaurant. I hadn't expected it to be overly busy on a Saturday lunchtime, but it was rammed with a large party enjoying the 'all you can eat' lunch buffet. I squeezed inside and loitered by the door, waiting for a member of staff to notice me.

Mrs Chen, the owner, made her way through the tables, her eyes lighting up when she saw me. Since

I'd last seen her, her hair had turned a silvery grey and she seemed smaller in stature but still the formidable woman I remembered.

'Milly!' she said, her arms opening.

I didn't have the heart to correct her, unable to believe she recognised me after what must have been two years since I'd last dined here with my parents.

'Hello, Mrs Chen, how are you?'

'Good, good, busy. How are your parents?'

'They are living it up in Torrevieja!' I said gleefully, but Mrs Chen looked momentarily confused.

'Spain?'

'Yes, they're still in Spain.'

'Wonderful, wonderful, we miss them. Are you hungry?'

'No, I'm here for something else.' I jumped as a loud cheer erupted from one of the tables. 'Do you have time for a quick chat? Sorry, I know you're busy.'

'Yes, yes, come where it's quiet.'

Mrs Chen led me towards the rear of the restaurant, to the passageway where the kitchen was.

'I was hoping I'd be able to look at your CCTV, if you have it?' I looked around, spying a dome-shaped camera attached to the ceiling in one corner.

'Has there been a crime?'

'No,' I replied, realising I hadn't come up with a reason why I needed to see it. 'Umm, my boyfriend was here on Wednesday night, with another woman, I think.'

'Oh goodness, child, hang on.' She patted me on the arm and disappeared into the passageway.

The party filling the restaurant let out another cheer and a helium balloon floated to the ceiling, while a tall man jumped to try to retrieve it. I stood awkwardly, wanting to melt into the bird-print wall-paper, but then Mrs Chen came back, waving me towards her. The door at the end of the passageway led into a storage room, where a dusty monitor and keyboard sat on a table surrounded by packets of food. The shelves along the walls were fit to burst and my stomach rumbled for Schezwan chicken.

Mrs Chen sat down and moved the mouse, the monitor springing to life. Surprisingly tech-savvy for a lady of her years, she navigated back through the security videos to Wednesday's date, dragging the time bar into the evening.

'Know what time?'

'I'm guessing around eight,' I said hopefully, scanning the tables looking for Jack. I spotted him in the top corner of the screen, only half of his face and that of his guest in shot. I stiffened and Mrs Chen glanced up at me.

'You see him?' she asked, narrowing her eyes.

'Yes, thank you, Mrs Chen,' I said, already heading for the door.

'Wait, Milly, here.' She grabbed a bag of fortune cookies from the table, pushing them into my hand. 'Don't leave it so long. Come eat soon, free dessert,' she said, a twinkle in her eye as I bolted out of the door.

'Thanks again,' I called back, rushing to the exit and tripping over a woman's handbag, who tutted as the contents spilled out onto the floor.

'Sorry, sorry,' I muttered as I kept moving, my neck mottled.

Outside on the pavement, I bent double, fearing I was about to be sick.

'You okay, love?' one of the betting shop customers asked me.

'Fine,' I managed, stumbling away, eager to get a moment to myself.

I veered to my left, around the corner where the entrance to the flats above the parade of shops was situated. Moving past the smell of the overflowing bins beneath the stairs, I carried on to the garages behind, where I plopped down on a low wall.

Jack was there all right, I didn't even have to see all of his face to identify him, plus he was wearing the jacket with the leather patches at the elbow in which I'd found the receipt. But the woman opposite him was not Grace Stewart. I had no idea who she was, but she had dark hair like Helena, not blonde. From the few seconds I saw, I could tell the meeting wasn't work related, not from the way the woman was dragging her foot up his trouser leg under the table. She looked familiar, but I couldn't place her; she wasn't Grace.

Everything had been thrown upside down. If Jack wasn't with Grace on Wednesday night, who was the last person to see her? Was the Joules coat more common than I'd thought and it had been Helena's all along? I had so many questions and part of me was glad I hadn't already made an anonymous call to the police dropping Jack's name, because what if I was mistaken. I needed to tell Megan; she'd know what to do.

As I got up and started to walk, something else dawned on me. I'd practically listened to him have sex with Grace, he'd said her name when she was in the room, I hadn't got that wrong. So that meant he was potentially sleeping with more than one woman and Helena's suspicions had been right.

16

The film about deep-sea divers was okay, but my head was elsewhere. The cinema was only half full, but Megan seemed to enjoy the intensity of the movie. I took some notes on my phone, in between shovelling in handfuls of popcorn, intending to write a review later to send off to Des, although it was hardly a priority for him, what with the news about the body. I had been a little late arriving because the bus hadn't been on time and when I'd met Megan outside the cinema, she'd known straight away I had something on my mind, but I'd put it down to being flustered we'd miss the film.

Afterwards, once we were seated in Wagamama's,

she fixed me with a hard stare and I knew the game was up.

'Okay, spill the tea.'

'As long as you don't get mad,' I replied after a long pause, and she frowned so hard, deep rivets appeared between her eyes. 'You know the house I've been staying in, where the guy is having an affair.'

'Yeah.'

'Well, the woman he was having an affair with is the girl who's gone missing.'

'Sandra's nail client? Grace?'

I nodded and watched Megan's mouth drop open.

'Oh my God, Mol, what if he had something to do with it?'

I explained what I'd found out, that they worked together at St Wilfrid's, but Jack had been having dinner with someone else the night Grace disappeared. I told her how I was originally convinced the burner phone with the contact 'Ian' had been used to converse with Grace, but now I wasn't so sure.

'What about the coat though, surely that's a massive red flag?' Megan asked once I'd revealed my discovery in the washing machine.

'It is, but again, I can't prove it's Grace's.' I paused to take a gulp of my Diet Coke. 'There's something else, but you cannot say anything to anyone. It'll probably come out later today or tomorrow anyway.'

'What?' Megan leant forward, nearly dipping her mousy hair into her bowl of katsu curry.

'A body was found, the name hasn't been released yet, but I saw a tent up and it was quite close to Church Road.'

'Holy shit, Mol, I think you need to come back to mine,' her eyes aghast, 'what if you're living with a monster?'

'I don't think so.'

Megan tutted. 'These people always seem so normal, Molly, then they turn. If you're found there, if you're discovered, what do you think will happen? You could get hurt.'

I changed the subject after letting her berate me for a few minutes, but at the end of our meal, Megan made her feelings known. She thought I was crazy to stay, but now I knew Jack hadn't seen Grace that night, I didn't believe he was a threat. When the bill came, Megan tried to pay, but I insisted, and when she invited me back to the flat for a movie and few glasses of wine as her flatmates were away, I agreed.

'You might as well crash, for tonight at least. I'll know you're safe... and you can borrow an iron for those clothes.' She winked at me as she shuffled into her coat.

'Oh piss off.' I laughed.

* * *

The evening was spent talking about everything but Grace and it was bliss not to have it hanging over my head for a few hours. Megan had a date with a guy she'd met online scheduled for next week, so we went through possible outfits, choosing what to wear before slumping down on the sofa to watch *You're Cordially Invited*, the latest Netflix offering. By the time the movie had ended, we'd laughed so hard our stomachs hurt, and we'd quaffed our way through almost two bottles of the local supermarket's finest rosé. We stayed up until the early hours talking. Eventually, I nodded off on the sofa, waking up with a cricked neck and a banging headache, covered in a blanket.

The flat was peaceful, Megan still fast asleep, and I made my way to the kitchen to see if she had any coffee whilst I waited for my phone to come to life. It was before ten, so the high street below was calm due to Sunday trading hours and it was strange not having to creep around. Tiny snores drifted from

Megan's room and I smiled, we'd had such a fun night together and part of me wished I'd taken my best friend up on her offer when she'd suggested renting a place, the two of us. But the pull of the dream camper van had been too much, and if I was honest, my lifestyle was a bit too nomadic for Megan. I had no desire to put down roots in Crawley, or anywhere for that matter.

As I waited for the kettle to boil, a message from Des appeared on the screen of my phone. I recoiled as I saw what he'd sent at six o'clock this morning.

Body is Grace Stewart.

So it was finally confirmed, Grace Stewart was officially deceased. Sally would be devastated at losing her only child, not to mention her husband, who was going through chemotherapy. The world wasn't fair; we were practically the same age and Grace's life had been snuffed out, but by whom?

I let the coffee I'd made grow cold as I stared out of the window of Megan's lounge, looking out onto the high street below, watching the workers scurrying to open their shops and the early consumers already heading their way.

Was now the time to go to the police with what

information I had, or would I be condemning an innocent man? Jack may be a cheating twat, but was he involved in whatever happened to Grace? I wanted to build a picture as much as I'm sure the police did. I also had Helena and Nathan to consider. Would blowing up his family and exposing his infidelity be the right thing to do? I squirmed with indecision, barely even noticing when a yawning Megan emerged from her bedroom in leopard-print pyjamas.

'Morning. God, I feel rough, do you?'

'Grim,' I managed, surprised to find my eyes suddenly welling up.

'What's wrong?' Megan rushed over to me, her loose topknot wobbling.

'It's been confirmed, the body is Grace and I don't know what to do.'

Megan wrapped her arm around me. The warmth of her body fresh from bed radiated comfort.

'You have to go to the police and tell them what you know.'

I sniffed; she was right but I wasn't sure I could do it. Maybe I wouldn't have to, someone else might know about Jack and Grace's affair. I didn't want to be the one responsible for ending his marriage.

Phrogging was cohabiting in secret, not getting involved in other people's lives, but I'd been thrust
into a missing person case whether I liked it or not.
One which could have potentially escalated to a
murder.

'I'll make some more coffee,' Megan said, leaving
to go to the kitchen, rubbing sleep from her eyes.

While she was gone, I grabbed my phone and
messaged Des.

> Do they know the cause of death
> yet or the time?

His reply came quickly, just one word: 'no'.

I couldn't imagine how Sally and Grace's father
felt, likely hanging on by a thread at this point now
their world had imploded.

'Do you have plans today?' Megan asked, returning from the kitchen with two steaming mugs of
coffee.

'No, I need to write that review before I forget
what the film was about, but my laptop is back at the
house.'

'Plenty of time for that. I'll make us some breakfast, shall I?'

I nodded, asking if I could have a shower, hoping

the hot water would cleanse the alcohol and misery from my head.

'Go ahead, you know where the towels are.'

When I returned, my skin pink from how hot I'd had the water, Megan handed me a bacon sandwich, smothered in brown sauce, which I consumed greedily.

'What are you doing today?' I asked.

'Chores obviously; the washing basket is over-flowing. Maybe a Netflix and chill afternoon. Hannah is coming round tonight. You're welcome to stay and join us.' Hannah was Megan's older sister, who was a little snobby. I looked down at my rumpled clothes, decision made instantly.

'No I need to get back at some point, see what is going on at the house. It's weird, I feel out of the loop here – not that I hear much when I'm there.'

'Just be careful, promise me you'll stay in touch by text.'

'I will.'

* * *

It was after lunch when I left, deciding to walk back to Church Road, hoping the fresh air would do me good. I prayed the Reillys weren't having a Netflix and chill day too, which would mean I'd be sitting in the garden all afternoon.

When I got there the driveway was empty with the Mercedes nowhere to be seen, so I ventured around the back as normal, pulling out my phone to see if I could find any clues as to where they'd gone. Helena's Instagram had new posts: four photos from yesterday's trip to Hever Castle with Nathan looking super cute dressed fully as a knight, his face obscured by a massive helmet. It looked like he'd got the sword Jack had promised him, his stance as he wielded it pulling at my heartstrings.

Today she had posted a reel, a Sunday roast with the caption 'Taking my folks out for lunch'. I had no idea where her parents lived but figured it was safe to go inside the house as, in the photo, I could see Jack's hand and Nathan's iPad on the table, so they were all together.

The first thing I did when I got inside was to check the washing machine for the coat, but it had vanished. It must have been moved yesterday afternoon or this morning. Fresh piles of laundry were stacked on the side in the utility room ready for ironing. Thinking Jack might have hidden the evidence, I was surprised to find the coat hanging up in the cupboard under the stairs, recently pressed, with the label cut out. Perhaps it had been Helena's after all. I guessed we'd find out eventually if Grace was wearing her coat when she'd gone missing.

Upstairs, the master suite was as I'd left it, my laptop and creased clothes stacked in the upper section of the far wardrobe. When I saw Helena had posted photos of a crème brûlée minutes before, I decided it was safe to iron my newly washed pile before I wrote the film review and updated my blog. It wasn't until I was halfway through ironing the last item, a pair of jeans, that I heard the key in the door.

17

'Ow, fuck,' Jack hissed as he touched the metal plate of the iron, obviously not expecting it to be burning hot. 'Did you leave the iron on?' he yelled back to Helena as I cowered behind the washing basket. This was it; I was about to be discovered and my brain rapidly tore through a list of excuses as to why I was there. What was a journalist doing in his house?

'I don't think so,' Helena shouted back as Jack unplugged it, before reaching into a cupboard to grab a cloth and some antibacterial spray.

'I think you fucking did,' he muttered, his tone venomous as he ran his hand under the tap. He had his back to me, still in his tweed jacket and brown brogues, looking every bit the country gent. I hadn't even had time to leave the utility room, or unplug the iron, barely having seconds to grab my clothes and squeeze behind the washing basket before he barrelled into the room. Thank goodness the ironing board had already been up as that could have looked extremely suspicious. Although I couldn't imagine I'd believe someone would sneak into my house to do the ironing.

'Nathan, are you okay, honey, do you still feel sick?' Helena cooed in the kitchen and I guessed that was the urgency. I had to remember not to trust Instagram as far as when things were posted.

'I'm going to put him straight in the bath, Jack.' Helena's voice was already drifting away as I imagined her carrying a poorly Nathan up the stairs. Hopefully he'd just eaten too much and didn't have a bug; I didn't want to get ill.

Taking my chance and holding my folded clothes in front of me like a shield, I emerged from the utility room into the empty kitchen. Cold air rushed in from the hallway and I could see the front door was swaying in the breeze. Jack's car door was stretched open and he was half in and half out, wiping down the seat. Footsteps padded overhead as the sound of taps running drifted from the bathroom. I couldn't go up to the master suite now and I didn't want to take the chance of hiding in the cupboard under the stairs, knowing Jack still had his coat and shoes on, so I opened the integral door to the garage. I could hide out in there for a while; they never put the Mercedes inside anyway.

It was dark and cold and for a second I panicked I'd left my phone in the utility room, but it was there nestled in my back pocket. I used the torch to guide my way, finding a plastic storage box at the back to sit on, behind a pile of packing boxes, a rolled-up tarpaulin and an old washing machine as I scrolled through the comments on my blog.

@FoxyPhrog: We need to know what happened!!!!

@Yourplace: OMG I live for this drama!

@SecretSquatter: If this happened to me I'd legit shit my pants.

I had to upload blog post number five. People were crying out for information, but here I was stuck in the garage waiting for my chance to go upstairs. I had no idea how long I'd be here and it was freezing, the smell of oil and bleach clogging my nostrils.

I scrolled through my phone mindlessly, looking again at Helena's Instagram posts. The food they'd had at lunch looked delicious and I was glad I wasn't hungry. Megan was a feeder and I never left there less than stuffed.

Jack burst through the door and I ducked down, nearly dropping my phone onto the hard concrete. Thankfully, he bypassed me and headed for some shelves down the side for what looked like car cleaning fluid. Helena appeared in the doorway a second later; they were obviously mid argument.

'I told you I didn't leave it on.'

'Well you must have done. Did you or did you not iron this morning?' Jack's tone was brusque.

'You know I did,' she sighed, 'you wanted your jeans ironed.'

'Well, there you go; it's not exactly a mystery, is it? Are you trying to burn the fucking place down before we've even been here six months?'

'For goodness' sake!' Helena's hand went to her forehead as though she could scrub Jack's jibe from her brain. 'Nathan's in the bath; did you get the stain out of the upholstery?'

'Almost, the garage will charge a fortune if I take it there.'

'He didn't do it on purpose, Jack, it was probably your bloody driving.'

'That's right, of course it was,' he said sarcastically. 'Isn't everything always my fault?'

Helena tutted. 'Not always. But on another note you still haven't sorted out the camera doorbell or an alarm, we need to make sure the house is secure.'

'Yes, boss.' Jack gave Helena a salute and she rolled her eyes.

'I'm going to get changed.' She whipped around and returned inside the house as I shrank lower on the storage box, grateful I was hidden.

Jack eventually found what he was looking for and disappeared back to his car. I took my chance to leave, knowing they were both busy. The front door was still wide open, did they not care about their heating bills? Venturing up the stairs, I listened for voices. Helena was in the bathroom with Nathan, laughing as he splashed, seemingly having made a full recovery from whatever sickness he'd had. I swept past the landing and up again towards the master suite as fast as I could, trying to keep my footsteps light, almost reaching the top when Nathan's words made my blood run cold.

'That woman was here, Mummy.'

I'd been seen. Nathan had seen me. My throat was thick and I couldn't swallow.

Helena took a few seconds to respond, but when she did, her voice was light, a forced joviality in her tone. 'Don't be silly, Nathan, the only woman here is me.'

'She left me chocolate, but sssshhhh, it's a secret,' he said in what sounded like a pantomime whisper.

Helena let out a nervous chuckle, dismissing Nathan's insistence the chocolate fairy was real. Thank goodness I'd got rid of the wrappers, which were... Shit! Still in Helena's bathrobe, along with the receipt from the Golden Lotus.

I debated whether or not to tiptoe back down to her bedroom and retrieve it from where the robe hung on the back of their bedroom door, but Helena came out of the bathroom, already unbuttoning her silk blouse.

I prayed she was going to put her pyjamas on or some loungewear, anything but the robe. I loitered at the top of the stairs, listening and trying to peak down to the hallway below. Eventually, she returned from her bedroom in sand-coloured loungewear and I breathed a sigh of relief. I'd get the receipt and wrappers later when they were watching television, but I had to be more careful and stop making stupid mistakes.

I retired to the wardrobe, sitting on blankets and my sleeping bag as I wrote the review of the diving film for Des. Once finished, I scrolled through social media, first X, then Facebook, where the news a body had been found had hit the local Crawley page. I devoured the comments, some suggesting it could be, but hoping it wasn't, the missing Grace Stewart.

I knew it wouldn't be long before her name was out there. The anonymous poster had supplied a fuzzy photo of the erected tent and yellow tape, mentioned the disused railway line but not specified where.

Below me, the front door slammed and Jack's footsteps jogged up the stairs.

'Car's done. How's the little man?'

'Fine, I'll come downstairs when he's finished in the bath.' Helena's tone was clipped, but Jack seemed calmer now the car was sorted.

'I'm going to use the toilet upstairs.'

'Just use our en suite,' Helena said.

'You'll only moan if I do.'

Through the crack in the wardrobe door, I watched Jack enter, his head bowed, eyes glued to his phone. He stood in the bathroom over the sink, his skin had a greyish pallor; was he about to be sick too? That was all I needed, stuck in a house with a tummy bug doing the rounds. I waited for him to close the door, but instead he slammed his phone down on the counter and stared into the mirror. A second later, his head drooped and his shoulders shuddered. Was he crying?

His loud sniffs confirmed as much and he wiped at his face, blowing his nose before the door closed, the tap was run and I could no longer see in. Had he seen the post on Facebook? Was it the news a body had been found which had affected him so deeply or the comments that it could be Grace? I was so confused by his actions; I couldn't work him out. Everything pointed to him: the coat, the affair, how he'd been with Grace the time she was here, grabbing her wrist and telling her to 'stop playing games'. But I knew he'd been with someone else the night she disappeared, unless he'd visited her afterwards?

The tears were real, private and gut wrenching to watch, but were they tears of sorrow, of loss or of remorse?

* * *

Blog Post #5

www.phrogging.com

Phew, not long ago I had another near miss that was too close for comfort. Hiding in the same room as the husband and for a few seconds, I thought it was game over. My heart was pounding so fast, I feared he might hear it; I've never felt fear like it. I wrongly assumed the family were out for hours. Turns out, posts on social media aren't always uploaded in real time and I was nearly caught trying to iron some clothes.

At the end of the day, we, i.e. phroggers, are not supposed to be in these houses, we don't belong and keeping ourselves hidden is how we exist simultaneously. I'd love to know, has anyone been discovered and kicked out or faced any violence when confronted? Has anyone been arrested or charged, perhaps with breaking and entering or theft?

Other than my near miss, it's been relatively peaceful. Last night, I stayed at a friend's and it was bizarre moving around so freely; it's like I've been conditioned to be in stealth mode all the time. The workmen haven't been back over the weekend, but I'm sure they will be in the coming week. Three more nights and I would have made it an entire week.

So, here's what I know you're waiting for... the next instalment in the mystery of the missing mistress. I know you're all invested in this ongoing drama, and I feel like I'm reporting from the front line. Whereas I arrived at this beautiful house hoping for a nice peaceful stay, it's turned out to be anything but.

Tragically, the mistress has been found deceased. I'm still reeling from this recent information and trying to work out what to do with it. I've done some digging on my own as to who could be responsible. Some paths lead to the husband, other ones lead away, but as far as I'm aware he wasn't the last person to see her alive. On the evening she didn't come home, he was elsewhere and I know that for certain, although I need to identify who he was with. Not only that, but on him finding out she had been found, he was visibly upset. Grief and shock, not guilt.

I know I need to do the right thing, but I'm not entirely convinced he was the one to harm her. I understand the implications of being so involved, but I also have to rely on my gut.

If the police get involved, I may have to leave, which isn't something I want to do, but I can't get involved in their investigation, nor can I hide what I know. So, as you can tell, I'm in two minds on what to do.

Will update more tomorrow, but in the meantime, those of you who have been caught... let me know what happened.

Appreciate all your support and comments, phroggers.

18

The comments on my previous blog were in the hundreds, so many wanting to know more, now invested in the mystery I was immersed in. I couldn't deny it felt good to know people were waiting with anticipation for my next instalment, it gave me a buzz I'd not experienced before and was kind of addictive.

I heard Helena ask Jack if he was okay when he went back down to the first floor, but he dismissed her, saying he was tired. Nathan was getting out of the bath and the smell of coconut bath foam wafted up the stairs. I breathed it in, longing to plunge beneath the warm water, it had been so long since I'd enjoyed a soak in the tub. Nathan said something I couldn't hear, but Jack's response made me shudder.

'Ghosts don't exist, son, neither do fairies.' His tone was playful and I imagined him giving his son a wink as Nathan giggled like the two of them were sharing a secret.

'Honestly, Nathan, you're being very silly,' Helen reprimanded.

'She was here, I saw her and she must have come back.' His young voice was defiant, but Helena's response was stern.

'Enough now, go and put your pyjamas on and we'll have a go at building the Lego set Nanny bought you.'

'What's he on about?' Jack whispered, barely loud enough for me to hear, their conversation carrying on in the hallway.

'He thinks the house is haunted.'

Jack scoffed and let out a laugh as my chest tightened. Had I been seen and not realised it?

'It doesn't help that you keep sneaking him chocolate,' Helen sniped.

'I'm not... Perhaps it is the fairy.' Something Jack must have did or his facial expression made Helena break into a laugh. It seemed I'd got away with it for now.

I waited until everyone was in the kitchen and I could hear the unmistakable sound of Lego being poured out of a box before creeping down the stairs to rifle through the pockets of Helena's robe. My pulse shot up when for a moment I thought Jack was about to come up, but thankfully he stayed on the ground floor and I was able to get back to the master suite without anyone hearing. I'd learned where all of the creaky floorboards were and knew to avoid them.

At least now I had the receipt and the chocolate wrappers. Nathan had no evidence to share with his parents he'd been visited by the chocolate fairy and I wouldn't be so stupid as to leave him another gift. I had to be more careful, there was so much at risk. I didn't know the family beneath me, what they were capable of and what they would do if they found me here? Would they call the police or deal with me themselves?

Back upstairs inside the safety of the wardrobe, I logged on to phrogging.com, the comments on my latest blog already racking up, even though it had just been posted. One comment made my scalp prickle.

@HomeSweetHome: You're in Sussex aren't you?

I shut the laptop lid with more force than I intended, a fluttering in my chest. How did they know where I was? Sussex was a big area, but it was one hell of a stab in the dark – could they be local? I'd hardy given anything away in the blog posts. Was I attracting online sleuths, as well as phroggers, or did the two go hand in hand?

I snuggled into the sleeping bag, my eyes heavy, debating on whether to have a nap. Tomorrow would be the start of a hell of a week. The media would release Grace's name, then everyone would know and I'd no longer be one step ahead of the curve.

If Grace's death was deemed suspicious, the police would investigate. Surely they'd interview her colleagues at work. Would Jack admit the affair or remain silent? If they didn't at least talk to him about his relationship with her, I'd have a decision to make: anonymously drop them his name or stay quiet and try to find out what happened myself. The first thing I needed to do was work out the identity of the brunette at the Chinese restaurant. Her face was so familiar, but I couldn't place where I'd seen her.

Was Jack having more than one affair or was the woman trying it on, and the snippet of the CCTV I witnessed was her being flirty?

I couldn't forget World Book Day was on Thursday and I'd have an access-all-areas pass to St Wilfrid's School, which I intended to use to my full advantage. At the least I'd be able to find out what the other staff thought of Jack, or get an idea.

With my stomach still full from Megan's feeding, warm and toasty in the sleeping bag, I fell asleep, waking hours later to find the sun had set. The house was in darkness and I was disorientated as I came to, hearing rustling coming from the other side of the wardrobe door. I willed my body to stay still, knowing any movement could give me away. I wiped the drool from my mouth. What if I'd been snoring?

The footsteps on the other side sounded light, unlike Jack's, but I guessed whoever was creeping around was trying not to be heard. I strained to look through the tiny gap in the wardrobe door, seeing only a flash of white satin, like an apparition had passed by. I jolted backwards, squeezing my eyes shut momentarily, praying I hadn't made any noise. It had to be Helena, but what was she doing up here? I hoped she wasn't sorting through the boxes because she had insomnia.

After a couple of minutes, I heard her going back downstairs and ventured out of the wardrobe, my bladder demanding a release. The power lead to a laptop had been left plugged in on the opposite wall. Had she been up here doing something in secret on her laptop? Why not use her office?

I checked my watch, it was five o'clock on Monday morning, early even for Helena. I'd slept for almost twelve hours, my head full of cotton wool and back stiff. It wasn't long before the delicious smell of coffee emanated from downstairs and I imagined Helena sitting at the kitchen table, nursing a steaming mug as the sun rose behind the house.

What had made her get up so early? I had a few hours to kill before the house would be empty, so I booted up my laptop. Des had sent me through an assignment last night, to cover and review a new Turkish restaurant which had opened in the high street this past weekend. Those ones I was more than happy to do, especially when a three-course meal and a drink was covered on expenses. Megan would be only too pleased to come with me, although she always cringed when I took photos of the food, like I was some influencer hoping to get a free meal. Thinking about food my stomach rumbled and I was looking forward to a relatively lazy day in the house with no one home.

Weekends were more difficult; families spent a lot of time at home, which meant I either needed to be out or hidden. It was lovely to have the reset of a night at Megan's and the smell of Nathan's bath last night made me tempted to have one today while the Reillys were at work and school.

I had some preparation to do, questions for World Book Day and I also intended to comb through social media to try to find the mysterious brunette Jack had dined with while I waited for Grace's name to be released. I wasn't sure what I expected, blue flashing lights and a detective to show up at the door putting Jack in handcuffs? No one knew about him and Grace; no one, it seemed, except me, and it weighed heavily on my mind. I had a responsibility to Grace and her parents to make sure her death was fully investigated, which they wouldn't be able to do if they weren't in possession of all the facts.

I scrolled through all the emails in my junk folder, deleting the sales and money-off coupons which had landed overnight, freezing when I saw a handle I recognised from a comment on my blog

post. I'd received an email from homesweet-
home@gmail.com. Opening it, I recoiled.

I know where you are. Crawley. The missing
girl is Grace Stewart... Ask me how I know.

That was it, no formalities or even niceties, it was
straight to the point. How on earth had @Home-
SweetHome got my email address; had they hacked
into my account? And how were they able to say
with certainty the missing girl was Grace Stewart?

Whoever it was wanted me to engage, but there
was no way. It made my skin crawl, like I was being
watched. Someone knew where I was, maybe not
exactly, but close enough. I swiftly checked the blog
post I'd uploaded last night to see whether they'd
exposed me on there, but there was no comment
from @HomeSweetHome. Not yet anyway.

19

I watched as the sun slowly rose, the mist outside evaporating, and the household woke one by one to start their day. Movement below began slow but soon ramped up the closer it got to half past seven when Helena was due to leave. No one came up to the master suite and I twiddled my thumbs, itching to get up and walk around; the wardrobe had been my prison for too many hours.

Once Jack and Nathan left for work and school, I headed downstairs, made some coffee, ate some of Helena's granola which was now half full, then ran myself a bath. It was decadent and reckless soaking away for an hour until the gardeners arrived, banging around in the back garden, their noise disturbing the peace. When I peeked out of the window in the Reillys' bedroom, I was pleased to find even more fence panels had been removed, with no sign of new ones in the garden.

As I got ready, charging my phone and laptop while I applied some make-up, my phone flashed, catching my eye. Des was calling.

'Hello,' I answered.

'It's Des, can you come into the office this morning?' He sounded gruff, which wasn't unusual, but my insides clenched all the same.

'Sure,' I replied, as brightly as I could before he hung up. What was I being summoned for? Either he had another crappy job for me or I was going to be torn off a strip, but for what I didn't know. He'd let me go with the Grace article and agreed to publish it on the website and social media pages of the *Crawley News*, so it couldn't be that.

I slipped out of the front door a while later, jogging to the gate and scooting over it. I wanted to get off the driveway as fast as possible in case someone asked me what I was doing there or the gardener came out to his van. I caught the bus into town and overheard two elderly ladies sat behind me talking about Grace.

'It's terrible, isn't it? This place is going downhill.

Young women are not safe to walk the streets at night anymore.'

'You're right. We never used to even lock our doors, Anne, how times have changed.'

'That poor woman's family, they must be going through hell right now.'

I quickly scanned Facebook, where Grace's name had been posted in the local group. *Crawley News* had reported the body of the female had been identified as Grace Stewart and the family had asked for privacy as they came to terms with their devastating loss.

My stomach sank. Despite knowing the news was coming, now it was out there, sadness surged through me. It was real: Grace was dead. There was no information posted on a cause of death and it looked like the nationals hadn't picked it up yet when I searched their website. Again, it wouldn't be long, a young single white female from a good background, they would deem it newsworthy.

Perhaps that's what Des wanted, everything I had on Grace so we could stay ahead of the curve, but when I arrived in the office at about half ten, he was holed up with Neil, who I could see gesticulating wildly through the glass.

'Shit's gone down this morning.' Jo Street, the

favourite of my co-workers, looked up from her monitor. She was tall, slim and always looked glamorous but had a hilarious potty mouth which made Des wince and me howl with laughter.

'What's happened?' I asked, looking first at her, then over at Des.

Jo took a large gulp of coffee from her flamingo print mug, as though she was steeling herself to tell me something awful. Her words spilt out in a mad rush. 'Well, first of all, I've got the hangover from hell. I mean, who goes out on a Sunday anyway, those mojitos will be the fucking death of me. Then this guy gropes me in the queue for the loo. I grabbed him by the balls and—'

'No, Jo, what's gone down here? Why is Neil doing the YMCA in Des's office?' I interrupted.

'God knows, but he's got a cob on about something, probably that poor girl. Another female lost to some misogynistic twat, no doubt.' Jo chewed her biro thoughtfully.

'Well, you still look bloody gorgeous with a hangover.' I patted her on the shoulder as I caught Des's eye and he waved me towards him.

'Cheers, I feel like shit.'

I left Jo and knocked on Des's office door, a small pathetic rap like I was a sheep going into the lion's den. As much as I didn't want to feel intimidated by Neil, he was so angry about something, I physically shrank.

'Her! She writes about bloody lollipop ladies and missing dogs!'

'Neil, that's enough. If they've asked for her, there's bugger all we can do about it and Molly's a fantastic reporter, she just needs a break.'

'What's going on?' I chipped in.

'Yeah, a break, on my bloody story!' Neil snapped, ignoring my question.

Des waved his hands, trying to calm Neil down, and sighed, looking at me with an amused glint in his eyes. 'Sally Stewart will only speak to you as far as the press are concerned.'

Des's words left me momentarily reeling.

'Well good luck with that. Family liaison is there now, you won't get anywhere near her,' Neil spat, his face almost puce.

'Okay, what's the angle? Grief story, murder plot, what?' I asked, Neil's vitriol spurring me on. I had to stay professional and try to push all emotion aside.

'Murder plot? How much have you told her?' Neil demanded.

'Neil, if you wouldn't mind stepping out, go and have a fag or something before you burst a blood vessel. You have your contact at the police, we're all going to have to work together on this one, okay?'

Neil stormed out, slamming the door and leaving the fitted blind swinging.

'Jesus.' Des rubbed the back of his neck. 'Take a seat, Mol.'

I slid into the chair, dropping my rucksack on the floor with a thud.

'As you know, the woman's body has been confirmed as Grace Stewart. Neil tried at the house, but Sally will only speak to you, so I need you to hotfoot it round there and get an interview, on record, another photo too.'

I nodded, although my eye twitched. How was I supposed to interview that poor woman whose whole world had just fallen apart? It was the one thing I hated about reporting, we were supposed to have no emotions, thick skin, we were there to do a job. It was something I'd always struggled with.

'Neil's contact at the station has let slip there's going to be a criminal investigation,' Des revealed.

'Has the medical examiner's report come back?'

'Not officially. Cause of death looks to be a broken neck.'

I grimaced, visualising Jack's large hands

squeezing the life out of Grace as she lay beneath him, powerless to do to anything.

'Caused by strangulation?' I asked.

'Apparently not, but...' Des paused to take a deep breath. 'Circumstances don't match up with anything accidental.'

'How do you mean? Was she sexually assaulted?' I rubbed my clammy palms on my jeans. It was too warm in Des's tiny office. I waited for him to speak.

'No, but... Not a word to anyone, okay?' Des pointed at me and I nodded so hard I feared my head might topple from my shoulders. 'Someone poured bleach all over her body.'

'What!' The saliva in my mouth turned to dust. There was only one reason someone would do that and it was in the vain hope of getting rid of evidence.

'Yep, I'm not even sure the parents have been informed of that at the moment, so be led by them, okay? We can't publish anything not from their lips, otherwise we'll be giving up our source. So this is your chance, kiddo, in with the big leagues now.'

I stood up on wobbly legs and slid my rucksack onto my shoulder. For some reason, it felt heavier than before.

'Do the police have anything yet?' I asked.

'Not that I'm aware.' I pressed my lips together, I

was right in the centre of the entire case with knowledge no one knew and I felt the pressure building in
my temples.

I turned towards the door until Des's voice
stopped me.

'Have you got anything you want to share? I
know you've been doing a bit of digging on Grace.'

My face grew hot, but I kept eye contact.

'Nothing concrete,' I said flippantly, 'but I'll keep
you updated.'

'Show Neil you deserve to be here, yeah. Make
me proud.'

I smiled at Des's twinkly eyes. Heaven forbid if
he ever found out I was knee-deep in the crime that
had been committed and had witnessed Grace's affair first-hand.

20

I mouthed goodbye to Jo, who was on the phone as I left, deciding to walk to Sally's and stopping off on the way to buy a small bouquet of white roses. Neil was right, if the police liaison officer was already there, they would be gatekeeping any access by the media. No doubt trying to block anything being printed; that's what usually happened. We were the bane of any police investigation, except for when they wanted our help, but I doubted they'd believe a small-fry reporter from *Crawley News* would be worth getting their knickers in a twist about.

On the driveway of Sally's bungalow was a dark Volvo hatchback that hadn't been there before, blocking in what I assumed was Grace's white Fiat

500. I loitered outside for a while, fearing it belonged to the family liaison officer, taking a pew on a wall across the road. At least I'd arrived before any other reporters, anxious there might already be tape cordoning the house off and journalists outside with their cameras. It would hit the national news for sure, especially when the details of Grace's death were published.

I waited for around fifteen minutes, planning in my head what I would say to the family liaison officer, when a woman in her early forties wearing a polyester navy suit left the house and climbed into the Volvo. She barely gave me a second glance as she drove past me. As soon as she was out of sight, I crossed the road and knocked on the door.

'Who is it?' Sally's voice came through the red painted wood and I imagined the liaison officer telling her not to answer anyone who stopped by uninvited.

'Sally, it's Molly, from *Crawley News*. I wanted to see how you are.' I kept my voice soft, trying to be as friendly and non-threatening as possible. The last thing I wanted was to spook her.

'Molly,' Sally greeted as she opened the door, and I held the flowers out in front of me, making sure to keep a respectful distance.

'I'm so sorry for your loss, Sally, for you and your husband.'

She took them, holding the blooms to her pink nose. Her eyes were red-rimmed and she wore no make-up. With her hair scraped back into a severe bun, she looked like a ghost of the woman I'd seen before.

'Thank you for the article you wrote... She was found soon after.'

I doubted I had anything to do with that but smiled politely anyway.

'Is there anything I can do for you? Either of you? Do you need any shopping or prescriptions picked up?'

Sally shook her head; she didn't need to say the words, I knew all she wanted was her daughter back and that was something I couldn't offer her.

'Okay. Do you think you might have time for a chat?'

Sally's weak smile slipped and I added, 'I would love to hear more about Grace and what the police are doing to find out what happened to her.'

'I'm not supposed to,' Sally said, her eyes filling. I'd blown it, but then she added, 'I can't see it'll do any harm.'

She drew the door back further and invited me

in, bypassing the kitchen altogether, where a stack of unwashed mugs sat on the side, stained with tea.

'I've been spending a lot of time in the annexe,' she said, leading the way out of the back door and down the garden path. I wasn't surprised, Sally likely felt closest to her daughter there, surrounded by her things.

It was warm inside and we sat at Grace's small table in the kitchen.

'Do you mind if I record this, to make sure I get it right?' I asked, setting my phone to voice record on the pink tablecloth.

Sally nodded. She looked like she'd lost weight since I last saw her, not that she had any to lose. Her face was gaunt and the dark circles beneath her eyes had taken up residence.

'When did you find out Grace had been discovered?'

Sally told me how the knock on the door came early on Saturday morning, a detective requested some hair from Grace's hairbrush so they could see if it was a match. They told her they didn't think it was a good idea to view the body and I guessed it was because of the bleach. I had no idea what those chemicals would do if left sitting on the skin for any amount of time.

'Yvonne, the family liaison officer, arrived with a detective on Sunday to inform us of the news. She's been here ever since; she's just popped out.' Sally's shoulders shook and I got up to retrieve a tissue from the side.

'Do they have any idea what happened?'

'Her neck was broken and I thought, she must have fallen. They told me she was on the disused railway line that runs up towards Worth Church, but then they said it looked suspicious.' Sally dropped her head into her hands, her next sentence muffled. 'I can't imagine anyone hurting her, she was loved by everyone.'

'I'm so sorry, Sally, I can't imagine what you're both going through.' I rested my hand on her forearm, my mind flashing to Yvonne and how long it would be before she returned and threw me out on my ear.

'It's devastating. Roy hasn't got out of bed since; he's given up.'

'Have the police asked about her friends, boyfriends?'

'I told them I didn't think Grace was seeing anyone; they looked around in here. I gave them a few of her friend's phone numbers and told them she worked at the school. They wanted a picture of her day-to-day life, but if I'm honest, I think they are as clueless as us as to why this happened.'

I nodded, knowing I had to give them Jack's name, looking into Sally's grief-stricken eyes – how could I not?

'They took her laptop, but her mobile phone is missing.'

I raised an eyebrow and quickly lowered it, that was new information. Had whoever hurt her disposed of her phone, knowing it might contain evidence? Jack's burner had messages on it, but were they from Grace?

'Was she clothed when she was found?' I asked gently, hoping for Sally's sake she was.

'She was, the only things missing were her keys, her phone and her coat.'

I cleared my throat, bile burning my chest. The smoking gun. Even once washed, surely the coat would still have Grace's DNA on it. Why on earth had Jack kept it, was he mad? But I guessed he didn't think his house would be searched, especially if no one knew about their affair. He hadn't bargained on a phrogger moving in and seeing things no one was supposed to.

'Sally, would you mind if I took a photo, perhaps one of you holding something of Grace's, a framed picture of her perhaps?' Imagining that was what Des would want.

'I look terrible,' she chuckled.

'I just want to get Grace's name back in print; we mustn't let the community forget her, we must keep pushing the police to find out who did this.'

'Okay,' Sally agreed, getting up to pick a photo of Grace, herself and Roy from the window ledge in the lounge.

I took my chance to peer into Grace's bedroom; the book of poems was still on her bedside table. Perhaps the police hadn't even looked at it, or maybe they'd taken a photo but not collected it as evidence. They must believe the crime hadn't happened here.

'Did the police tell you where they think Grace died – was it by the tracks?'

'They thought she was moved, dumped there like a piece of rubbish.'

I took the opportunity to snap a photo of Sally, while her eyes were full, ready to spill down her cheeks, hating myself.

'I'll do everything I can to keep her name out there. I'm covering World Book Day at St Wilfrid's on Thursday, maybe I can speak to the headteacher, suggest a memorial or something. I imagine she was much loved by the students and the staff.'

'She was.' Sally looked past me out of the window at nothing in particular, a finality in her tone. There was nothing more for me to learn today.

'I'll let you be. Will Yvonne be back soon?'

'Oh yes, she only popped out to get some milk and bread for us, I've nothing in, you see, otherwise I would have offered you a cup of tea.'

'That's okay. Thank you for seeing me.' I picked up my phone and put it in my rucksack, hoping I'd be away before the family liaison officer returned. 'Take care, Sally. I'll pop in later in the week and see how you are.'

I wasn't being disingenuous, I did want to see how she was doing, her and her husband, but the thought of not exactly profiting from her grief but exploiting it made me sick to my stomach.

21

Outside, the fresh air was cleansing and I inhaled deeply. The misery in Sally's house was intoxicating, as I knew it would be. As I walked back to Church Road, I sent the voice recording and photo I'd snapped over to Des to check whether he was happy for me to go ahead and write it up.

I knew I had to contact the police; if nothing else, to give them Jack's name. But I wasn't about to call the police from my mobile number and the only phone boxes now were in the centre of town, unless I called from Jack's landline. Did inputting 141 in front of the number you were dialling really hide your display? It used to and it was hardly as if they'd trace the call.

Church Road was covered in pink blossom, blown from the trees in the wind, although it still felt too cold for March. I was longing for sunnier days and shorter nights, craving the warmth but not enough to fly out to my parents in Torrevieja. They had offered to pay for my ticket for a long weekend and I would visit, but there was too much going on in Crawley to leave now.

At number six, the landscaper's van was still in the driveway and as I debated what to do, a dog walker passed me with barely any spatial awareness, nearly knocking me off the pavement.

'Do you live there?' the old man asked, pointing at Jack's house as his black Labrador sniffed my hand.

My back stiffened and I struggled to keep my voice even. 'No, I'm a... friend of the family.'

'So much work. First it was inside, now it's the garden, there's no peace,' he complained, flattening the collar of his wax jacket. Tiny hairs sprouted from his nostrils as he flared them.

'I think it'll soon be finished, they're just making the house their own. Are you a neighbour?' I was trying to be as cordial as possible in spite of his grumpy demeanour.

'I live next door.' He waved towards the next

house, although I couldn't see much of the building due to the giant hedge between the two properties. 'How many of you live there?' he asked loudly and I sensed he was hard of hearing.

'Only three, why do you ask?'

'Well, there's so many comings and goings – girls going in during the day or loitering outside, like you.'

I took a step backwards. What was he suggesting? Ignoring my irritation, I fished for my phone, finding the photo I'd scanned of Grace from my first visit to Sally's.

'Was she one of them?' I asked, as he squinted down at the screen.

'Yes, I've seen her. She's the girl that's gone missing, isn't she?'

I nodded. 'Have you reported it to the police?'

He frowned at my question. 'No, why do you think I should?'

'I think any information will help them, don't you?' I suggested as genially as I could manage. If the police had another call citing Church Road, maybe they'd take mine seriously.

'Yes, perhaps you're right. I'll phone them when I get in. Anyway, tell your family to keep the noise down. It's not good to be hearing banging and smashing at my time of life.' He gave me a bizarre salute and carried along the path to his house, the dog lagging behind.

I'd have to be careful; he was surely a curtain twitcher or maybe he walked his dog up and down the street all day long, spying on his neighbours because he had nothing better to do. I sighed, turning back to number six glancing at my phone and realising I'd missed a call from Des. I called him back.

'Hey, great interview, I've just listened to it.'

'I'm not sure I'm cut out for this, Des, it was awful.'

'Don't be ridiculous, you got inside and you got your story, that's what we do.'

'I felt so heartless,' I admitted, kicking at the kerb with the toe of my trainer.

'Did you offer her words of comfort? Were you kind and supportive?'

'Yes.'

'Well, there you go. Did you lie to her?'

'No!' My jaw tilting skyward at the accusation.

'Then you've got nothing to feel bad about. Great work. Write it up and I'll stretch to an extra drink for you when you do the Turkish restaurant review.'

I chuckled at Des's offer, a poor attempt at 'if you scratch my back, I'll scratch yours'.

'Okay, Des, will do.'

When I hung up, the gardeners were getting in the van, muttering something about fancying McDonald's for lunch, and I hotfooted it around the back to see if there was still a way in. To my horror most of the fence panels had been replaced by sturdy ones with trellises at the top except for two where no panels had been erected yet. It seemed they had been busy this morning, perhaps they'd received a delivery of panels whilst I'd been out. Thankfully with two still down I got inside the garden and into the house with ease.

Upstairs, I dropped my rucksack and climbed onto the chaise longue, ready to write up the interview with Sally. With my legs stretched out and laptop at the ready, I glanced over at the bathroom where the door stood ajar. Was the phone still in the plastic bag hidden inside the cistern? Like an itch that needed scratching, I got up to find out.

The phone was still inside, half submerged, and I switched it on to attempt the passcode again, in case by some miracle I could get it open. As expected, I got it wrong three times in succession, so it locked me out. As I was about to switch it off and return it to its watery hole, it vibrated in my hand, Ian's name flashing up on the screen. I gasped, almost dropping the phone in the bowl as I stared at the screen, deciding whether to answer. Throwing caution to the wind, I slid the bar across the screen, pressing the button to mute my end. I heard breathing at first, not heavy like a threatening call, more a faint huff, and it sounded like they were walking, I could hear footsteps on concrete. A second later, a wary female voice said, 'Hello?'

In a panic, I ended the call when I heard the engine of the Mercedes pull onto the drive. Panic soared through my veins and I was all fingers and thumbs as I tried to turn the phone off and stuff it into the bag. The front door clicked open at the same time as the cistern clinked into place.

Back in the bedroom, my laptop and rucksack were still on the chaise long and I hurriedly put them in the wardrobe before climbing inside and sliding the door shut. Panicked perspiration bloomed in my hairline and I sank down to the floor, trying to listen for movement coming from downstairs. It had to be Jack, but was he alone?

I'd been crouched for less than two minutes when there was a feeble knock at the front door and the pitch of a female voice could be heard. Who was it? I heard the tinkling of laughter, someone apologising for being late, but little else, nothing I could decipher two floors up. Ten minutes later, I heard the unmistakeable moans of pleasure, but knowing it wasn't Grace downstairs, I had to restrain myself from going to see who exactly Jack was diddling today. God, the man couldn't keep it in his pants because I didn't believe Helena was downstairs, having popped home from London for a quickie with her husband.

So he had been sleeping with Grace behind his wife's back and now she was gone he was seeing someone else? My jaw dropped as I listened to the woman squeal so overly dramatically I bet the grumpy neighbour next door could even hear. Was Jack that good in bed or did she think she was auditioning to be in an adult film? I couldn't believe my ears or the gall of that man. How many women did Jack have on the go? I swallowed the bad taste in my mouth. He was disgusting and his poor wife had to be told. An affair born out of love I could understand, but he seemed to be on a quest to screw as many women behind Helena's back as he could.

Jack was charming, handsome even, but what was it about him which made these women throw themselves at him, knowing he was a husband and a father? Why would they agree to secret liaisons at his family home? Had he even considered Nathan at all, the consequences it could have on his marriage or his future with his only son?

I wasn't worldly; in my twenty-two years, I'd had exactly two boyfriends and zero one-night stands. I knew nothing about casual sex and hook-ups; Megan had sometimes made me blush when she told me about them. For me, sex was intimate, not an exchange for mutual gratification. You had to care about the person, but my best friend poked fun at me and called me old-fashioned. Everyone was swiping right to find their next conquest, but I couldn't think of anything less personal. I knew I was the odd one out, my mum had often told me I had an old head on my body, but I longed for the day I'd be romanced and taken out, not selected from an app like someone buying a new pair of trainers.

Eventually, the theatrics stopped downstairs and I no longer had to listen uncomfortably red-faced to something that should have been private. Jack never came up to the master suite and not long later I heard the pair of them leave the house, but by the time I climbed out of the wardrobe and got to the window the only thing I saw was a flash of brown hair walking over the bridge, then Jack alone in the Mercedes pulling out of the gates. I'd missed my chance to see who Jack's latest conquest was.

22

Was the woman walking over the bridge the mysterious brunette who Jack dined with at the Golden Lotus, the same woman who was on the burner phone under the alias Ian, calling to announce her arrival maybe? I'd thought Ian was Grace, but maybe I'd been wrong all along. Unless he'd used the same contact for both of them, but that didn't make sense. Maybe he'd swapped the numbers, Grace could have been the first 'Ian', but whoever the brunette was, he could have replaced Grace's number with hers. It seemed heartless considering the circumstances and my head hurt thinking about the logistics involved in having so many affairs going on at once. He had to be an expert liar, which left me unsettled.

I hadn't got that impression at all when I'd met him at St Wilfrid's School. He'd been charismatic and gentlemanly; the librarian Claire appeared to like and respect him. I'd seen and heard things in the house that led me to believe Jack wasn't all he made himself out to be. I guessed we all wore a mask of sorts, but not to such an extent.

I wrote up my interview with Sally, listening to the recording on repeat, hoping I'd been compassionate. Guilt gnawed at me because despite the interview being legitimately sought and written with no embellishments or scandalous headlines, I was still exploiting the Stewarts' grief at their lowest moment.

Des got in contact as soon as I sent it over, promising it would be front-page news unless there was a major development in the case by publication on Friday. It made me feel worse that I bubbled with excitement at the thought of having my name on the front page. Yes, it was only the local weekly rag, but still, all the articles and features were going towards my portfolio and may mean a tabloid might take me seriously when it was time to move on.

In my response, I asked Des if there were any updates from the police or news on the medical examiner's report, but he stated it was too early. Neil couldn't be seen to harass his source at the station, otherwise he could lose them altogether. We were at the end of the line, being drip-fed information just ahead of the public.

I was a little too eager for the police to tie what evidence they had together, but they weren't in possession of all the facts, I had to get Jack's name to them. If the bleach hadn't contaminated the DNA, there would have to be some to find on Grace's body, wouldn't there? A quick swab from Jack would either determine it was him or clear him outright. If he didn't do it, he'd be eliminated and I could rest easy.

I used the bathroom and went downstairs to make some toast, knowing I'd be ravenous later if I didn't eat something now. When I couldn't put it off any longer, I picked up the landline, typed in 141 and dialled Crawley police station. Panic set in, was there some way I could disguise my voice? My heart pounded when it rang and an automated voice listed options for me to choose. I pressed the corresponding digit to speak to the front desk and after it rang seven or eight times, I was subjected to hold music.

Eventually, after pacing for ten minutes, a female picked it up.

'Good afternoon, Crawley Police, sorry to keep you waiting,' she said brightly.

'I have some information pertaining to Grace Stewart,' I masked my voice in a deep timbre which sounded like I was pretending to be a man.

'Okay, are you willing to speak with me or should I try to contact the team working on that investigation.'

'You,' I blurted. Sweat pooled beneath my armpits as though a spotlight was shining directly on me. I didn't want to be asked any questions, I just wanted to tell them what I knew.

'Okay,' she said, a little taken aback.

'Jack Reilly worked with Grace at St Wilfrid's School. They were having an affair.' I heard the scratch of the woman's pen as she wrote the information down and with my anxiety reaching a fever pitch, I hung up. I could have told them about the coat or the burner phone, but those things weren't evidence exactly, unless DNA was found on the coat. If they didn't think Jack was a suspect for Grace, potentially I could make another call. If they did, I was sure they'd issue a warrant to search the house.

That led to another problem. If they came in

here to tear the place apart, it wouldn't only be the coat and burner phone they'd find, they'd find me too. I couldn't allow myself to be caught in the house, barely anyone understood what phrogging was about. I'd be some homeless weirdo who liked to sneak into people's houses and live in their wardrobes like I was popping off for a weekend trip to Narnia. But I'd made the call because I wanted to do the right thing, for Grace and for Sally. I'd forever be haunted by the desolate look in Sally's eyes today.

* * *

The rest of the afternoon seem to go at a snail's pace, the gardeners returned just before two, but luckily I was upstairs. I stayed glued to social media, reading comments and posts about Grace. Dawn Cottrill, Grace's fellow TA, had been on Facebook, advertising a crowdfunding campaign for Grace's funeral costs. It seemed presumptuous. Most of the comments were sending condolences, a few were outraged women citing females walking home alone were targeted.

I checked all the news websites, but only the BBC local page had used a snippet of my interview with Sally and credited *Crawley News*. It was on our site already, first contact made with the parents of the girl found in a ditch. Helena hadn't uploaded anything since yesterday's lunch photos and there was no statement on St Wilfrid's website either. I suspected it had been a mournful day at the school now the news was public.

@HomeSweetHome had sent me an email, another one-liner, and boredom made me bite.

Oh come on… indulge me.

I replied. *Why?*

I didn't have to wait long for a response, maybe twenty minutes.

Because I want to show off. I wasn't going to post where specifically you are, not on the public site.

The comments sounded threatening in tone, but I had no doubt @HomeSweetHome was some teenager sitting in their bedroom who'd stumbled upon the site by accident. They'd never phrogged in their life!

I closed the laptop, partly amused, yet irritated all the same. I had been intending to write another blog, but perhaps it would be better to stay quiet and see what developed. Had the neighbour kept to his word and phoned the police too? If he had, they had to act and I also had to start looking for alternative accommodation.

I dozed off whilst reading a dog-eared copy of *The Language of Flowers* by Vanessa Diffenbaugh – a novel I'd adored since secondary school – waking to Jack's voice on the stairs.

'Fancy pancakes, Nathan? We've not had them since Pancake Day.'

'Yes! I won't tell Mum,' Nathan insisted as though it was a given.

'Get changed and you can help. I just need to pop upstairs and grab something.'

With my eyes crusted with sleep, I rubbed at them frantically, going rigid when I heard him enter the bedroom and head straight for the bathroom. He removed the phone and switched it on, tapping at it before wandering back towards the wardrobe. I held my breath; the footsteps had ceased, but I had no idea what had caught his attention until I heard the laptop lead being unplugged. I slowly shifted, cranking my neck to look through the tiny gap to find him staring at the lead in his hand, forehead crumpled. It must have been Helena who'd been up here, using her laptop in secret while Jack slept. What was she looking at?

Jack was distracted by the phone in his hand emitting a short buzz and he sniggered as he read what had come through.

A minute later, the phone was put back inside the cistern and he was unbuttoning his shirtsleeves and rolling them up.

'Get the eggs out of the fridge, my boy,' he called as he descended the stairs, the glee in his voice obvious.

With Grace out of the picture, it seemed Jack was quick to immerse himself in another affair. Had he not cared about her at all? I had to find the brunette and warn her. She might not know Jack and Grace had been sleeping together. What if she went missing too? I scoured social media, searching through photos of the teaching staff at St Wilfrid's, then the enormous list of Helena's friends and her photos waiting for one of them to jump out at me, but it was futile. Without a name, I was screwed.

At six o'clock, Helena arrived home earlier than usual and Jack served dinner. It smelt like a Thai green curry and my mouth salivated at the aroma. I should have had more than granola and toast today. After dinner, I heard plates being loaded into the dishwasher, then Helena came up to run Nathan a bath. Nothing seemed out of the ordinary and I'd settled in for the evening, drafting another blog post when at around half past seven there was a sharp rap at the door.

Curious, I crept out of the wardrobe and over to the window, eyes widening when I saw a black car parked across the gates. Voices I couldn't make out came from below and I moved to the top of the stairs, cranking my neck to try to hear what was being said.

'Who is it?' Helena shouted, telling Nathan to be quiet as he splashed around in the bath.

Jack came halfway up the stairs, his voice calm but the tremor unmistakable.

'It's the police, they want to talk to me about the missing woman from school.'

23

'Why?' Helena couldn't hide the incredulity in her high-pitched whisper. 'Are they arresting you?'

'No, no, just a chat, but I'm going to go with them, okay. I don't want Nathan asking any questions, tell him I've popped out. I'll be back in a bit.'

Helena mumbled something in response to Jack's whisper, but I couldn't make out what she'd said. A minute later heavy, footsteps left the house and Helena went back to Nathan with forced joviality in her voice, suggesting they play Mario Kart when he was done in the bath.

I stared out of the window of the master suite, watching Jack joking with the two men as he climbed into the car and it drove away. Why hadn't they interviewed him at the house? Was he trying to protect Nathan or didn't he want Helena finding out who he'd been with the night Grace disappeared? He must have told her about the missing teaching assistant, if not her name, as she didn't question him further, but it was strange he said missing and not deceased. With it being in the public domain, Helena could easily find out, if she didn't know already.

At least the police had taken my call seriously, but I was frustrated I couldn't eavesdrop. I had to make sure I was downstairs when he came home, if he returned, to listen to what he said to Helena. Up here, I wouldn't hear anything.

Before I let anxiety get the better of me, I headed for the stairs, knowing Helena and Nathan were still shut in the bathroom. I could hear the water draining down the plughole and knew I didn't have long until they both came out. When I reached the ground floor, the smell of creamy curry drew me to the kitchen. One bowl had barely been touched and another plate with half-eaten potato shapes and chicken nuggets smothered in ketchup lay beside it. Perhaps they'd tried to get Nathan to try the curry with little success, reverting to the childhood staples.

'More for me,' I muttered, grabbing a spoon. I loitered at the entrance to the kitchen, the bowl in my hand, shovelling it in, one ear listening out for what was going on upstairs. I knew the Mario Kart game was on the system in Nathan's room and if I was lucky they would both stay up there. Either way, I needed to find a place to hide out of sight for when Jack came home. I left the bowl where I found it, hoping Helena would think Jack had scraped it into the bin, and gulped water direct from the tap. The drain gurgled as the last of the bath water flooded down the pipe and I heard the bathroom door open, Nathan's footsteps running into his room.

'Put your PJs on and I'll be there in a sec,' Helena called from almost directly overhead. She had to be in her bedroom. I looked around for places to hide, glad I'd remembered to pocket my phone before I came down. I couldn't imagine waiting for hours in the utility room crouched behind the laundry basket, nor freezing to death in the garage, plus I wouldn't hear much from either of those locations. The cupboard under the stairs would have to do.

I stepped inside, closing the door and ducking beneath the line of hanging coats, using the torch on my phone to see where it was safe to tread. Rows of shoes covered the floor, but as the cupboard ran under the stairs, it narrowed on the left-hand side and I squeezed into the gap, with my legs tucked up to my chin, hidden behind the hoover. It wasn't comfortable and I considered finding somewhere else, but above me the floorboards creaked as Helena descended.

* * *

Jack didn't return for almost two hours. In that time, I had cramp twice, my bladder was almost bursting and the curry had given me indigestion. Jack came in just in time to give Nathan a kiss goodnight before joining Helena in the kitchen. I heard the pop of a cork and wine being sloshed into glasses. I envisaged them sitting at the table, Helena at one end with an eyebrow raised, waiting for Jack to spill. I guessed he'd either denied everything or admitted the affair but supplied his alibi. Perhaps I should have mentioned the burner phone and the coat after all, but at the end of the day if he had a cast-iron alibi and Grace's estimated time of death had been established, if they didn't match up what more was there to talk about.

My skin itched in frustration, not knowing everything. I wanted all the puzzle pieces so I could find out what had happened to Grace, who had hurt her and why.

Eventually, Jack spoke in answer to Helena's question of 'What happened?'

'They wanted to ask how I knew the missing girl Grace Stewart asked about the school, the staff.'

'So they're pulling in everyone then? The head-teacher too?'

'I guess. I told them I didn't really know her well, but she seemed like a pleasant girl.'

'It's awful; do they think it was an accident?'

'They didn't say, I don't think they wanted to tell me too much. She disappeared the night I had that work thing last week, when I called Sam over because you got caught up at work.'

I tried to listen to every inflection in his voice, to gauge if he was lying, but he sounded composed, even genuine.

'They requested a voluntary swab, which I gave them, then they let me go home.'

'You let them swab you?'

'Yeah, why wouldn't I?' Jack said.

'So nothing ever happened with this Grace?' Helena's voice wobbled.

'No, darling, I promise.'

I gritted my teeth; he was as smooth as silk, lying came easily to him.

'You're telling me the truth, Jack, aren't you?' Helena's throat croaked as though she was already crying.

I shuffled in the cupboard, knocking the hoover with my knee... It tipped and I reached out to grab it but wasn't fast enough. The handle crashed into the door and I shrank back, nearly peeing myself at the racket it made.

'What was that?' Helena asked. 'Was it Nathan?'

Footsteps came into the hallway and I pressed myself as far back as I could, folding my body against the wall, adrenaline making my teeth chatter. The stairs above my head creaked as the Reillys climbed up to check on Nathan. Less than a minute later, they came back down.

'Garage?' Jack opened the integral door, letting a waft of chilly air inside.

One of Helena's scarves had fallen off a hook and I dragged it towards me, covering as much of my body as I could. The door opened, the hoover hit the ground and Jack's shadow blocked out the light.

'Hoover,' he said by way of explanation, picking it up and shoving it back in the cupboard. I winced as the head rammed me in the stomach. Sweat poured down my forehead, sure Jack was about to whip the scarf away and reveal me hiding, but instead the door was closed, plunging me back into darkness.

'So what do they think happened to her?'

'I don't know. Like I said, they didn't give me any details.'

'And you didn't have an affair with her?' Helena pressed, the pair of them standing outside the door.

Jack sighed. 'No. I love you, Hel, our little family, the three musketeers. Why would I want to risk all of this?'

'Because I can't do it again, Jack, not again. I'll leave and I'll take Nathan with me.' Her voice was slightly muffled, like he was holding her close and her face was pressed into his chest.

'You have nothing to worry about, you're the only one for me.'

I swallowed the bile in my throat; the man was an absolute lothario and Helena was either refusing to see it or she was clinging on to her marriage by her fingernails.

'If that's the case, Jack, then who the fuck do these belong to?' Helena's voice was shrill, spitting vitriol like she'd gone from nought to sixty in a flash.

I wished more than anything I could see what was going on the other side of the door. What had

Helena showed Jack that caused her to shriek and shocked him into silence?

'Because they aren't mine,' Helena shouted.

At once, I knew exactly what she held in her hand. The underwear I'd found beneath their bed, the lacy pink thong that didn't seem like it was Helena's style.

'I've never seen those before,' Jack choked out and I imagined his skin icily pale, confronted with evidence which was pretty irrefutable.

'In our fucking home, Jack!' Helena's voice was getting louder, and from the sounds of it she'd shoved him, because he grunted. 'No wonder you're dragging your feet getting a camera installed – worried about what I'll see, are you?'

'Ssshh, Nathan's upstairs,' he hissed, trying to regain control, but Helena had lost it, storming up the stairs, yelling about changing the sheets and that Jack would be sleeping on the sofa. He followed her up, trying to explain it away as a misunderstanding, that he had no idea where they'd come from. I listened as thumps of bedding landed on the hallway above, thrown from the bed. Jack's soothing voice tried to de-escalate his wife, to limit the damage, but she was incandescent.

A minute later, Helena's footsteps stomped

downstairs, I imagined her carrying sheets, Jack just behind her. They stopped right outside the cupboard.

'This is your last chance, Jack Reilly, do you understand? I will not be made a fool of. Whatever this is, or was, ends now because if I find one of your whores in my house, I will walk away with everything – our son, the house, the car. You will have nothing.'

I silently gasped. I'd always thought Helena was blind to his philandering ways but maybe she'd looked the other way, up until now.

Her footsteps clacked towards the kitchen on the parquet floor, yet I still heard Jack's breathing, standing outside the cupboard.

'For fuck's sake, Grace,' he hissed in a low voice, laying claim to whose underwear it was.

I held my breath, waiting for him to move away, but he remained, gathering his thoughts, maybe thinking about the brunette and how he'd have to end things. One way or another.

24

The atmosphere was frosty in the Reilly household for the rest of the night. Jack and Helena barely spoke. After their showdown, the television went on for an hour but I couldn't tell if they were in the same room. Eventually, Helena went up to bed, but Jack's footsteps didn't follow. I didn't move until gone midnight and by the time I'd unfolded myself from the understairs cupboard every muscle in my body ached. The atmosphere in the house felt oppressive.

I had no idea where Jack was, but the lounge door was closed and no light leaked from beneath it, so I crept up to the master suite, surprised to hear Helena snoring softly as I passed her bedroom. She must have taken a sleeping pill to knock herself out, because how she'd sleep otherwise after the earlier confrontation I had no idea. I used the toilet, my bladder fit to burst, but having been confined to the cupboard for so long, I was reluctant to get into the wardrobe straight away so stretched out on the carpet and booted up my laptop.

Des hadn't emailed me and there was nothing of interest on the socials, except Dawn's fundraiser, which had hit five hundred pounds already. I cleared out my inbox of junk and stared at the earlier email from @HomeSweetHome practically begging me to ask how they'd found out I was in Crawley.

'Okay, I'll indulge you, let's see what you've got,' I mumbled to myself, clicking reply. It would be interesting to see if @HomeSweetHome had genuinely worked out where I was or if they were fishing, but it was one hell of a guess.

How? I typed and clicked send.

My last blog post had more and more comments requesting an update, some suggesting I'd fallen foul to the perpetrator. So much conjecture, so many people hypothesising, it was easy to see how these things spiralled out of control. I knew I had to write an update; the readers were getting frustrated with my radio silence, but I wasn't sure what I was willing to disclose. If @HomeSweetHome had discovered my location, perhaps I'd been too open with my information already.

It was now the early hours of Tuesday, so I'd managed a week at Church Road, despite all that had gone on, although I was aware my time in residence was now limited.

Megan had called earlier but no voicemail had been left. I didn't want her to worry, so, although it was late and I knew she'd be asleep, I messaged her, letting her know I was fine but couldn't risk talking over the phone. I jumped when my phone flashed and she responded straight away. She'd been sent on a last-minute sales course to Southampton and wouldn't be back until Friday, calling earlier because she'd wanted to FaceTime to show me the plush hotel she was staying in but agreed to send photos tomorrow instead.

Going back to my emails, I saw @HomeSweet-Home had responded. Didn't anyone sleep? I could almost hear the glee within the words.

Algorithms... simple.

I took the data you gave me – missing girl (now deceased) – disused railway line – weather – newly bought property – and ran it through an algorithm. It gave me two location options: Crawley, West Sussex and Silloth, Cumbria. I had a feeling it would be the former.

I read it again in amazement, who was this guy?
So are you some kind of hacker or a computer geek? I typed.

The latter, I guess. My name is Harry, I'm twenty-one and at university in Plymouth. Gets kind of boring around here if you're not into getting wasted or high and chasing skirt.

Interesting, so he wasn't attracted to the usual university social life.
Ever phrogged? I asked.
Harry's reply wasn't instant this time.

No, but I want to, when I'm out of here.

I knew it! He was a voyeur doing his research, cruising the phrogging websites before he took the leap, but maybe Harry from Plymouth could help me out.

So you can't hack into stuff then?

What do you want to know? came his reply.

Let me think about it and I'll come back to you, I typed.

I still don't know your name.

I stared at Harry's message; how much was I willing to reveal?

Millie.

It was close enough and I wasn't about to trust some guy I'd never met before, even if he could pinpoint where I was phrogging, down to the town at least.

So what happened to Grace Stewart? he asked. I paused, staring out of the window, unnerved at how much Harry knew, including Grace's name. I considered my reply, unsure how to respond, eventually typing.

I don't know, but I'm going to find out.

I closed my laptop down, eyes heavy, rolling onto my back and staring out of the skylight into the night sky. It was good to stretch my limbs and enjoy the plush carpet, instead of being folded into a tiny space. I watched the planes fly across, coming to and from Gatwick, their lights flashing, the silence of the house a comfort.

What would tomorrow bring? The police had spoken to Jack but hadn't taken it further, yet. Helena had found Grace's underwear and she was one more infidelity away from calling time on their marriage. Which meant Jack had another mistress to get rid of.

Who killed Grace? If I went with Occam's Razor theory, the simplest answer being the correct one, it was Jack and he had to have met up with Grace after dinner at the Golden Lotus with the mystery brunette. He had the coat after all. It was the most likely scenario and he had motive. She was pressurising him to leave Helena, which I didn't believe was ever on the cards, and perhaps she'd pushed him too far. It seemed more plausible than Grace being randomly attacked and killed whilst walking home in a safe neighbourhood and her assailant pouring bleach over her. That theory didn't explain the coat either, unless it wasn't Grace's.

My brain ticked through the endless possibilities until I grew sleepy and eventually I packed the laptop into the wardrobe and went to bed.

* * *

The next morning, Jack's presence in the master suite woke me up, his light footsteps across the carpet. He retrieved the phone from the cistern and pocketed it, tossing the plastic bag into the bin in the bathroom, before going for a jog. Was he getting rid of evidence, anything that connected him to Grace?

At just after six, with the house quiet and the rest of the family still sleeping, I took a chance and crept downstairs to look for the green Joules coat. I hadn't seen it last night in the cupboard, but it had been dark. After a second, I found it. It had been moved off the peg, rolled up into a ball and shoved behind the hoover, Helena's scarf discarded on top. Why had it been moved and why hadn't Jack disposed of it if it was Grace's?

A pot of coffee had been freshly made in the kitchen and I helped myself to a cup before tiptoeing back upstairs. Helena's alarm went off soon after and the usual morning routine began. I was surprised she hadn't called in sick, but it was business as usual. Jack and Nathan left the house at their scheduled time and I was about to climb into the shower when Des sent me a message, asking me to call him when I was free.

'Great stuff on that article, getting loads of comments and views, Mol, well done. Keep in touch with the Stewarts okay, we might need to do a follow-up.'

'Sure, will do,' I said, appreciating the praise. 'What information has Neil managed to get? Do they fancy anyone for Grace's murder yet?'

'They're only just classifying it as a murder investigation, they've spoken to a few people, but there's no one in the frame, to my knowledge.'

'Any DNA news?'

'The medical examiner's report has been published, but nothing was found in terms of the perpetrator because of the bleach – whoever it was poured a lot on her.'

'Oh God, did Sally have to identify her?' My heart broke for the poor woman.

'Parents were advised not to, they confirmed it was her with a DNA sample. Cause of death officially was...' I could hear Des turning pages of his notepad before he read aloud, 'A fracture of three of the cervical vertebrae in the neck, compromising neurological supply to the respiratory muscles and innervation to the heart. Currently they don't have much to go on.' I let that sink in for a moment, the medical terminology sounded so impersonal, like Grace was a shell, and not a person but ultimately, she'd died from a broken neck and not from strangulation. It sounded more accidental than planned.

'Perhaps they'll find some DNA. Was she seeing anyone?' My frustration mounted, dancing around with Des, trying to conceal what I already knew. 'Her mum didn't think so,' I added.

'Doesn't look like it. Neil is writing up a piece now, but currently it's a mystery. We're going to ask the public for information, with the police's blessing, see if it'll open up new leads. I'll keep you informed.'

'Okay, thanks for letting me know.'

'No problem, kiddo, keep up the good work. Oh and don't forget the Turkish place, the owner is hassling me. And I've sent you over a request for a piece on the pothole saga.'

I groaned.

'I know it isn't exciting, but the community are rallying together and petitioning the council to do something about it now.'

'Is it one of those pieces where I need to stand there like a moron with a measuring tape, or do you want me to plant a shrub in one?'

'Great idea,' he chuckled.

'I'm on it,' I replied with zero enthusiasm in my voice. There was no chance I'd let my success go to my head working for Des.

'Anyway, gotta go, catch you later.' With that, he hung up.

* * *

I left Church Road after ten to run some errands. I needed to get some shopping and visit the infamous pothole sites in Crawley Des wanted me to write an article about, although how I'd make that stretch to five hundred words I didn't know. At lunchtime, I popped into the Turkish restaurant and booked a table for that evening. The staff were welcoming and pleased to take my booking, not remarking on my 'table for one'. I got a good vibe from the place and the restaurant was almost half full, which was a surprise for a Tuesday lunchtime.

After my visit to three pothole sites, all in the town centre, dodging traffic to try to get a good shot and measure the depth, I spent a bit of time talking to the local residents. Most complained at the amount their council tax had gone up yet their cars were being damaged by the insufficient repair of the town's roads. With a few quotes and photos, I headed to the library to write up what I had, intending to email the local councillor I'd got a quote from for another piece to see if he'd talk to me again. I also needed to get another blog post up.

An hour later as I finished my second latte and waited for the ancient computers to upload the next blog post, I checked my socials and logged into the *Crawley News* email account on my phone. The name that popped up on the screen turned my veins to ice. I had an email come through from jreilly@stwilfs.sch.org which had to be Jack. In the subject line, one word was written: 'Grace'.

* * *

Blog Post #6
www.phrogging.com

Firstly, I must apologise for taking so long between posts. A lot has been going on here. The main thing is I haven't been discovered – or murdered, for that matter. I'm safe and I can't believe it's only been a week since my arrival. It seems like I've been living here forever and I hope the family don't suddenly decide they need the space I'm hiding out in. Not now I've got comfortable. I know some of you have been asking where I've been sleeping, I don't want to give too much away, but suffice to say you can think of me like Harry Potter.

I've had some questions you guys wanted answers to. Firstly, how do I go to the toilet. The answer is quietly! I have a bathroom only a few steps away from where I'm sleeping that is not really used by the rest of the house. I only flush when everyone is out, and it's the same with showering, only when the coast is clear and I dry everything thoroughly after-wards. I've used their machine to wash some clothes once so far, when the family were out for the day.

@SecretSquatter asked if I've ever deliber-ately moved something or tried to mess with the family. The answer is no! That's not what we're here for. I don't want to terrorise these people, I want to live harmoniously.

Some of you posted about the experi-ences you've had being caught phrogging and, to be honest, they petrified me, so I'm hoping I don't come face to face with the family because I don't know how they'd react. Especially with what's been going on with the mistress. There's not much news to report, but it looks like the police are investigating her death as a crime. I did contact them anonymously and told them he had a relationship with the victim. They came to the house, took him away to interview but let him go, so I don't think he's being considered a suspect, or maybe not yet. I need to trust they know what they're doing.

Either way, his marriage is hanging by a thread. From what I gather, this hasn't been his first affair and not only that he's got another one on the go now too. The tension in the house is near boiling point. There's one thing I cannot get out of my head. Someone killed that poor woman and cut her life short, they tried to cover their tracks and they are still out there, evading capture. What if I'm living with them?

25

'What the hell,' I muttered. Why had Jack emailed me?

I clicked into the message, my brain already conjuring up lots of theories; he knew I was in their house or that I'd seen him and Grace together. My breathing shallowed as the words on the screen swam before my eyes.

Hi Molly,

It's Jack Reilly from St Wilfrid's; we met when you came to visit in preparation for World Book Day. I wondered if you had any time to chat about Grace Stewart. I'm sure you know she was a colleague of mine. I saw your article on the Crawley News website after visiting Grace's parents. It would be good to catch up and talk Book Day plans before Thursday too.

Thanks in advance, Jack

I leaned back in my chair, eyes narrowing. His email was weird, to say the least, although I was relieved I hadn't been found out. I mentally kicked myself because I was sure if he knew I was living in his house the last thing he'd do was send me an email. I guessed by Grace's name in the subject of the email he was hoping to grill me for information on what I might know about the ongoing investigation. Neil's piece hadn't gone live yet, but it likely would later today, even though there wasn't much to report as far as the crime went.

My body tingled with apprehension; would he go on the record? Could this be another angle, an interview with Grace's colleagues? Des would be delighted. I reread Jack's email, smirking at the mention of World Book Day planning, inserted like an afterthought. I couldn't deny I was intrigued, mainly at how he would act. Meeting him would give me the opportunity to ask some personal questions, but I'd have to be careful not to let on I knew

anything past his and Grace's professional relationship.

I tapped out a response.

Hi Jack,
Good to hear from you. I'm looking forward to visiting St Wilfrid's for World Book
Day on Thursday. I do have some time free
later today. I'm reviewing the new Turkish
restaurant in town, it's called Marmaris and is
in the square. I'll be there from seven o'clock
if you wanted to stop by.
Molly

My skin was electrified. I was playing a risky
game with a potentially dangerous man, but our
meeting would be in public and had been cemented
in writing for the authorities to find if I suddenly disappeared. I wished Megan was around, she'd help
me figure out how to play it. I had to look at it like
another job, I was there to glean information from
Jack, like carefully pulling a thread from a sleeve,
whatever it took. He would likely be on his guard
and I'd be on mine too.

His response was quick and only one line, *See*

you there. I squirmed in my seat, it felt like a date, something it absolutely wasn't.

But what if you've given him that impression?

I hadn't, my email hadn't been flirty, it had been professional and to the point. I would be at the restaurant doing my job, sampling the food to review. If he came along to talk while I ate, that was fine.

I looked down at my crumpled jeans and frowned. It might not be a date, but I needed something to wear that didn't look like I'd slept in it.

I'd hardly spent any of Mum's guilt money, so I left the library and hit the shops, treating myself to a black floral dress I could wear with tights and boots. It would come in handy for the summer and in the meantime I could dress it warm for spring. It was smart but casual and didn't look like I was trying too hard either because I didn't want Jack to think our meeting was anything it wasn't.

Jesus, Mol, it's not like he's going to come onto you, I told myself, but I knew he was a lothario and maybe it was the chase he enjoyed. I was the right age range, going by his dalliance with Grace. Either way, after tonight I'd have a better understanding of Jack Reilly than I'd had before.

I headed back to Church Road, my phone

pinging with an email from the councillor, supplying me with some standard spiel to put in my article. It meant when I got back I could deliver the article early to Des and concentrate on tonight.

When I returned, the landscapers were back and all of the new fences were in place, so I wasn't getting in through the garden. I sat in the overgrown jungle staring at the barricade before traipsing around to the front. I dug the key I'd had cut out of my bag, almost at the house, but had to dart behind a bush when Jack came past me in the Mercedes, the gates of the driveway swinging open.

'Shit,' I hissed, putting my hand in a muddy puddle as I slipped. Now how was I supposed to get in? I loitered at the end of the road, weighing up my options and cursing myself for not getting back before Jack brought Nathan home.

The next-door neighbour grumbled to himself as he walked past me with his Labrador, but he didn't speak or even smile and I doubted he'd recognised me from before.

At the entrance to the narrow road leading to the church was a bench and I sat, eating a chocolate bar I'd bought earlier and debating what to do next. My phone flashed and I saw Megan was trying to Face-Time me.

'Finally!' she said and I grinned at her eye roll.

'Hi, how's the course?'

'Sod the course, check out this room, girl!' Megan panned the phone around, showing me every inch of the beautiful suite with a view that glimpsed the harbour.

'Lush!' My eyes widened, envious at her good fortune.

'I know, I got the director's room as she couldn't make it. Talk about staying in the lap of luxury.' She squinted at the screen. 'Where are you?'

I knocked at a piece of overhanging foliage. 'I'm stuck outside. I can't get in the house at the moment and I've got to go out tonight to review the Turkish restaurant in town,' I moaned.

'Ah that's a shame; I would have come with you.'

'Well, Jack sent me an email. I've got so much to fill you in on, but he might be joining me.'

'What? Mol, don't do anything stupid.'

I laughed at the look of horror on Megan's face. 'Chill, it's nothing, it's not a date.'

Megan turned away from the screen.

'Damn it, someone's knocking, I've got to go. Listen if you need to, crash at mine.'

'Really?' I replied hopefully.

'Sure, I'll text ahead and let them know you're

coming. At least you'll have a proper bed for tonight. I'll ring you tomorrow.' Megan blew me a kiss and ended the call.

Perhaps it was my lucky day as well. I got up and brushed the dried mud from my hand before making my way to the bus stop to head back into town.

When I arrived at Megan's flat, via a detour to the supermarket to buy some groceries as a peace offering, Cassie opened the door, scowled and immediately walked away. She had her headphones in and I guessed she was in an online meeting. Megan told me she worked from home and I heard her mention something about balance sheets as she went back into her room and closed the door.

'Hello to you too,' I mumbled, dropping my rucksack on the sofa and heading into the kitchen to stack my purchases on the side. I made the both of us a cup of tea, but as Cassie was still on her call, I left the mug outside her bedroom door before flopping onto Megan's bed.

Her room was painted a dark purple with fairy lights strung up from a few Christmases ago that had never been taken down. Pictures of us and her flatmates adorned the wall, along with flyers from events we'd attended; On the Beach, the festival in

Brighton, Glastonbury – something we'd sworn never to do again – and the Isle of Wight festival. Summers were made for camping in tents, partying on the beach and drinking copious amounts of cider as we watched the sun go down.

I longed for summer to come, the rest of the year felt overly sensible with too many adult responsibilities and bills to pay. Megan was climbing up in the sales world and I was one step above being the tea lady at the local newspaper. I sighed as I took in a whiff of fabric softener from the crocheted blanket Megan's mum had made her which covered the bed. I beamed from ear to ear. A night here was the equivalent of a night in a plush hotel and I was grateful for Megan's offer.

'For fuck's sake!' Cassie yelled and immediately I knew what I'd done.

'Sorry, Cass, I made you tea.'

'Well, I fucking know that, I'm standing in it.'

Megan's flatmates weren't bad people, they just didn't want to share their tiny space with another body, one who didn't contribute much to the running of the place, hence the bag of shopping. I'd bought cake, milk and bread, a couple of microwave meals and a bottle of wine for them to use. I understood their point, and the eye rolls whenever I rocked up didn't go unnoticed, but I tried not to let them sting.

'Here for the night then?' Cassie appeared in the doorway, peeling off a soggy tea-stained sock.

'Yep, but you won't know I'm here, I promise.' I held my palms up. 'And I bought you and Lou some bits as a thank you.'

'Thanks,' Cassie nodded. 'Don't bring anyone back okay,' she grumbled, although her voice had softened.

There was no chance of that.

26

As the evening approached, I found myself getting nervous, my appetite waning, which was frustrating with a free meal up for grabs. Jack might not even show up, but I still took advantage of Megan's shower and when Cassie went out to meet Louise, the other flatmate, for dinner, I put a load of washing on and hung it on the airer in her room. I'd even be able to iron it tomorrow once it was all dry.

I sat in front of Megan's tiny dressing table, knowing she wouldn't mind me borrowing a bit of make-up or a spritz of perfume. I even gave her hair straighteners a whirl and the Molly in the mirror looked like she'd had a makeover. Was it too much? Would Jack think it was all for him? I hoped not, but in the back of my mind I questioned why I'd made so much of an effort. Did I want Jack to find me attractive, would it help get me the answers I craved or was I so desperate for attention that even some from a married man would give me the boost I desired? I forced those unhelpful thoughts away, I'd always been an over-thinker, but I needed to focus on the task at hand.

The flat was empty when I left, the restaurant only a five-minute walk away, another reason why staying at Megan's was so appealing. Butterflies flapped in my stomach and I pushed open the door to Marmaris, half expecting to see Jack already there. I was warmly welcomed and seated at the back in a booth, where a waiter stood to take my drinks order.

'May I suggest a cocktail? We have two for one on a Tuesday night.' He handed me the menu, which I scanned, quickly requesting a mojito, which was delivered a few minutes later with a basket of warm bread and two dips. My stomach rumbled, appetite returning, and I inhaled the bread, then drank the first cocktail far too quickly and moved straight onto the second. I scanned the restaurant; it was reasonably busy with a friendly atmosphere and I pulled my notebook out of my rucksack to record my surroundings.

The music was a traditional Turkish medley but played at the perfect volume to accompany the chatter around me. Despite my initial nerves, I soon relaxed, dining alone, but every so often my gaze would be drawn to the window to see if Jack was outside. Surprised to find myself feeling disappointed when he wasn't. My main course, mixed shish kebab with rice and salad, was delicious, helped by the fact I was halfway through my fourth cocktail and craved carbs to soak up the alcohol.

'Hi.'

I looked up to see Jack standing beside the table, water dripping from his hair and down his face. He swiped it away and I caught the glint of his wedding ring.

'It's raining?' I said without thinking, my cheeks flaming.

He smiled and gestured to the booth. 'It's chucking it down. May I?'

'Yes of course.' I dabbed at my mouth with the napkin, heat rising from my chest up my neck, where I knew the skin would be mottled. I shouldn't have had those cocktails.

'Sorry I didn't mean to interrupt your dinner.' He shook off his damp jacket and laid it to the side before leaning back on the plush turquoise cushion, dabbing at his face with a napkin.

'It's fine. Like I said, I'm here doing a review. Can I get you anything?' I asked as the waiter materialised.

'No, no... um actually, I'll have a drink please. Bourbon, plenty of ice.'

I smirked at the grown-up nature of his drink, so different to mine which was overflowing with mint leaves and had an luminous green straw.

'So, how can I help you?' The alcohol made me bold.

His eyes slid towards my notepad, reading my notes on the restaurant. 'You like it then?' He nodded towards it, ignoring my question.

'So far yes The food is delicious.' I pushed my plate across the table. 'Try some.'

He picked up my fork without batting an eyelid and stabbed a cube of chicken onto it. My lips parted as he slipped it into his mouth, strangely intimate knowing I'd used the fork a few minutes earlier, but he clearly didn't care or maybe this was his act.

'You're right,' he agreed, grinning, 'it's divine.'

The flush burned my neck again, like I was being cooked from the inside. His green eyes flashed wickedly and for the second time since I'd been in his company I understood why women gravitated towards him. I couldn't put my finger on what exactly was appealing. His eyes were an attractive hue and his face pleasant, but there was something about his manner which drew me in, his confidence maybe.

'So, Grace?' I coughed, desperate to switch my brain off and move to the topic we both wanted to discuss.

'Yes. How are her parents? I've been thinking about them a lot.' He sounded genuine, pausing to draw a hand across barely emerging stubble. 'I have a young son and I can't imagine what they are going through.'

'They're broken, as you would expect.' My voice came out a little curt, shifting into reporter mode. 'How well did you know Grace?'

Jack chewed his lip, about to speak, but the waiter delivered his bourbon and a fresh basket of bread, which he immediately delved into. Was he nervous, wanting to do something with his hands, or just hungry?

'She was a teaching assistant, as I'm sure you know, but she wanted to move into pastoral care. I was mentoring her, I guess you could say.'

That's one word for it.

'Were you close?'

I caught Jack stiffen ever so slightly. 'Profession-ally yes. There hasn't been much reported on how she died, do you know what happened to her?'

So that's why he was here? He wanted to find out what I knew about the crime. If he'd committed it, why was he asking? Unless it was deflection. It seemed a lot of effort to go through, I wasn't police, just a lowly reporter, my opinion didn't matter.

I drained the last of my mojito, my bladder sig-nalling the urgent need to be emptied. 'I'm going to the ladies',' I announced, standing up, my legs like Bambi on the ice.

God, now he thinks I'm a lush.

I walked as confidently as I could towards the op-posite corner of the restaurant to where the toilets were situated, contemplating how to answer his question.

Should I tell him what I knew, what would likely be printed in Neil's article? Maybe it would gain his trust. Although he'd already lied to my face about his 'professional' relationship with Grace, who's to say he wouldn't lie again.

I stared at my reflection in the mirror as I washed my hands, the dolled-up version of myself with an alcohol glow frowning back at me. Those mojitos had been strong, it wouldn't be a good idea to have another.

When I returned to the table, Jack had ordered himself another bourbon and my plate had been removed. Was he driving?

'They are bringing us some baklava.' He leaned forward conspiratorially. 'I think they know you're doing a review.'

I smiled, hoping Des wouldn't look too hard at the bill when I put it in for expenses.

'Do you know where Grace was found?' I asked, seeing if I could catch Jack in a lie.

'Only from what was reported, the disused railway line, but it goes on for miles.'

'She was found by Worth Church.'

'That's near me!' His eyes widened. Either he was one hell of an actor or he didn't have anything to do with Grace's death.

The waiter arrived with his tray containing our dessert and another two cocktails for me. I frowned at Jack, who shrugged. I hoped he wasn't trying to get me drunk and extract information from me. I reached for one out of politeness, intending to drink it slowly.

'Do they know what happened to her?' He repeated his question from earlier as soon as we were alone again.

'Apparently she broke her neck,' I said, leaning back and folding my arms across my chest.

'So she fell?'

I shook my head.

'Then what happened?' he pressed.

'They don't know.' I could feel the truth bubbling up. 'Someone poured bleach over her.' The words tumbled out before I could stop them from my alcohol-loosened lips.

'What!' Jack's outrage wasn't an act, he shook his head and dropped it into his hands.

Without thinking, I reached over and touched his arm in a gesture of condolence. 'I'm sorry.' Guilt made my throat thick. I'd been too cavalier, said too much without thinking of the consequences. Maybe he loved her. Maybe he didn't hurt her at all.

27

Jack sniffed, lifting his head and I saw his eyes were glazed with tears which threatened to fall. I hid my shame behind my mojito, the sharpness of the lime snapping my focus back. I shouldn't have any more to drink.

'That's awful,' he choked out, his hands balled into fists, his knuckles a milky white.

It was now or never; he'd got what he wanted from me but I'd learnt little in return. In for a penny, in for a pound. 'The police interviewed you, didn't they?'

'How do you know that?' he snapped, snatching up his glass and almost necking the whole thing.

'I have connections.'

'Well then, you'll know I was elsewhere, having dinner with a colleague.'

So the mystery brunette was another work buddy. I hadn't found her photo in the list of teaching staff on the website.

'Can you think of anyone who'd want to hurt Grace?'

Jack's frown lines deepened, and he shook his head. His strawberry blond hair was almost dry, trying to curl on top where he had the most length. 'I have no idea; I told the police that.' He swirled his glass, the ice rattling. 'Did you go to her house, were there any clues there?'

Besides the inscribed book of poems? Well, Jack, I'm not sure. Was that what he was worried about, evidence of their affair? Was his concern about who hurt Grace or whether he was about to be exposed?

'Not that I saw,' I eventually replied. Without realising it, I'd polished off my fifth mojito and I pushed the other one out of reach. The alcohol was impairing my judgement. I tried a baklava in the hope the syrupy pastry might help sober me up.

'Shall we get out of here?' Jack signalled to the waiter and before I knew it, he was pulling his wallet out of his jacket pocket. I waved him away a little too forcefully.

'No, I'll get it, I'm claiming it back on expenses.'

'Put the bourbon on a separate bill, would you, mate?' Jack instructed the waiter who approached. 'I don't want you getting into trouble with the boss.' He grinned at me, a sharklike smile meant to reel me in. The grief he'd displayed for Grace had been short-lived and I remembered he was already onto another woman.

'I need to get home,' I said, retrieving my phone so I could pay.

'We could go somewhere else, grab another drink in The Old Bank?'

'Isn't it a school night?' I spat, unable to keep the sneer out of my voice.

His eyes darkened. Clearly, being rebuffed wasn't the norm for Jack.

'It is,' he conceded. 'Okay well, let me take you home, my car is parked around the corner.'

I snorted, as if I would get into a car with him. For one thing he could be a murderer and secondly he'd be over the limit after the bourbon.

'I can walk, Jack, it's fine.'

The waiter arrived with the bill, card machine in hand. I waved my phone at him to indicate I was ready to pay and Jack helped himself to one of the mint chocolates left on our table.

'But we haven't even discussed World Book Day.'

I paid, leaving a generous tip, and the waiter gave me the receipt before he turned to Jack with the bill for the bourbon. I stood, speaking directly to the waiter who'd finished with Jack and was now smiling graciously.

'I just wanted to say, the food was fantastic, thank you so much.'

'Yep, we'll be back.' Jack appeared beside me and tried to help me on with my coat, like we were a couple. I shrugged it on awkwardly, not liking where this was going.

He followed me out the door as I attempted to walk without swaying. Although intoxicated, I didn't fail to notice the pressure of his hand lightly at my back.

'You really don't have to walk me; it's only five minutes away.' I giggled to myself, on another night, unbeknownst to Jack, we would have been going back to the same place.

'It's fine.' He rubbed his hands together to keep them warm. 'At least the rain has stopped.'

The air was damp and filled with the smells of the surrounding restaurants we passed. It had poured down while we'd been inside Marmaris and the pavements were slick as we navigated our way around a queue of teenagers outside the kebab shop.

'So much for spring, eh?' Jack tried to continue the conversation, but I wanted to get back to the safety of Megan's flat so I could crawl into her bed, frustrated I hadn't been able to shake off Jack's offer to walk me home.

'I'm so bored of the rain,' I admitted eventually.

'World Book Day should be fun,' Jack said, clearing his throat. 'My son is going as Dog Man, as, I believe, half the boys in his class are.'

'Cute. Are you all prepared for the big event?'

'Oh, Claire is all over it, that woman is a machine. The kids love her.'

I couldn't help but smile at his praise for the colourful librarian as he regaled how many children she'd single-handedly taught to read since she'd joined St Wilfrid's.

'We're here,' I announced, when we reached Megan's front door. I stood awkwardly, waiting for Jack to speak, but his gaze moved from my eyes to my lips and for a second he looked as though he might try to kiss me. I fumbled for Megan's key and he took a step back, the moment passed.

'Thanks for agreeing to meet with me, Molly, I appreciate it.'

'No problem.'

'I had a nice time.' His eyes slid back to my lips, then lowered to my chest for a second. I tried not to shudder, pulling my coat tighter around me.

'Me too,' I replied quickly, checking my phone, 'will you get back in time to put Nathan to bed?'

I didn't recognise I'd said something out of turn until Jack's face changed. His eyes narrowed and he looked at me quizzically, his chin jutting forwards.

'Umm, no, I'm probably too late.'

'Oh okay,' I stuttered. 'Well drive safe.' I turned my back and slid Megan's key into the door, but Jack hadn't moved from his spot on the pavement.

'See you Thursday,' he said, slowly as though he was contemplating if he would, while I stepped inside and closed the door. I slid down to the welcome mat, air rushing out through my cheeks.

'Fuck!' I banged the back of my head hard against the PVC, hoping Cassie and Louise were still out and not about to come downstairs and see what the noise was. I couldn't believe I'd been so stupid. Jack hadn't told me his son was called Nathan, yet I'd opened my big, fat mouth and now he was wondering how I knew. If anything it made me look as though I'd done my research, because I liked him or perhaps I wanted to become the next notch on his bedpost. Inwardly, I cringed at the faux pas.

Although, did it matter what Jack thought as long as it wasn't the truth? I highly doubted he had any suspicion I was secretly living in his home. If he imagined I had a crush on him, that was fine, I'd let it play out as long as he didn't make a move, because if he did, there was the possibility I might scream bloody murder. There was also the possibility he might murder me.

Squirming with embarrassment, I sighed and got up, half crawling upstairs, relieved to find the flat empty. I quickly washed my face and drank a pint of water before climbing into Megan's bed like I'd won the lottery. Her double divan with its soft mattress and plump pillows was a stark contrast to the Reillys' wardrobe and I could sleep in any position I wanted, able to fully zone out and stretch my limbs without keeping one ear alert for any visitors. Writing up the review could wait; I wouldn't be able to concentrate or produce anything worth reading.

It turned out to be the best night's sleep I'd had in months. Even when I was staying at Megan's before, I'd been on the sofa, which was lumpy as hell. She'd always offered to share her bed, but I hated putting her out almost as much as her flatmates hated having an extra guest on their sofa. I woke to the noise of the kettle and guessed it was Louise who was up, because no light shone through the curtains and I knew Cassie rose late. I rolled over to check my phone, finding a multitude of notifications from practically everyone I knew. Rubbing my eyes, I scrolled through them.

Megan had sent a few texts checking I was okay; the last one was sent after I'd fallen asleep, but she'd made Cassie come into her room to see if I was there. I must have been dead to the world. I quickly responded, apologising and promising I'd fill her in when she was back on Friday. Mum had called and left a voicemail asking me when I was going to fly over to visit, and Des had messaged to let me know Neil's piece had gone live. I had emails from @HomeSweetHome to read too. If only I could get my brain to function after way too many cocktails the night before.

I was tempted to roll over and go back to sleep for another couple of hours, knowing the only thing I needed to do today was write up the review for Marmaris and do a little preparation for World Book Day tomorrow. My mouth was like sandpaper but quickly became the Sahara when I saw an email arrive in my inbox from Jack.

28

I checked the time; it was a quarter past six. He had to be going for a jog. I imagined him lacing up his trainers, checking his phone for messages. Had he put the burner phone back into the cistern?

I opened the message, my palms sweating.

Thanks again for meeting me. Looking forward to seeing you tomorrow for World Book Day. Let me know if you get any updates on Grace's case.

By the way, how did you know my son is called Nathan?

Jack

Memories of letting that slip last night came rushing back and I pulled the duvet over my head. How could I explain knowing what his son was called, it was hardly in his biography on the school website. Then it came to me. *Just be coy, Mol, you don't have to tell him everything.*

I tapped out a reply.

Because I <u>always</u> do my research.

I almost put a winky emoji, but my reply sounded flirtatious enough as it was. If that's how this was going to roll, I'd have to go with it.

Satisfied with my response I messaged Mum some random dates towards the end of March for a visit I could hopefully postpone when it got closer and clicked the link in Des's message to Neil's article on the *Crawley News* site.

The body of a woman found by a dog walker last week in Crawley has been identified as missing local woman Grace Stewart.

On Friday 28 February, West Sussex Police were called to a section of the disused railway line in Worth, where the deceased, Grace, a twenty-three-year-old teaching as-

sistant, was reported missing after not returning home.

A police spokesperson said their thoughts
were with the family at this 'difficult time'.

Grace's death is being treated as suspicious and the force has reached out to the
local community for anyone who might have
seen Grace in the lead-up to her disappearance.

That was it, hardly an exposé. No mention of
how Grace died, the bleach or the fact they believed
her body had been moved. My stomach churned at
how much I'd revealed to Jack which wasn't in the
public domain. I should have kept my mouth shut;
in fact, I shouldn't have met with him at all. I was
playing with fire and I knew it. Because of me, now
he knew all the details the police had, which meant
he was one step ahead of us all.

The heat under the duvet evaporated, replaced
by a chill which was not down to Megan and her flatmates trying to keep their energy costs down.

I heard Louise head for the bathroom and a
minute later the shower was running.

Throwing off the duvet, I crept into the kitchen
and made a coffee with the hot water remaining in

the kettle and slunk back to Megan's room. I wanted
to keep a low profile, knowing neither Cassie nor
Louise would be thrilled about me staying and definitely not using their milk and coffee supplies.

I sat up, plumping the pillow against the headboard and retrieved my laptop from my rucksack. It
would be easier to respond to my emails on there
and I wanted to see what @HomeSweetHome had
to say.

Millie, did you find out what happened to
Grace?

Then another a while later.

Are you okay?

I chewed my lip before responding.

Can I trust you?

@HomeSweetHome, or rather Harry from Plymouth, was bound to be asleep, he was a university
student and it was early on a Wednesday morning,
so I turned my attention to the review for Marmaris.
I tried to conjure up the taste of the delicious

chicken shish which had been tender and full of flavour, but unfortunately the only thing on my palate was the remnants of the mojitos I'd consumed and the acid burning in my belly. Even the coffee was making my stomach churn. I'd surreptitiously taken some photos of the food before Jack arrived so used them as inspiration for my glowing review.

Once finished, I sent it off to Des, along with the photos and my expense form, seeing I'd already had a response from Harry.

Of course. I told you. I didn't post where you were on the public site even though I could have.

He was up early, but he could have a lecture at nine or maybe he was a morning person.

Okay, when you have time, can you send me everything you can find out online about Grace Stewart?

His response was almost instant.

I don't have a lecture until eleven so I can have a look now. I've just seen it's a murder investigation. If you give me the name of the guy where you're phrogging, I can look him up too.

I didn't want to go that far, not yet. I had no idea if I could trust Harry, but like he'd said, he could have outed me in the comments on my blog, but he hadn't. I had to give him points for that.

I replied, choosing my words carefully, not wanting to alienate someone who could possibly help.

I will, but not yet. Like you said, it's a murder investigation and we have to tread carefully. They've already interviewed him and there's been no arrest, I don't even think he's a suspect, but I'm sure he's involved somehow.

It didn't take long for him to reply.

Okay, I understand, but I get the feeling you aren't telling me everything. I'll start the search on Grace and let you know what I find.

I typed a quick thank you and deleted the emails from my inbox.

The whole day stretched out before me, but I rolled over and dozed until all the movement around the flat ceased. I wasn't sure if Cassie was shut in her room or whether she'd gone out, but when I ventured to get some toast, no one materialised to glare at me. My clothes were almost dry so I used the iron and folded them neatly back into my rucksack. It was like the Tardis in there and luckily most of my outfits consisted of interchangeable jeans, T-shirts and leggings.

I had a shower and washed my hair, concerned it smelt a little too much like the Turkish grill from last night. I perused Megan's wardrobe, spying a cute burgundy corduroy skirt and lightweight jumper I could wear to St Wilfrid's tomorrow. We were almost the same size, although Megan was taller. I didn't think she'd mind, but I called her, anyway, leaving a rambling voicemail about Jack and asking if I could borrow the outfit. Not wanting to start my preparation for World Book Day I gave the flat a quick tidy up and a hoover, washing and drying up the breakfast plates. I placed a twenty-pound note on the side, scribbling 'thank you' on a scrap of paper. At least I'd contributed something towards my stay this time.

When I booted my laptop back up, Harry had

emailed despite it being less than two hours since we'd last communicated.

> My search is done. If you give me your number, I can talk you through what I've found.

I wasn't going to fall for that, but my curiosity was piqued.

> Give me yours, I'll call you.

He did and I dialled 141, knowing it would come through to him as 'No Caller ID'.

'Hey, Millie.' Harry's voice was deep yet gentle, not at all what I was expecting.

I cleared my throat. 'Hi, Harry, nice to meet you.' I let out a laugh, trying to cover my awkwardness, and I heard Harry chuckle at the other end.

'How about we switch to a video call,' he suggested and I recoiled.

'I'm not sure about that! Well, you can if you like, but I'm not showing my face.' My phone indicated Harry's video was trying to connect and I swiped to accept, making sure my camera was off.

Harry's face popped up, a floppy dirty blond

fringe which hung down to baby blue eyes. He had a manly jawline with a cleft chin that put Henry Cavill's to shame. My cheeks flamed and I was grateful Harry was unable to see.

'So,' he said, quickly launching into what he'd found, displaying his laptop screen, 'have you ever done a reverse image search?'

'Once, for, like, trainers or something.'

'Well, I did for Grace. Because other than her Instagram, which doesn't yield a lot, she didn't have a massive online presence. She might have been on Snapchat, but I can't access that.'

'Go on,' I encouraged.

'Okay I'll start at the beginning. Grace Mary Stewart, born tenth of January 2002 to Sally and Roy Stewart at East Surrey Hospital. Raised in Crawley, went to St Wilfrid's School, then college to study childcare. No significant others to mention, Instagram posts mainly tag friends Dawn Cottrill, Sandra Caldeira and Elaine Boyle on nights out, otherwise it's all memes about teaching or positive quotes.'

I thought Harry had finished but he'd only paused to take a breath. His excitement through the screen was palpable and my eyes widened with every word.

'Hobbies include swimming, volunteering at a dog rescue place in Godstone and reading, a big fan of the poets apparently.'

My smile grew as I watched Harry gesticulate.

'Bank account at HSBC, still living at home with her parents, annexe in the garden apparently, father undergoing treatment for bowel cancer, massive fan of the series *You* and has a major thing for some dude called Penn Badgely, which sounds made up.'

Harry finally stopped and leaned over to take a drink of water from his bedside table.

'Wow, that's amazing.' I was unable to believe what he'd found in such a short space of time.

'That's not all. You know I mentioned reverse image searching?'

'Uh-huh.'

'Check your inbox.' Harry grinned at the camera as I refreshed my email to see what he'd sent. The image slowly downloaded onto the screen and I enlarged it to full size. It was a photo of two girls posing with their enormous McDonald's order in their car.

'It's called a mukbang apparently, I went down a wormhole of hashtags.'

'Okay,' I squinted at the screen, 'I don't understand – what am I looking at?'

'Top left corner.'

Outside the car, lit up by the glowing street light, were two figures on the pavement. One of them was Grace and I recognised the other one too.

29

'Jack,' I breathed, letting the name slip out, but Harry didn't pass comment.

'Look at the expression. They're arguing for sure.'

'Okay, that's great but—'

Harry interrupted me, unable to contain himself. 'It was posted a week ago, on Wednesday the twenty-sixth of February at 6.42 p.m., look there's even a date stamp on the Instagram filter they used.'

I gasped and Harry stared straight into the camera, nodding, his eyes alight.

'The night she disappeared.' I bit my bottom lip as I squinted at the picture.

'Was it? I know she was reported missing on the Thursday but...' It was my turn to interrupt.

'Her mum told me she wasn't in the annexe on Thursday morning, her bed hadn't been slept in.'

'Her mum?' Harry frowned and I knew I'd said too much again. I wasn't any good at keeping secrets, it turned out. Maybe it was time to lay my cards on the table. Harry hadn't asked for anything in return for my favour and the more I spoke to him, the more I believed I could trust him.

'I'm going to switch my camera on.' Glad I'd done my hair and make-up today, I positioned the phone and my face popped up on screen.

Harry smiled and I swear his face coloured a little.

'Hi, Millie.' He brushed his hair out of his eyes.

'It's Molly, actually,' I grimaced. 'I'm sorry.'

Harry shrugged. 'It's okay.'

'I'm a reporter for a local newspaper.' His eyes narrowed at first, as though he'd been set up, and I rushed on, trying to explain myself. 'But this hasn't been for a story,' I twirled my finger in the air, 'I've just got caught up in this case because I'm phrogging in Jack's house and he was having an affair with Grace. I witnessed their... interaction,' I said, choosing my words carefully.

I went on to tell Harry everything from the beginning, starting with how I found out about the affair, to the burner phone, the coat which had been
hidden and the fact Jack had slipped under the radar
because no one knew about the pair of them, until
my anonymous tip to the police. I admitted I struggled to believe he was responsible, but equally was
sure he'd had something to do with Grace's disappearance. Harry soaked it all up, his eyebrows
shooting up his forehead.

'I can't believe you met him, twice! It's so mad
and he has no idea you're phrogging at his house. It's
like everything you have, all the evidence, it's all circumstantial.'

'The coat isn't, but it has been washed. It has to
be Grace's, therefore it must still have some DNA
on it.'

'Then give it to the police, or tip them off and tell
them where it's hidden.'

I sighed, frustration mounting. 'I did call the police, gave them his name, told them about the affair.
They've spoken to him and I'm guessing he's
denying all of it. If there's no witnesses or record of
them communicating, then potentially he could get
away with murder!'

'She must have had DNA on her body, surely?' Harry held his hands up, as exasperated as I was.

'Apparently not, because – and like my phrogging at Jack's, this goes no further.'

He nodded, waiting for me to continue.

'Someone doused Grace in bleach.'

Harry leant back against his wooden headboard, running both hands through his sandy hair, the both of us at a frustrating impasse.

'I've got to get ready for a day full of lectures, but let me think about it. I'm sure there must be some way we can connect them. The photo isn't really clear, not of this Jack bloke anyway.'

'Can you send me the name of the person who posted the mukbang, so I can look them up?'

'Will do, talk to you later, Molly.' Harry signed off and I got up from Megan's bed, needing to stretch my legs and burn off some of the adrenaline powering its way around my system.

Talking to Harry had been like unleashing an explosion, but it was good to finally get everything off my chest and out into the open. If Jack was responsible for Grace's disappearance he deserved to be locked up. Once tomorrow was over, I wouldn't have any reason to see him again and I had no choice but to actively start looking for a new place to live. Imagine if he discovered me, he'd think I was stalking him. I had over half of the money I needed for the camper van so it would be a few more months either sofa surfing or phrogging before I could buy my own bed on wheels.

Going back to Megan's bed, I saw Harry had sent me a link to Instagram, where I could find the woman who'd posted the mukbang. She was a college student enrolled in a hairdressing course, but I couldn't find any connection to Grace. Harry was right, the photo had an old-fashioned time stamp filter on it, courtesy of Instagram. It was minutes from Jack's house and also a short walk from where Grace was found and meant there was a real possibility Jack was the last person to see Grace alive.

So he killed her, then went out for dinner? the sarcastic voice in my mind butted in. Who knew what anyone was capable of, psychopaths walked the streets among us anonymously every day, maybe Jack was one of them. I remembered our brief goodbye at the front door last night, how close he'd stood as I'd feared he would try to kiss me. A cold shiver ran the length of my spine. Maybe I'd escaped the same fate.

Wanting to free my mind, I googled mukbangs and was pulled down a rabbit hole of watching videos where people ate large quantities of food and filmed it. I typed up some notes, knowing I could turn it into an article to tout to magazines if it was a new trend coming in from America.

Around lunchtime, I reluctantly got ready to go, making sure Megan's room was spotless and the rest of the flat yielded no evidence I'd been there. I'd put a load of washing on that Megan had piled in a corner of her room and stuck it on the airer, trying to be helpful. She'd responded to my earlier message and said it was fine to borrow the skirt and jumper, so that was one less thing to worry about. I'd still not prepped for World Book Day, the event hanging over my head like a black cloud. Des emailed me that Michael, the freelance photographer, would meet me at St Wilfrid's School at ten. When I could put it off no longer, I reluctantly headed out of the door.

I didn't want to return to Church Road, but only had a couple of hours to get inside before Jack and Nathan came home. Knowing the fence was now up and most of the garden work completed, I'd likely have to use the key I'd cut and risk going in the front door. If the side gate was open, I could let myself into the back, which would be better.

I called Mum to give her an update on life as I walked, the wind cold on my ankles, looking at all the houses I passed, sizing up their phrogging suit-ability and keeping a mental note of any For Sale signs. Mum and dad were shopping at a local market and I could hear the hustle and bustle of the sur-rounding crowds as she half yelled down the phone.

'Honestly, I'm fine, Mum. I've been staying at Megan's.'

'It's about time you got a proper place, instead of crashing at hers,' she scolded.

'I'm saving for the camper van, you know that.' I sighed, knowing Mum was wishing she had a more stable, level-headed daughter she didn't have to worry about.

'It's not safe for a girl to be sleeping on the streets!' she despaired, despite the fact I'd told her I'd be inside a locked van with the curtains drawn. 'Where will you shower?'

'Mum, I just want to try it!'

'Okay, but I think you're mad!'

'Did you get the link I sent you?' I asked, changing the subject.

'Oooh yes, your dad was so proud. Your name on the front page, that's amazing, Molly.'

I beamed, walking a little taller at the praise.

'One day it'll be on the front page of a tabloid,' I said with utter conviction.

'We have no doubt, then you might have enough money to buy your own place.'

I grimaced, the conversation always led back to putting down roots, buying property and grown-up things I had no intention of pursuing. My parents had never understood my hedonistic nature, despite their penchant for travel.

'I've got to go, Mum; I'm getting on the bus,' I lied, not willing to continue the conversation. Having my parents in Spain made things easier in some ways, their disapproval could only be felt down the phone and I had the choice when that happened.

When I turned the corner into Church Road still trying to recover from Mum's sour tone, I blanched when I saw an ambulance with blue flashing lights outside the Reillys' house with a first responder car behind.

'What the hell's happened?' I muttered as I broke into a jog.

30

When I got closer, I saw the patient was the grumpy neighbour next door and he was being wheeled on a stretcher into the back of the open ambulance. I slowed to a walk, trying to catch my breath. His black Labrador was in the window of the lounge barking and my heart lurched, but I used the distraction to whizz past and enter the code for the gate for number six, which was four fives, thinking it would look much better than me climbing over. The number was pinned to the wall in the hallway by the front door in case any of the Reillys forgot, even though Jack had a remote control for his car. Hopefully there weren't too many people looking out of their windows right now and even if there was, all their focus would be on the ambulance and not on me.

The driveway was empty and I hurried to the door, checking the camera doorbell displayed no sign of life, and used my key to gain entry. My heart thudded against my ribcage at the brazen entrance to somewhere I shouldn't be. The house was cold; despite the sunshine outside, it wasn't high enough in the sky to warm the lower levels. I slipped my boots off and carried them through to the kitchen. Everything looked the same as it always did, tidy, clean lines and polished floors. How Helena kept up with it whilst working I had no idea because I'd only seen the cleaner come in once, unless she'd been whilst I'd been out.

I had a look in the fridge, but there was nothing but fresh ingredients, so I resorted to the snack cupboard and found a Cup a Soup packet in the back.

Taking the steaming mug and a packet of crisps wedged beneath my arm, I juggled my boots and climbed the stairs, already dreading the confines of the wardrobe after sleeping in Megan's bed.

'Shit!' I hissed, slopping hot soup onto my hand when I reached the top and saw boxes of flat-pack furniture had been laid out in the centre of the room. The Reillys had bought a bed, which meant they had to be moving up to this floor. Or maybe it was going to be Helena's room alone after she'd found the underwear?

I put the mug down and slid open the wardrobe, my stomach sinking further when I saw my bed space had been filled with stiletto shoes in clear boxes. Above hung Helena's clothes from the rail. The other wardrobe hadn't been filled yet, but I had an uneasy notion it wouldn't be long.

Outside, the garden had been finished, the new wooden fence glowed in the sun, with a soil surround ready for plants, a small rockery created where my entrance from the overgrown mess beyond had once been. I cursed; now what was I going to do?

I checked the airing cupboard, but it was teaming with towels and sheets as it had been the last time I'd looked. Nathan's bedroom had little free space and the office upstairs only housed the beige sofa and small desk; no places to hide. The only realistic space to sleep was the cupboard under the stairs, where I doubted I'd get comfortable, or the garage, where I'd freeze to death when the temperature dipped. There was nothing for it, I'd have to go back to Megan's, but as I was about to grab my things the front door opened and Jack came in.

My stomach lurched, how had I not heard the car? I rushed out of the office and up the stairs two at a time, knowing Nathan's little legs would sprint up to his bedroom any minute. I took my soup and rucksack and squeezed inside the small compartment of the other sliding wardrobe that was yet to be filled with Helena's things.

As expected Nathan thundered upwards and I sank down to the carpet, discombobulated. I wasn't in my normal space and was unable to relax, fearing I'd be discovered. What if Jack came up to assemble the bed? What if Helena decided to move the rest of the stuff up when she came home from work? I chewed my nails, anxious at what was to come, but now I was stuck. Unless they went out again, there was no way I'd escape the house without being seen.

Two hours went by with me straining to listen to every movement from below, as though I'd been transported back to my first night, but everything went as it usually did. Jack cooked dinner, a Chinese dish by the smell of it. Helena came home, and even from up here I could sense the atmosphere was frosty. Every time I feared there'd be a creak on the stairs, none came, and I remained the only person on the second floor for the entire evening. When it came time for Nathan's bath, I drew back the door and stuck my head out, trying to absorb every inch of conversation between husband and wife that floated up.

I wasn't sure what I'd missed while I'd been away, but things hadn't much changed between the pair. They seemed to bark at each other rather than talk, so much so Nathan whined they didn't love each other anymore.

'I'll get the bed built at the weekend,' his tone clipped, 'if it will make you feel better.'

'I don't know what to tell you, Jack,' Helena said in a hushed whisper outside the bathroom door. 'You had dinner with another woman just last night, you came home smelling of alcohol. You're clearly checking out of our marriage and you must think I'm a doormat if you expect me to put up with it.'

I chewed the inside of my cheek as nausea washed over me.

'I didn't *have* dinner, I met with a reporter, we were having a chat, that's all, partly about Grace – I wanted to find out if my name was going to be in print. I know her because she's doing a piece at school for World Book Day.'

'You were seen, Jack, at the restaurant! Rosie, who gives me a lift to the station, was out last night.'

I winced at the venom in her voice.

'Seen doing what exactly?' he said. 'Sitting across the table and talking. She was there reviewing the place. This is exactly why I didn't mention it, I knew you'd turn it into something it's not.' Jack's frustration was mounting.

Nathan splashed louder in the bath, like he was trying to drown them out.

'Don't try to turn this around on me.'

'You're blowing it out of proportion,' Jack said, 'it was innocent, damage limitation. The rest of the staff already seem to know I've been questioned by the police and I wanted to know if my name was going to be published.'

'Oh, don't be ridiculous, it's not as if they've named you as a suspect.'

'That might not matter when it comes to the newspapers, the head is worried about the reputation of the school being tarnished with the publicity, that's why I sought out Molly. Do you want me to lose my job?' Jack sighed, the fight in him evaporating. 'I promise you, Hel, you have nothing to worry about.'

I wished more than anything Helena would grow a backbone and get rid of him, take Nathan and find someone who deserved their love, but her affections seemed committed to a man who couldn't keep his dick in his pants. I was almost positive if I'd invited him inside for a drink last night, flirted with him and made a move, he wouldn't have turned me down. The ring he wore on his left hand obviously meant little to him.

'Despite what the police may think, I *know* you had a fling with Grace. I meant it when I said it's your last chance, Jack. If I find out you've been sniffing around any other pretty young twenty-some-things, you'll be out the door so fast your feet won't touch the ground.'

I smirked. *Go, Helena.*

It would be interesting to see how he'd play it tomorrow, whether he would be professional and courteous with me or lecherous. I was eager to gauge what his colleagues thought about him, watch his interactions with the female faculty and see if I could sniff out the identity of the mystery brunette. In fact, I still had to prep and write down some interview questions for Claire, the librarian. Sliding the wardrobe door shut, I booted up my laptop and got to work.

I finally relaxed when it got to bedtime and the house grew silent, my mind wandering to the old man next door and if someone was taking care of his dog. Helena retired to bed alone and I assumed Jack stayed downstairs; neither came up to the second floor. I finished my preparation for World Book Day and checked my emails but had nothing from Harry.

When I checked my blog post I'd received more comments than I expected. Surprised to find readers were still invested in my phrogging experience despite my lack of regular posts. Maybe it was time to give them a bit more information, something they could get their teeth into.

* * *

Blog Post #7
www.phrogging.com

Hi Phroggers. Again I'm sorry to be posting late. I really did want this to be a nightly blog, but it's been a bit difficult recently. It's been just over a week since I've arrived, but I have spent a couple of nights away from the house due to various circumstances.

Annoyingly I've returned today to find the area in which I've been sleeping looking like it's going to be inhabited soon. Flatpack furniture has arrived and I think perhaps the wife, or the husband, will be exorcised from the marital bed, if you catch my drift. To say things are rocky would be an understatement, but it's the kid I feel sorry for, especially with a philandering dad who, it seems, can't keep his hands to himself.

I met him, out in the real world, which was bizarre to say the least and let me tell you, he's on the lookout for the next notch on his bedpost, I'm sure of it. The police haven't been back, so I guess they aren't treating him as a suspect. No one knows they were to-gether, his wife suspects, but it seems I'm the only living witness who saw them and I wish I could prove it, but I can't. It would be my word against his.

From what I understand, the investigation into the mistress's death seems to have stalled. Without going into too much detail, whoever hurt her made sure there was no DNA evidence to find. I need to look for somewhere else to live fast and maybe I should put this behind me, but the thought of no one being held responsible for the death of this poor, young woman haunts me daily. Her parents are broken and I could potentially hold the key to it all.

Is it time for me to come clean, tell the police what I've been doing and face the consequences? Should I do the right thing even though I'll get into trouble and risk losing my job? It's weighing on my conscience the fact I've kept quiet up until now, I've made an anonymous tip, but it hasn't led anywhere. The police haven't been able to put the pieces together. So I'm torn, phroggers. What would you do if you were me?

31

I uploaded the blog and dropped Des an email asking for any updates on the investigation. He knew I was like a dog with a bone, so it wouldn't surprise him. I wanted to get hold of Neil too, but he was hostile at the best of times and likely still hadn't forgiven me for approaching Grace's parents before he could slither his way in. I hated being out of the loop and if I didn't have the World Book Day event tomorrow, I'd go into the office looking for answers. Perhaps I would, as soon as I could get out of there. I had debated about confiding in Des, but I was so worried he'd chastise me and it would set me back professionally, I'd decided to keep quiet.

I logged off and curled up into my sleeping bag.

The empty section of the sliding wardrobe was slightly smaller than the one I'd previously been sleeping in and I struggled to get comfortable, Megan's luscious bed now a blissful memory. Maybe Mum was right. I was a grown woman sleeping in someone's wardrobe, it was ridiculous, but I'd stubbornly stuck to my guns, knowing my savings were creeping up and I'd soon be able to afford the camper van.

I slipped into a fitful sleep, waking as usual with the sounds of a frantic morning coming from below. Helena was yelling at Jack not to forget Nathan's art project and, Jack was shouting at Nathan to hurry up and get dressed into his Dog Man costume. All the noise was giving me a headache and I was an entire floor away. I had a stiff neck and my back was killing me, I couldn't wait to unfurl my body and stretch my limbs.

Finally, everyone left and I emerged to go downstairs and make a coffee, I'd need it today. Knowing I was going to be surrounded by boisterous kids, dressed up and excited at the prospect of being let out of their lessons filled me with dread, but I'd smile and suck it up, get my article and Michael's photos like a good reporter.

With time slipping away, I had to get my backside into gear, so I jumped in the shower and got ready, pleased with how Megan's skirt and jumper looked as I stood in Helena's full-length mirror. I should make more of an effort on a daily basis. I spent as much time as I could afford on my hair and make-up because today was a test of sorts. I was intrigued how Jack would be with me, especially after my email, which could have been perceived as flirty. I'd been a bit abrupt towards the end of the night when we'd met, mainly because I wanted to get rid of him despite his insistence at seeing me home safely. He'd given me the creeps, but we'd be in broad daylight, in a school filled with other people, so I had nothing to fear.

I left the house via the back door and through the side gate, hurrying down the driveway and hopping over the low double gates. Last night I'd written a note to put through next-door's letter box in case the old man was back from hospital, or any relatives needed help with the dog. I slipped it in, listening for sounds of barking, but the dog wasn't in residence. Whatever happened at number six, I could still be around to walk or feed the poor mutt if need be.

I wouldn't have time to walk to the school so decided to jump on the bus, checking my emails while I waited for it to come bumbling down the road.

Harry had sent a quick email to say he was working today at a coffee shop and would write more later but hadn't been able to stop thinking about a way to connect Jack and Grace. I knew the feeling, it was all I'd been thinking about. I tapped a quick reply, thanking him for his help.

Scrolling down, Des had responded to my email asking about the investigation and I eagerly clicked to open it and see what he'd written.

Grace's house broken into late Tuesday night they think, nothing was taken. Might be worth dropping by. No leads from the police as of yet. Neil is on standby, but nothing to report on investigation.

Holy shit! Someone had broken into Sally's house or did Des mean Grace's annexe? Why would they break in if nothing was taken? I didn't have Sally's number, nor did I have time to make a detour, but I'd visit on the way back from St Wilfrid's if I could get past the family liaison officer.

By the time I got to the school and buzzed in at the gates, I flattened down my flyaway hair and tried to present myself as cool and collected when I got into reception. Although when I approached the desk, I suddenly lost the ability to speak. Behind it, asking me to sign in so she could issue me a badge, was the mystery brunette I'd been searching for.

'I'm sorry, have we met before?' I asked when I'd regained my speech, signing the visitor form.

'I don't think so.' She smiled, flashing a wide and welcoming smile. I looked down to see her name badge. Ivy Fanning. Was Ivy Ian in Jack's burner phone?

The receptionist was pretty, the same big brown eyes and full lips I'd seen on Mrs Chen's security footage where she'd been sliding her foot up Jack's leg in the Golden Lotus restaurant.

'Is Jack, sorry, umm Mr Reilly available?'

Ivy narrowed her eyes at me as she judged whether I was a threat.

'Take a seat, I'll call him for you.' Her tone was crisp, the friendliness evaporated, and it was clear she had a thing for him.

I positioned myself facing the desk so I could see Jack approach. His eyes glinted at Ivy as he came down the stairs. He even winked at her and my throat closed up. Ivy was his current bit on the side, that much was obvious, but was she in danger?

'Thanks, Ivy,' he said, his voice syrupy before he finally turned his attention to me, awarding me his warmest smile. 'Molly!' He greeted me as if we were old friends and my insides squirmed.

You're going to have to act your socks off here, Mol.

'Jack, lovely to see you.' I plastered a smile on my face.

He approached as though he was expecting air kisses but held his hand out at the last minute, clasping mine as he shook it. The feel of his skin on mine almost made me baulk.

'We're all set up and ready for you, let me escort you to the library. Claire has done an amazing job. One of the authors is already here, as is umm, Michael is it, the photographer?'

'Wonderful.' I pulled my notebook and pen from my bag. 'Did you get home all right the other night?' I asked, loud enough for Ivy to hear as we climbed the stairs, revelling in the huff I heard behind me.

'Of course. Have you heard anything else? News seems to have dried up, I do hope they are investigating thoroughly.' He sounded pompous and I couldn't help but retort.

'I'm sure they are. In fact, I believe they've got a number of leads they are pursuing.' Not remotely feeling guilty about my lie, it was enough to wipe the smug smile from Jack's face momentarily before he recovered.

'Good, good.'

'I was hoping to speak to the headteacher today.'

'Oh?' Jack stopped at the top of the stairs and stared at me.

'About some sort of memorial. The kids adored Grace, didn't they?'

Relief washed over Jack's face. He was hiding something and not just whatever was going on with the receptionist. I had to find out what.

'They did. That's a great idea. I'll introduce you to Mrs Cunningham, she's bound to stop by the library at some point.'

As we walked, Jack reeled off the list of activities they had planned for the students, beginning with the first author talk and signing, followed by some games, a quiz, costume competition and a raffle. The day would finish with the last author talk and book swap. The majority of younger students we passed in the corridor were dressed up as characters from books, I spied a lot of Harry Potter and Road Dahl.

When we got to the library the author talk was already in full swing, with lots of pupils sat in rows of chairs and on the carpet. I spotted Claire, the librarian, behind the author, dressed in an impressive

Dr Seuss's Cat in the Hat outfit with a fully painted face. Michael was moving around, crouching and taking photos.

'They're rapt,' I whispered to Jack as we stayed at the rear of the library and I took notes of the programme, listing the author's name and the book she was reading an excerpt from.

Jack leaned closer, his hot breath melting into my hair. 'Do you know what I love about it? Whatever a child is going through, at school or at home, there is always a book that can help, a character going through a similar situation. It's important they aren't alone. Even when they don't feel they can talk about it or share their feelings, there's an outlet. It's why I'm so happy to be involved, I really advocate reading as a powerful tool whilst children grow and mature.'

'I agree.' I was a little taken aback by Jack's sheer commitment to the cause as he beamed at the children applauding the author. Was there more depth to the sleazebag than I thought or was Jack a conniving actor?

32

Michael came over to say hello and show me the shots he'd got so far, while Jack made his excuses, saying he had a couple of meetings but would return in a short while. The pair of us immersed ourselves for the morning, I did a quick interview with the author of a new sci-fi series, a lovely man in his fifties who had the children hanging off his every word. Then I spoke to a few year seven children who were reading *Captain Underpants* and *Goosebumps* and thought they were hilarious. Michael got some excellent shots of the author signing and, afterwards, the games Claire had arranged for the students. Before I knew it, it was almost lunchtime and I needed to go to the ladies'.

I left Michael with Claire, the pair talking animatedly about their dogs, and escaped with the children down the corridor, hoping I'd stumble across a toilet I could use. The layout seemed to have changed in the six years since I'd been there.

'Hello, can I help you.' I'd been looking at every door for a toilet and almost bumped into the tall wiry woman who'd approached from the other direction. She wore black rimmed glasses and her forest green suit was expertly fitted to her narrow frame. Her voice was polite but stern as she attempted to find out who I was and what I was doing roaming the school's corridors.

'Sorry, I'm Molly, from the *Crawley News*.' I held up my visitor badge. 'I'm here covering World Book Day. It's going fantastic in there,' I gestured behind me, 'but I was just looking for the toilet.'

'Ah, welcome, Molly, I was going to pop in, but here, let me escort you to the ladies'.' She turned on her heel and walked so fast I had to widen my stride to keep up. When we reached the toilet, she turned and I saw her name badge read Mrs Cunningham.

'You're the headteacher?'

'I am.' The corner of her mouth tilted upwards. 'Did you want to interview me?'

'Yes, and actually there's something else I want to discuss with you, if you'll wait two minutes.'

I dashed inside, trying to be quick, and when I came out, Mrs Cunningham and I had a brief conversation about World Book Day before I offered my condolences on the loss of Grace. I explained I'd visited her mother, who had given me permission to write a piece on Grace, and asked whether she'd consider putting some kind of memorial up. Mrs Cunningham was stoic, although I could see Grace's death had come as a shock, her chin quivered when she told me how much the students adored her. In regard to the memorial, she already had plans for a plaque to go up in the corridor outside the classroom Grace assisted in so the students could see her face every day.

Once our conversation ended, the headteacher admitted she was keen to get to the library and see what Claire had planned for the rest of the day. I asked her to help me find Jack as I had some more questions for him, and she led me further along to his office. His door was open and a curvy brunette leaned against the frame, her hip jutting out in a too-tight pencil skirt. Mrs Cunningham raised an eyebrow as she approached.

'Ivy, are you on lunch?' Her voice was acidic and Ivy whipped round like she'd been poked with a cattle prod.

'Just finished.' She hurried down the corridor, awarding me an icy stare as she passed, like it was my fault she'd been caught loitering.

'I have Molly for you,' Mrs Cunningham said to Jack, who waved me in. He didn't bat an eyelid at Ivy's apparent infraction and the headteacher didn't raise it, instead she told me how nice it was to meet me and that she was looking forward to seeing the coverage in the *Crawley News*.

'Making friends?' Jack smirked once his boss had left.

'Always,' I replied, clasping my hands together, my palms already damp. I was keen to see Jack's office, to learn what I could whilst I was here but being alone with him put me on edge. 'She's going to put a plaque up for Grace, outside the classroom.'

'I thought she might, it's a great idea and will keep Grace's face in the children's minds. They've found it difficult to comprehend she won't be back.' His voice tapered off and he looked past me for a second, perhaps conjuring up her image.

'Are you ready to head back to the library? It

looks as though I need a chaperone.' I attempted to laugh, but it came out more of a croak, unable to ignore the urge to be around others.

Jack's focus snapped back to me, sizing me up. 'You look nice today, Molly, that colour suits you.' He came around the desk like a tiger on the prowl and I willed myself not to recoil. 'But I don't think this leaf goes with your outfit.' Jack laughed, leaning over me so I could inhale his leathery aftershave. I felt the lightest touch on my hair as he carefully plucked out the leaf. My legs wobbled like they were on stilts until my attention was drawn over Jack's shoulder to a piece of paper on the desk tucked beneath his keyboard. The header was visible in capital letters, a pretty typeface. It wasn't a sheet of paper as I'd first thought but the page of a book. *Love Poems*. I gasped and Jack stepped back, believing I'd let out of the sound because of some chemistry we shared, or the proximity of our bodies, a signal he could persevere in his seduction.

'Maybe, Molly...' He paused, his voice so low it was almost a growl. 'You should take me up on that drink.'

I looked up at him, our faces too close and his green eyes mesmerising, reminding me of Kaa from

The Jungle Book. It was like he couldn't help himself but I had to keep him on side.

'Maybe...' I stalled, 'I will.' As if on cue, a student bolted past the office shouting and Jack immediately stepped out to reprimand him, giving me enough time to snatch up the page and slip it in my back pocket.

I ground my teeth together. Even without looking I knew exactly what it was. He'd torn out the inscription he'd written in the book he gave Grace and I'd solved the mystery of the burglary. Jack was so desperate to make sure there was no connection to Grace, he'd broken in to steal it.

'Sorry about that,' Jack said, as soft as silk.

'It's okay.' I tried to look seductive but feared it was more constipated. 'Perhaps we should get back to the library,' I soothed, my ears pink.

Jack's disappointment was swift but he relented and gestured for me to go first into the throng of students making their way to class.

My skin prickled as we walked past a steady stream of oncoming children and some staff, who all smiled politely or said hello to Jack. No one had given me the impression they didn't like him, perhaps maybe Mrs Cunningham, but that could have been directed at Ivy.

'Hiya.' Dawn approached, surrounded by a gaggle of smaller children.

'Oh hi, Dawn!' I beamed at her.

She marched on, rolling her eyes at the children she was trying to escort somewhere, and I could see she had her hands full.

'You know Dawn?' Jack's forehead creased.

'A little,' I admitted, hoping it unsettled him. I wanted him to feel as though the web was closing in, as I was sure he wasn't telling the police everything. It didn't matter; I was going to make Neil give me his contact because it was time to tell them all I knew. If they were still convinced Jack was innocent afterwards, then I'd done all I could.

Back in the library, Michael was chomping on a sandwich while the kids were perusing the books available for the book swap. Jack headed over to talk to Mrs Cunningham and I didn't see much of him for the rest of the afternoon, but I was happy to lose myself in the event, knowing I'd easily have enough to fill a spread. We stayed until the winner of the costume competition was drawn and I made sure to get names of the students we'd had permission to photograph before thanking Claire for inviting us.

Michael had come by car and offered to run me back to the office, where I was keen to see Neil before he left for the day. When we got there, it was like a morgue.

'Where is everyone?' I asked Jo, who blinked up at me from behind her coffee mug.

'You know they don't tell me anything,' she said, shaking her head. 'Morons, they think the world revolves around them. Neil even asked me to grab him breakfast this morning, like I'm his bloody personal assistant.'

I burst into laughter; Jo's glare could cut ice.

'And what did you say?'

'I told him if he asks me again I'll shove his breakfast bagel up his arse.'

I bent over double. Jo had such a way with words, but her delivery was exceptional, she barely batted an eyelid.

'Sexist prick,' she added for good measure. Neil was 'old school', so he thought any female in the workplace was at his beck and call for whatever whim he desired. Jo was a fantastic feature writer who held a degree in English Literature, whereas Neil was a two-bit hack who they only kept on because of his established local connections.

Behind me, the double doors flew open and Neil emerged, red-faced and sweating. Des was a step behind and nodded hello as he passed.

'Want me to pop out and get you an afternoon snack, sweetie?' Jo called across the office.

Neil glared at the pair of us as we both sniggered behind our hands.

'Right, I better go and see what's got their knickers in a twist.' I sighed.

33

I followed Neil to his desk, perching on the end. Clearing my throat, I borrowed a little of Jo's confidence and leaned closer to him, wrinkling my nose as I caught a whiff of stale sweat.

'Neil, I need you to get me in front of your police contact.'

'Absolutely not.'

'I need to talk to them,' I hissed through gritted teeth.

Neil's face turned from red to crimson and he swung around in his chair, manspreading so wide as though his testicles were too big to close his legs.

'You think I'm giving you *my* contact,' he snorted, 'so you can needle your way in with him like you did with the Stewarts? Sure thing, Mol, how about my job too?'

'Stop being ridiculous. I need to talk to him about Grace, there's things they don't know.'

'So tell me and I'll tell him,' Neil said, a little too calmly after his outburst, but I could see the hunger in his eyes.

I shook my head, like I was going to fall for that one. 'It's fine, I'll go to the lead detective on the case instead.'

I marched into Des's office, flexing my fingers. Why was everything such a pissing contest?

'How did today go?' he asked.

'Great. St Wilfrid's put on a brilliant event; the kids were lapping it up. Michael got some fab shots and I'll write it up later today.'

'Nice work, kiddo. Planning on stopping by the Stewarts' on your way home?' Des raised an eyebrow, a smile creeping onto his face.

'You know me too well.' I grinned. 'You don't happen to know Neil's contact at Crawley police station, do you?'

'Huh,' he scoffed, putting his hands on his hips, suit jacket bunching at the shoulders, 'if I did, I would have got rid of him years ago. He keeps his cards close to his chest does Neil.'

'Worth a try.' My shoulders sagged and Des clapped a hand on my back, almost knocking the air out of me.

'That's what I like to see, you're hungry for it now, name on the front page and all that. I said you'd go far, Mol, I could see it in you from day one.'

'It's not like that, Des, I mean, yes I want it, but it's about Grace's case. I hate having to wait to be drip-fed information.'

'Patience is a virtue, but I don't think they have anything, that's what Neil says. I tell you what, see what Mrs Stewart says about the burglary, we can put a small piece in about it, no news on Grace's case but tragic family in mourning suffers another crime, whack in some statistics and it'll go up front, page two maybe.'

'Okay, boss. Oh and can you push my expenses through, I'm skint!'

'Christ, Mol, what do you do with all the money we pay you!' To my horror, he opened his wallet and pulled out a crisp fifty-pound note.

'I can't take that, Des,' I said, shrinking away, but he grabbed my hand and forced it into my palm.

'It's a retainer,' he winked. 'I'll still approve your expenses.'

He drove me crazy, but Des was the softest bloke

with the loudest bark I'd ever met. It wasn't that I didn't trust him enough to tell him my secrets, but I knew he wouldn't look at me the same way when he found out I was phrogging.

'Thank you.' I raced out of the office as my eyes misted over at Des's kindness. I hadn't eaten all day and salivated at the thought of grabbing a subway roll on the way to the Stewarts'.

* * *

The meatball sub wasn't the best choice and especially not while walking and juggling that, my rucksack and a small bunch of lilies I'd picked up. As I got closer to the Stewarts' bungalow, I mopped myself up with napkins as best I could and sucked on an extra-strong mint.

Steeling myself for a brisk snub from the family liaison officer, I knocked on the red door, but it was Sally who answered, immediately inviting me in and offering me a cup of tea. I accepted gratefully and we sat in the kitchen.

'These are for you, Sally.' I pushed the white lilies across the table and thanked her for my tea. 'How have you both been?'

She slid onto the seat opposite, her clothes hanging from her shrinking frame.

'Taking each day at a time, that's all we can do, focusing on Roy's treatment plan, but he's given up – to be honest, we both have.'

I reached over to place my hand on Sally's. 'You mustn't give up, Sally, you have to stay strong and fight for justice for Grace.'

'We're just numb and the fact they still haven't caught whoever did it, well I can't fathom that he's still out there, wandering around with no consequences. What if he hurts someone else.' She swiped a tear away from her cheek, concentrating on a groove in the pine table.

'Have they told you anything? Do you still have a family liaison officer?'

'Yvonne is still with us, she's gone to a meeting at the station, about the case. It seems they are struggling for leads; it's like Grace disappeared off the face of the earth until she was found in that ditch. They've questioned one local man, but he has an alibi. That's all I know.'

I remained quiet, surely at some point she'd bring up the break-in. I needed Sally to believe I'd popped in to see her because I cared, and I did of course, but it wasn't my only motivation.

The silence between us lengthened, Sally stared at her tea, leaving it untouched. She seemed desolate.

'Sally,' a male voice, obviously Roy's, called from upstairs, and Sally jumped up.

'I'll just see what he needs,' she said.

I stood too. 'Do you mind if I get some air?' I asked, gesturing to the back door. Sally nodded and left the kitchen and I ventured into the garden. The annexe was locked, but where the glass should be at the top of the door, a piece of plywood covered it. I moved over to the window, squinting through the glass to see into Grace's bedroom. The book of poems lay on the bedside table, looking untouched, but I knew better.

I had the torn-out inscription in my pocket. I'd checked while I was waiting for my subway order. *I am like a fish in love with a bird wishing I could fly away.* Jack hadn't written his name, but I knew it was his hand. Any handwriting expert would be able to confirm it and it was motive, for the break-in anyway, and if the police could substantiate my claim about their affair perhaps they'd look at Jack harder.

I pulled out my phone and snapped a quick photo of the annexe, the broken door in the centre.

'What the hell do you think you're doing?' I spun

around to see a giant of a woman at the back door, already stalking down the path. 'Delete that photo right now. You need to leave, how you can harass this family after what they've been through.'

'I'm not harassing them, I came to see Sally,' I said, trying to keep my voice calm, but I deleted the photo.

'What? You think because you bought her flowers it gives you the right to exploit her for a story?'

'That's not what I'm doing, I'm trying to keep Grace's name out there, asking the public for help, leads that might mean you'll catch whoever did it.' My neck mottled, but I stood as tall as I could, shoulders back, I had nothing to be ashamed of.

'Please leave and don't come back.' Yvonne, the family liaison officer, waited with her arms folded for me to move past her and she practically rushed me through the house and out of the front door. I felt bad not saying goodbye to Sally, sure Yvonne would poison her against me as soon as I was gone.

'I need to talk to someone on the case.' Turning to Yvonne, I put my foot back in the door so she couldn't close it.

'Are you for real?' She glared at me, her pointed nose pink at the tip.

'I have information, about the case. I want to talk to the lead detective. I'll only talk to them. I think I know who did it and I have evidence.' My words faltered at the end. What I had was circumstantial, but if they could get the coat, it might have Jack's DNA on, as well as Grace's.

'Sure you do,' she scoffed.

'I do, and if you don't do anything, you're letting the man responsible get away with it.'

'Fine, give me your details, reporter Molly.' She smirked and I wanted to punch her in the face. She'd assumed I was the same as Neil, a hack, who would sell their own mother for a story, but that wasn't me and I was insulted at the insinuation.

I dug around my rucksack for a card. Des got them printed up for me when I first joined and I remembered feeling like I'd made it. 'Here, ask them to call me, but I want to meet them face to face.'

'Please leave the Stewarts alone to grieve in private.' Yvonne shut the door in my face and I was disappointed I had nothing to send to Des. However, I had accomplished two things today; I'd seen Jack for the man whore he was and I'd asked to meet with the police. I was doing everything I could to get them to shine the spotlight on Jack, I just had to get them to listen to me.

34

I checked my watch, it was after three and I began jogging back to Church Road, worried I'd missed my opportunity to get into the house before Jack and Nathan returned. There were still no signs of life from the house next door, but I'd left them my number and I assumed if they needed help or someone to dog sit, they'd call. Thankfully, the driveway to number six was empty and I looked around before I climbed over the gate, which was far quicker than entering the code and waiting for it to open. The side gate was locked, so I used my key to the front door, nearly releasing my bowels when a car approached, slowing on the small bridge over the disused railway line.

'Shit, shit, shit!' I hissed as I tried to turn it, but the key was unyielding. I thought I heard the squeak of a hinge, picturing the gate opening behind me and Jack driving in, wondering who the hell the woman was trying to get into his house. Reluctantly, I looked over my shoulder, ready to pretend I was visiting, but the car I'd seen had driven past, sticking to the twenty-mile-an-hour speed limit so many residents ignored.

Finally, the door opened and I slipped inside, closing it quickly behind me, still shaken from what I'd perceived as nearly being caught red-handed. I guessed I didn't have long before Jack would be back, so ran straight to the kitchen to grab a couple of snacks before going upstairs. In the master suite, I shrivelled at the sight of a fully built bed pushed up against the window where the chaise longue had been.

'Holy shit, someone's been busy.' Was Helena so demanding she'd paid someone to put it together today while I wasn't here, had another tradesperson been in? Either way, the room was going to be too crowded for me soon. There was no mattress on the wooden frame and I guessed it was on order. As soon as it arrived I'd have to go, if not before.

My old bed slash wardrobe looked as though it

hadn't changed and thankfully the smaller side was still empty, Helena hadn't got around to filling it yet. I plugged my laptop and phone in to charge and used the bathroom, not knowing when I'd have another opportunity.

It was now four and Jack still wasn't back. Perhaps he'd taken Nathan out to dinner or he had some after-school club. Reluctant to venture back downstairs, I took advantage of not having to cramp myself into the wardrobe so early in the day. I almost wished there was a mattress to stretch out on, but the chaise longue, now against the wall opposite the wardrobe, would have to do. The sun streamed through the window, warming my face as I relaxed, knowing I had the mammoth task of writing up the World Book Day article but putting it off a little bit longer.

I had to write another blog post too, the one I'd posted last night had hundreds of comments, mainly phroggers warning me off telling the police everything, at least about living with the Reillys. Some had been arrested with breaking and entering but none had been charged, most being let off with a warning because the CPS didn't want to prosecute. Even thinking about being arrested made me break out in a cold sweat, it wasn't a path I was willing to go down, which meant I had to avoid being caught at all costs. Some of the commenters advised making another anonymous tip about the potential evidence at the house but told me to make sure I was out first. I needed to find a new home, but scouring Rightmove hadn't come up with any properties that would work and my thoughts turned again to next door. Was the family looking after the elderly neighbour's dog? Maybe the old man was already home from hospital as no one had rung or messaged me yet, but the property would be a dream stay.

I could feel myself nodding off when a buzzing came from the floor and I saw my phone was ringing. It was an unknown caller.

'Molly?' The voice was more of a growl than anything else and I pictured the man behind it frowning down the phone.

'Yes.'

'This is Detective Russell, I heard you wanted to speak with me.' At least Yvonne had passed the message on because I wasn't sure she would.

'In person, yes.' I tried to keep my voice steady and professional, but I already felt intimidated by the gruff voice.

'Are you free now?'

'Is tomorrow morning okay? I can meet you in

Starbucks on East Street, say around ten?' Detective Russell hesitated. It was clear he wanted what information I had now and I couldn't blame him for that, but if I left the Reillys', it would mean sneaking out and sneaking back in. It wasn't as easy as before with all the fences now in place.

'Okay, sure. See you then.' He hung up before I'd had a chance to ask how I'd recognise him.

With my relaxation disturbed, I headed downstairs to the cupboard where I'd last seen the coat. I wanted to be quick; I had no idea when Jack and Nathan would be home. Rummaging through the cupboard and behind the hoover, the coat was nowhere to be seen. The lacy pink underwear was gone too, in the bin probably. All the tangible evidence I'd seen which connected Jack to Grace had been removed, the phone too, if he'd even used it to contact her. I couldn't be sure anymore.

I had nothing to give to Detective Russell tomorrow, other than Jack's torn-out inscription and my insistence I'd seen the other items and knew they existed. I had the photo from the mukbang, if Jack could be identified. Harry was right, it was all circumstantial and if Grace's body held no DNA other than her own, Jack was in the clear.

Deflated, I opened my laptop and checked my

emails. I'd had one from Mum, sending some photos of her and Dad having a day trip to the beach, floating on a lilo in the sea, but further down my pulse quickened when I saw Harry had finally got in touch.

Hey Molly, hope you're okay. Sorry I haven't been in touch much, had an intense day of lectures yesterday and today I had a shift at the coffee shop. I've only just finished! Did you show the police the Instagram photo? I really want to call, but I don't have your number. Harry x

The email was sent an hour ago, so I typed a quick reply.

Hey, I'm meeting the police tomorrow, I'm going to tell them everything – well almost everything. I'm nervous, but I need them to connect the dots. We now know he saw her the night she went missing, that has to mean something. All of the evidence is gone. The photo is all we have left.

I met him again for an event yesterday where he works, it was something I was covering and he was overfamiliar, to say the least. I think he broke into Grace's house, well an- nexe, because he'd written an inscription in a book on her bedside table. I found the page torn out on his desk. It has to be him; he's getting rid of all his connections to her.

I was halfway through writing up my article on World Book Day when Harry responded.

Then we'll find a connection. Tell me his name, let me help you.
Stay safe, Molly. X

After chewing my nails and staring out of the window for five minutes, I relented and sent Harry Jack's full name. What harm could it do, maybe he'd be able to find something the police weren't looking into because Jack had an alibi as far as they were concerned.

Distracted from the article, I checked Helena's Instagram and found a recently posted selfie of three giant ice cream sundaes at Creams, a dessert-only restaurant. It had the caption, *Dessert then cinema to see* Dog Man... *a perfect afternoon spent with my men.* Helena must have got off work early for a midweek treat and at least now I knew what time they'd be home. I checked the cinema times; Dog Man was showing at five o'clock, so it was doubtful they'd be home before seven. I swiped back to the photo of the sundaes and the caption insinuating family bliss. I knew better and it was likely Helena was posting trying to convince herself as much as everyone else they were happy. Maybe she was trying to warn off whoever she thought was trying to steal her man?

Knowing I had at least a couple of hours to kill, I finished the article and took a shower, drying it down afterwards, and ate some leftovers of last night's noodles I found in the fridge. Another hunt through the cupboards, looking for any space where Jack could hide the coat came up short. Perhaps he'd taken it to the refuse tip or maybe he'd burnt it. I washed up everything I'd used and put it away, consistently checking Helena's Instagram posts. I didn't want to get caught out again like I had last time. She'd taken a photo of her and Nathan in the dark cinema, faces hidden behind boxes of popcorn.

I spoke to Megan on the phone at length, filling her in on the events of the past week. She pretty much told me to pack everything up and head to hers, she was returning from Southampton tomorrow and I could stay with her for the foreseeable future. The concern in her voice warmed me, but I assured her I was fine and safe.

It wasn't until the Reillys came home that I wished I'd taken her up on her offer. The yelling began outside on the driveway and carried on as they entered the house.

'Nathan, go and watch your iPad, put your headphones on.' Helena barked her instruction and his footsteps sounded up the stairs before his bedroom door slammed shut.

'You're an absolute psycho, you know that,' Jack shouted.

'That's what you've turned me into. I saw you texting someone in the cinema, who was it?'

'You're crazy, I've told you there's no one else, for fuck's sake, Hel, you need to drop this.'

I squirmed inside the wardrobe, wishing I was anywhere else.

'You're a lying, cheating bastard.' Helena's scream was guttural and followed by a loud smack and a grunt. Had Jack hit her?

35

'Get off, you're hurting me.' Sounds of a struggle came from downstairs and I heard something smash on the parquet floor. I slid the wardrobe open, already on my feet to rush down and intervene. Even if it meant exposing myself, I wouldn't let him harm her.

'Get out, get out,' Helena sobbed, and I heard the front door open and slam shut, shaking the foundations, before I crossed the room to reach the stairs. Seconds later, the Mercedes engine revved and pulled off the driveway so fast the tyres screeched in protest. I watched Jack leave through the window and the sound of clinking glass carried from the kitchen. I imagined Helena sat at the table, pouring herself a large wine, her shoulders wracking with sobs. I wished I could go downstairs and console her, to tell her she wasn't going mad. Jack was gaslighting her and I knew about two of his affairs. I hadn't seen Ivy at Church Road but I'd certainly heard her.

My blood boiled at what he was doing to his family, something I had no business being in the middle of, but here I was and I couldn't stand by and watch him blow up Helena's world. She deserved better than him and tomorrow I'd make sure Detective Russell looked at him properly, then I'd write a piece for *Crawley News* which would make sure his reputation was shot.

An hour later, two of Helena's girlfriends arrived and once she'd bathed Nathan and put him to bed, the party began downstairs. It was a constant stream of music from powerful female vocalists with lots of laughter, singing and slurred voices. I was surprised Nathan hadn't complained he couldn't sleep. None of them came upstairs and I ventured out to sit on the chaise longue and listen to the drunken revelry below. It had been a long and tumultuous day, and all I wanted was to crawl into my sleeping bag, but the party carried on way into the night. With no alternative, I used it as background noise, spending time replying to the comments from the last blog, wanting to wait until I'd spoken to Detective Russell before writing a new one.

Lastly, I wrote a tiny column for Des on the break-in, quoting Sally's words from earlier: 'We're just numb and the fact they still haven't caught who-ever did it, well I can't fathom that he's still out there, wandering around with no consequences, what if he hurts someone else.' I'd worded it so it sounded like I'd interviewed her about the break-in and apolo-gised to Des I didn't get permission to take a photo, explaining my run-in with Yvonne. I also asked him to fact-check it with Neil because he had the police contact and I didn't, although maybe tomorrow I'd have one of my own.

It was almost two in the morning when the party ended and the two women staggered out to a waiting taxi. I heard Helena throw up in the bathroom below before she went to bed and I dreaded to think how she'd feel tomorrow. Jack stayed out all night, but I wasn't surprised – who knew if he'd come back at all.

I was woken up by a loud buzzing and slipped out of the wardrobe to look out of the window at the drizzle. A lorry was trying to get the gate open. Helena trod down the stairs and I was sure I heard a groan when she realised the time. We'd all slept late; it was almost eight and I guessed she'd called in sick for work, which would make life difficult for me getting out of the house.

Helena must have pressed a button as the gate swung open and the lorry came onto the driveway, two men hopping out of the cab to open the rear doors. My heart sank when they pulled a plastic-wrapped double mattress out of the lorry and carried it towards the door. I hurried back into the wardrobe as footsteps climbed the stairs.

'Thank you so much. I would never have got it up the stairs by myself.' Helena's voice sounded croaky and I watched through the crack as the two men dumped the mattress onto the wooden frame. Nathan bounded in and jumped straight on it, bouncing up and down.

'Careful there, little fella, you don't want to slip,' came a soft voice.

'Can I get you a coffee to go, to say thank you. I'm sorry I didn't hear the buzzer at first.'

The men agreed and trotted down after Helena; their voices drowned out by the thump of Nathan's jumping.

'Nathan, you need to get dressed for school,' Helena shouted back up the stairs, 'we're late.'

I breathed a sigh of relief. At least if Nathan was going to school I'd be able to get out of the house, but there would be no shower for me this morning.

I waited until the men were gone, expecting Helena to run through the shower, but from listening to her bellowing at Nathan, it was clear she was chucking some clothes on to do the school run. Jack wasn't back and Helena must have called a taxi as one beeped its horn from the road outside, signalling its arrival, and they hurriedly climbed in. As soon as they left, I got dressed relatively smart in jeans and a pastel cardigan, spraying perfume and giving my hair and teeth a quick brush before making my escape.

Half of me wanted to stay and see what Helena would do when she got back, but I packed all my things in the rucksack just in case it was too risky to return later. Would she climb back into bed for the day in a haze of hungover depression or would she find out where Jack had spent the night? I doubted he'd allow one of those apps that tracked his location, or maybe he'd switched his phone off when he left. It wouldn't surprise me if she got on the phone to a solicitor specialising in divorce. It was going to be an interesting night ahead either way if I decided to return, especially as I was about to hand over everything I knew about Jack to the police.

* * *

I got to Starbucks for half nine and ordered a double-shot latte, my knee jiggling under the table. I wasn't sure if it was nerves or the extra caffeine, but adrenaline rocketed around my system like a speeding train. Keeping my eye on the door, I went over the notes I'd prepared, not wanting to get tongue-tied and forget anything.

Because I'd sat at the back, I didn't notice the burly man in a suit approach my table. He had silver hair cut in a short back and sides, his face was clean-shaven and he had car keys dangling from his fingers.

'Molly?' It was the same voice as on the phone.

'Detective Russell.' I stood up to shake his hand. He asked if I wanted a coffee, but I declined and he got in the queue, allowing me the chance to calm my nerves and size him up. He wasn't tall but he was stocky. I aged him around fifty, maybe younger, and he wore a wedding band. Was he Neil's contact? He could be. If so, would Neil have prewarned him I'd be in touch?

'You said you had information for me?' Detective Russell slid into his seat without any further introduction or small talk and I guessed he wanted to get straight to the point.

'Jack Reilly,' I said, rolling my shoulders back, 'you need to look at him again.'

He gave a vague nod to indicate he was listening, taking his time to add a sachet of sugar to his cappuccino and stir it.

'We did, he's clean.'

I laughed, but it came out more of a snort. 'He's anything but clean!'

Detective Russell narrowed his eyes at me and I already knew what he was going to ask before the words slipped from his mouth. 'What is your relationship with Mr Reilly?'

'I don't have any relationship with Jack Reilly, but I'm going to tell you some things and you're going to need to believe me.'

He leaned back in his chair and flattened his tie against his stomach, waiting for me to continue.

'He was having an affair with Grace; I witnessed the two of them together and I can prove he saw her the night she disappeared.' That got his attention.

I lifted my phone and showed him the post of the college students' McDonald's mukbang, pointing to the top left corner where Grace was clearly visible.

'This was taken, as you can see, at 6.42 p.m. on Wednesday the twenty-sixth of February. That's Grace, and Jack, and that,' I pointed at the photograph, 'is Church Road where Jack lives.'

Detective Russell squinted at the picture. 'How can you be sure that's Jack; he's a bit blurred. Plus he was dining with a colleague on the other side of town that evening; he has an alibi, we checked it out.'

I snorted again, unable to help myself. 'The woman he was dining with is more than a colleague, believe me. He's a serial adulterer! Maybe he did something to Grace before he went out for dinner,' I replied.

'I'm not sure that fits in with the time of death, but I'll look into it. Did anyone else see him with Grace?'

I shook my head and saw his attention waning.

'There's more,' my words rushing out. 'At his house, somewhere, is a coat, I'm pretty sure it's Grace's. It's a green Joules coat, she's wearing it in the photo, but I know it's since been washed.'

Detective Russell's eyebrows raised. 'How did

you know about the missing coat? We haven't released it to the press?'

'I know because she's wearing it in the photo and
I've seen it at their house! Also, there's a book of
poems on Grace's bedside table, it had an inscription
written inside. It's Jack's handwriting and I found
this' – I pulled the page out of my pocket and placed
it on the table – 'on his desk where he works, so he
had to have broken in to retrieve it.'

Detective Reilly frowned at the crumped paper
and I pressed on.

'They were having an affair, no matter how much
he's denied it, and now he's getting rid of everything
that connects the two of them.'

'Do you have a vendetta against Mr Reilly?'

'No,' I said, a little shrill, causing customers to
stare. The vein in my forehead pulsated with frustration. Why wasn't he taking me seriously? 'At his
house he had a burner phone, I don't know if he
used it to contact Grace, I think he now uses it to
contact Ivy, the so-called colleague he was dining
with. She's the latest one he's having an affair with.
There was underwear at the house too, it's not his
wife's, I think it's Grace's but don't know what happened to it because she found it. Speak to her, she's
practically said he's got form for adultery.'

'So you're a friend of the wife's then are you?'

I slapped my hand on the table. 'No, I'm nothing to do with either of them, but I'm telling you, he's your man.'

His frown deepened and he interlocked his fingers, leaning forward in his seat. 'Well, Molly, mind telling me how you know all this?'

36

That shut me up, even though I knew the question would come eventually. I sipped my coffee which was now cold, mouth like sandpaper.

He waited for me to fill the silence, speaking again when I didn't. 'Because it sounds to me, if you don't know them personally, you must be an amateur sleuth.'

'I'm not,' I insisted, a little insulted, 'I'm a reporter for the *Crawley News*.'

'Ah yes, the FLO told me.' He smirked, but I ignored the jibe, he clearly didn't like us as a whole.

'I can't tell you how exactly I know these things, but you need a warrant to search his house, because I'm sure you'll find items in there that will link him to Grace. If nothing else, you've got the photo and the inscription he wrote in her book.'

'This,' he held the page up, 'what you've just given me? For all I know you could have broken into the Stewarts' house and taken it. It might not be his handwriting at all.'

I squeezed my eyes shut; they bulged beneath the lids. This wasn't going anywhere. I could tell Detective Russell wasn't convinced, but I couldn't admit I'd been phrogging, not only to protect myself, but if a case against Jack ever went to trial on the basis of how I'd discovered the evidence, it would be torn apart in court. The police had to set things in motion.

Detective Russell leaned forward in his seat, eyes locking onto mine like a heat-seeking missile. 'Surely as a reporter,' he said with a note of derision, 'you know how difficult it is to get a warrant? We can't go searching people's houses on a whim, there are procedures to follow.'

'Okay, I understand, but I'm telling you, keep looking for a link. That's him in the photograph, he saw Grace, therefore he lied if he told you he didn't. You can interview him again, ask him about the book of poems, check his handwriting, there must be something.'

'We're looking at all lines of enquiry, not only Mr Reilly,' was his automatic response. This was a waste of time. 'Thank you for your information, Miss Hudson. Please don't hesitate to get in touch if you find out anything else. My direct line is on there.' The detective pushed his business card across the table and drained his coffee before getting to his feet.

I didn't reply as he weaved his way through the tables to the exit. I'd done all I could, but it seemed Jack could get away with murder. Not only that but Detective Russell had pocketed the torn-out page and taken it with him. I had no physical evidence left in my possession.

I pulled out my laptop to see if Harry had come up with anything and he had by way of a half page of information on Jack Reilly. I scanned the text carefully, his full name, date of birth, the fact he didn't have any companies registered in his name and his social media profile was non-existent. It was comprehensive, but there was nothing there that would connect him to Grace. I thanked Harry and tried not to let my frustration show in my email. As an afterthought, he'd suggested coming up to visit so we could meet properly. I stared at the screen in astonishment. It wasn't as if I could put him up somewhere, I didn't have a spare room – hell, I didn't even have my own room.

I ignored his suggestion and opened an email from Des, who thanked me for the small column on the burglary and assigned another story to me, this one about the town hall being torn down to make way for housing. I wasn't in the mood to start it today and instead ordered another coffee and took my time writing my eighth blog piece, wishing I had more to tell those who were following my journey. Perhaps I'd ask them for ideas; it was how I'd discovered Harry after all.

When there was enough caffeine in my bloodstream, I dragged my feet along to the supermarket, not particularly inspired but needing to grab some bits. I imagined Neil's smug face when he heard I'd been in touch with the lead detective, spouting nonsense. I wished I could show them all it was true, but they were so blinkered. Did they have someone else in the frame, was that it? There could be plenty of information I wasn't privy to.

I put breakfast bars, biscuits, chocolate and crisps in my basket, easy food I could munch whilst hidden away, but I wasn't sure what exactly I was going back to. I doubted Jack had left for good, in which case, now the mattress had arrived, Helena could be in the master suite tonight. It was time to move on, put Grace behind me and find somewhere new to stay.

As I queued at the checkout, my phone rang, I juggled answering it after I'd paid, trying to put my shopping in a bag.

'I'm back!' Megan screeched down the phone, her excitement contagious.

'Yay! Can't wait to see you.'

'Come round… we can have a lazy day and go out for dinner, or order in. I have so much to tell you.' I knew that meant Megan had hooked up with someone in Southampton and was bursting at the seams to tell me all the gory details.

I laughed, my mood lifting instantly. 'On my way. I'm in the supermarket, do you need anything?'

Megan asked for bread and milk so I made my way back around and picked them up, along with a box of doughnuts for us to share.

Megan's flat was only ten minutes on foot and she squealed when she saw me, pulling me into a hug which sent the doughnuts flying. Before long, the pair of us were lounging on the sofa gossiping and Cassie had come out of her room twice to tell us to keep the noise down.

'Cassie, chill, it's Friday, come and join us, there's

a doughnut here with your name on it.' Megan whirled the chocolate ring around on her finger, but Cassie disappeared back into her room and slammed the door.

'She hates me!' I whispered.

'She hates everyone.' Megan giggled.

It was nice to listen to Megan's exploits and forget this morning's meeting with Detective Russell, which had got under my skin. She'd met another sales representative, Adam, who she'd previously only spoken to on the phone but had got on well with and apparently he was gorgeous in the flesh.

'I barely slept in that luxurious room.' Her cheeks flushed. 'In fact, I barely got any sleep at all.' Megan proceeded to show me a photo of him, one she'd taken covertly, and another they'd taken as a selfie after one too many drinks at the bar.

I'd never heard her so smitten as she drawled on about his chiselled face and wavy dark hair she wanted to run her hands through again. She didn't have to wait long as they'd planned to meet up next weekend because he only lived forty-five minutes away in Chichester.

My chest tightened, it had been over a year since I'd even been on a date, so focused on work and saving for the camper van. Perhaps I should let

Harry visit after all, remembering the jolt in my stomach when his face flashed up on screen for the first time. I wished I'd taken a screenshot so I could show Megan now, sure she'd approve despite the slight age difference between us.

'So tell me what's been going on here. Shit, I forgot you had dinner with Jack. I'm sorry, Mol, I've been so immersed. Tell me everything!'

I relayed the events of the past week; all she'd missed, including my slightly awkward dinner at the Turkish restaurant with Jack and his flirting on World Book Day. I told Megan everything that linked him to Grace, watching her eyes bulge incredulously, and how frustrated I was that he could have done something to her and not be held accountable. I showed her Harry's emails, and how he was trying to help, and although my meeting with the detective this morning had made my blood boil, I was finding it hard to walk away. How could I give up on Grace, or Sally, when it felt like I was the only one who cared about the truth.

'Do you think the wife's in danger?' Megan shuffled closer to me and draped the blanket across our knees. It was already late in the afternoon and the sun was slowly dipping behind the buildings across the road from Megan's flat.

I remembered Jack's outburst, him storming out, the sound of a hand hitting skin before Helena threw him out. A week and a half ago, I had to stay upstairs while I listened to their lovemaking, how much had changed in such a short time.

'She could be,' I admitted, 'she knows about his affairs, or she thinks she does, enough to cause arguments. She's paranoid about it.' I paused, considering for a moment. 'I think he hit her last night before she told him to leave.'

'Bastard! And did he? Leave?'

'Yeah, he didn't sleep there last night. She had some friends over and got wasted.' I imagined Nathan, shut in his room with his headphones on, trying not to listen to them tear strips off each other. How much had he seen, not just last night but since the affairs began? It wasn't fair on him. Nathan was too young to be exposed to this stuff.

'At least she has friends she can lean on then. Imagine what'll happen if he gets arrested.'

'I doubt he's going to; they would have done it already.'

'Why don't you write an exposé, out him online or something, force the police to act?' Megan said thoughtfully, licking icing from her fingers.

'I'll get sued that's why, not to mention fired.' I

laughed. 'If only I could do something to force the police into action. It's so frustrating.'

'I hear you, girl, but I know what will make you feel better.' I caught the glint in Megan's eye, I knew what was coming. 'Chinese!'

* * *

Blog Post #8
www.phrogging.com

Hi Phroggers. I think this might be my last post from this location. It's not safe, the marriage is crumbling and arguments have turned physical. It's always surprising what goes on behind closed doors and I guess it was naive of me to assume I'd be living in a happy home.

The flatpack has been built and tonight there might be a new tenant in what was my room, so I'm contemplating not going back. Last night, the husband left after a row and didn't come home, but I'm assuming he hasn't gone for good. You know I mentioned meeting him out in the real world in my last post, well that happened again, this time under a strictly professional basis.

My opinion of him hasn't changed, as much as he seems to be able to charm those around him, to me he's still a sleazeball who can't keep it in his pants. He was a little too friendly, seemingly happy to cross the line, and it took every ounce of restraint not to run for the hills. Anyway, it was an interesting day and I found out who his latest conquest is. The mistress has been forgotten and he's moved on to someone new.

I took your advice and reached out to the police, but it didn't go well. I didn't tell them how exactly I knew the things I did, but I gave them evidence to back up my theory he is involved in the woman's death. I told them he was having an affair with her, but unfortunately they assume I'm some online amateur sleuth clutching at straws and I wasn't taken seriously. I've done all I can, I gave them a connection and, thanks to outsider help, managed to place him almost at the scene. Potentially he's the last person to see her alive so surely they have to look into that.

There's still no news on the investigation;

the police gave me the stock answer of 'looking at all lines of enquiry' when I practically begged them to search the house. I know there's more secrets in there than me hiding in a wardrobe.

So it looks like I'll be looking for a new location for my next phrogging journey, but I will keep you updated as it's been a blast having you along for the ride.

37

We ordered Chinese to be delivered as I didn't fancy venturing out and Megan was shattered from her week in Southampton. Cassie eventually emerged from her bedroom come office to eat with us and after a while she seemed in better spirits. While we were waiting for the order to arrive, Louise messaged on the flatmate group chat to say she was going out straight from work, so the three of us lazed on the sofa eating prawn crackers and duck rolls while we watched a terrible movie about a first date gone wrong. I tried to be present, but the later it got, the more my mind drifted to what was going on at Church Road and the atmosphere in the Reilly household.

Had Jack returned and smoothed things over or had Helena packed his bags, leaving them outside on the driveway? Was Detective Russell doing his due diligence on Jack's whereabouts that Wednesday night, tracing his movements on CCTV? Although there was little surveillance in the residential areas, he might see him when he got into Tilgate, there had to be cameras on the parade of shops where the Golden Lotus restaurant was situated. Maybe he was preparing to haul him in again and suggest he was lying about the last time he saw Grace?

Megan nudged my knee a couple of times, noticing me staring off into the distance. I couldn't even blame the cheap bottle of wine she'd found in the fridge; I'd barely touched my glass. Unease continued to prickle my skin, the sound of a palm hitting skin still echoing in my ears. I hoped Helena was okay, Nathan too, although I was pretty sure Jack wouldn't dare hurt him. Even so, it was as though they were unprotected because I wasn't there, to witness and intervene if things got too heated. I almost snorted at the thought, it was so ridiculous.

At around ten, Cassie fell asleep in an awkward position which was sure to give her a neck ache and Megan was grinning at her phone, her attention focused on a text conversation with Adam. All the while, my stomach churned. Not knowing what was happening was the worst as my imagination went into overdrive. In my mind, I pictured blue flashing lights, sirens and police tape, Helena's broken body being wheeled down the driveway.

'Wanna hit the sack?' Megan asked as she watched me bite my nails down to the quick.

'Sure.' I glanced over at Cassie occupying half the sofa, she'd begun to snore.

'It's fine, you can sleep with me.'

'If you can manage to stay off your phone long enough,' I teased.

We got into bed and I stared at the ceiling, willing sleep to come. One thing kept niggling at me. If Jack had harmed Grace, why had he been trying to contact her when she was reported missing? It wasn't for my benefit, he didn't know I was watching. It was the one thing I couldn't reconcile. Was I missing something?

* * *

I woke before Megan, sliding out of bed and into the lounge, where the rumpled blanket still lay on the sofa. Cassie must have woken up in the night and returned to her bedroom. I made some coffee, unable to believe I was up before eight on a Saturday morning, and cleared away the remnants of last night's Chinese, lighting a candle to get rid of the smell. I settled into the sofa, snuggling under the blanket, and scrolled through my phone, catching up on social media. Dawn's crowdfunding campaign for Grace's funeral costs had surpassed two thousand pounds and *Crawley News* had shared another article written by Neil on the investigation. I clicked the link and waited impatiently for it to load, but there was nothing new, just a rehash of what was already out there in the public domain.

Out of curiosity, I looked up Ivy Fanning, but her profile was locked down on Facebook. Instagram had a wealth of photos though, mostly of her trying to look sultry using various filters. Brown hair brushed over a naked shoulder and lips parted in surprise as if she wasn't aware she was taking her own photo. Jack didn't feature in any of them, but the night before last, she did post a photo of two glasses of red wine on a mahogany coffee table with the caption 'Love having visitors'. It wouldn't be too much of a leap to assume Jack had spent the night there if he wasn't at home.

When I opened my emails intending to delete the junk which had come in overnight, I saw Harry had sent me three emails, the earliest at five o'clock that morning. What on earth was he doing up so early? The first two were variations of 'call me'. The third one a rush of words with barely any punctuation.

I have a hacker friend he's looked up jack and earlier this week he upped the life insurance on his wife to a whopping one million I think she's in danger.

I stared at the screen unblinking. It was a little obvious wasn't it, upping Helena's life insurance if he had plans to harm her? Wouldn't it be the first place the police would look in terms of motive? I dialled Harry's number from my mobile, reading the email again. When he picked up, there was lots of background noise.

'Molly!' Harry said, breathlessly.

'Hey, Harry, where are you? I can barely hear you.'

'I'm getting on the train.'

My stomach dropped. 'To go where?'

'Some mates of mine wanted to go to Brighton for the weekend, so I decided to tag along. Anyway, I need to talk to you, did you get my email?'

I heard a loud siren in the background and Harry's voice breaking up.

'I got it, I don't think we need to worry.'

'There's more. Jack's old girlfriend, from high school. She went missing and was never found.'

My spine straightened, an icy shiver running down to my tailbone.

'I think I'm going to get cut off, I'll email you now and I'll ring when we get to Brighton.'

'Okay,' I replied, my throat dry.

'Stay safe, Molly.' Harry hung up and I refreshed my email every few seconds, waiting for whatever it was he'd found. Finally, the link arrived, an old newspaper clipping from 2004 in Sutton, now classed as London, but back then it was a Surrey suburb. A slightly fuzzy photo of a petite blond holding some L-plates in front of a maroon K-reg Ford Fiesta, grinning at the camera.

I scanned the article, absorbing every word. Seventeen-year-old Tanya Bishop had disappeared in September 2004, last seen out with friends at a local pool hall playing snooker. She left at ten o'clock to go home but never arrived. Boyfriend at the time Jack O'Reilly stated he was worried for her safety, but she'd had some issues with depression. At the bottom of the article was a small photo of Jack and

Tanya together and despite the extra O in his name, the likeness was uncanny. Clicking back to the information Harry had previously sent on Jack, I saw he was born at St Helier Hospital, Sutton, Surrey, but I hadn't noticed the extra letter in his name.

So Jack had moved to Crawley at some point, either with his family or as an adult, and changed his name, dropping the O so he was just Reilly. Why? Was it to remove the connection to the disappearance of a former girlfriend?

I googled Tanya Bishop but little was found. It looked as though she'd never been discovered. Her disappearance could have nothing to do with Jack, but equally it could mean he had form. My breathing grew shallow. I had to warn Helena.

I rooted in my rucksack for Detective Russell's business card and forwarded the email to him. He had more proficient ways and means to search Jack's background than I did. I made sure to delete Harry's information before sending it. Again it was circumstantial evidence, but wasn't it all about building a picture. The one forming of Jack was becoming less favourable with every new piece of intel.

Slipping into Megan's bedroom, she was still out for the count and I picked up my clothes and shoes like I was creeping out the morning after the night before. I used the bathroom to quickly shower, brush my teeth and get dressed before leaving a note explaining my early departure.

It was almost nine and the streets outside were already filling with morning shoppers. I darted between them, munching on a cereal bar as I debated whether to wait for a bus or walk back to Church Road.

The traffic was light, but I decided to walk, I'd already be arriving unusually early on a Saturday morning which was strange enough, but I also had to think of a reason for my impromptu visit, which was going to be more of a welfare check. I'd never met Helena before, yet I was about to drop a bombshell about who the man she'd married really was.

38

The further I got from the town centre where Megan lived and closer to Worth, the traffic lulled. I passed dog walkers and people heading back from the local newsagents with their milk and morning papers clutched under their arms. It was peaceful, if not a little cold, the tip of my nose numb from the elements. My pace quickened as I imagined scenarios of what might have happened at the Reilly house last night, what scene would I potentially discover? How much did Helena know about Jack's past and his affairs? Would my visit be the last straw and make her throw him out permanently and if so, would it tip Jack over the edge?

With a house like theirs they obviously did all

right for money and I knew Jack's meagre salary in education, renown for being substandard, wasn't carrying the load. Helena had already said she brought in the lion's share. If they split up and got divorced, would she take everything away from him like she'd threatened, even his son? Was that the motive for Jack to increase her life insurance, because he knew she was slipping away?

I licked my dry lips, trying to stop the incessant questions pummelling my brain. My stomach gurgled at the prospect of knocking on their door, still undecided as to what my excuse would be for showing up so early on a Saturday morning.

When I had number six Church Road in my sights, calves aching from speed-walking up the hill, my limbs itched with apprehension. I shook my body and tried to relax my muscles, which were moving into fight-or-flight mode. My chest was tight with knots as I approached the driveway, noticing the gate was wide open and the Mercedes nowhere to be seen. Had Jack already been kicked out, or maybe he hadn't been back since she'd told him to leave?

My throat was parched and scratchy as I made my way up the drive, a stone stuck in the grooves of my trainers, making noise on the resin. I tried to tell myself I was a professional, that's why I was here, for work, and I could blag it like I'd done so many times before.

I rapped on the wood and stood back, cowardly hoping the family were out but my shoulders clenched when footsteps approached. The door swung back and Helena stood in her loungewear and slippers, looking striking as always, even dressed down. She'd applied her make-up and straightened her sleek bob. She was gorgeous, why she wasn't enough for Jack I couldn't understand, but perhaps no single woman was. Her expression, although quizzical, wasn't unfriendly and I was pleased to see her in one piece with no obvious signs there had been an altercation in my absence. In fact, the Reilly residence seemed calm and peaceful. Maybe I'd jumped the gun and doubt began to creep in.

'May I help you?' she asked, her face passive with a hint of a smile.

'Umm, yes, I'm Molly Hudson, a reporter at the *Crawley News*. I was doing a piece at St Wilfrid's School this week that your husband helped organise.'

Helena's eyebrows rose a little and I pressed on.

'I'm sorry to bother you so early, I actually had some questions for a follow-up piece I'm hoping to submit this weekend.' I had no idea where the words came from, but they spilled out of my mouth before I could rein them back in.

'Ah, I see. Jack is out at the moment, but do come in, I'm sure he won't be long.' She drew the door back and I stepped inside, slipping my trainers off by the door automatically. It seemed he hadn't been booted out after all.

Helena turned back from heading into the kitchen, realising I wasn't behind her, and looked down at my socked feet.

'Oh you don't need to do that, come through. Would you like some tea, or a coffee? I'm Helena by the way,' she added as an afterthought.

'Nice to meet you, and coffee would be great, thank you.'

I followed Helena through to the kitchen, the place looking the same as it always did, a show home. My nerves jittered, how on earth was I going to approach this? After hearing Helena berate Jack for having dinner with me, even though that wasn't technically what we were doing, I expected some animosity from her, but either she hadn't made the connection or now she'd seen me in person, realised I was no threat to her marriage. I wasn't sure whether to be offended or not.

I stood awkwardly, watching her move around the worktops with speed, using the fancy coffee machine which growled and whirred, circulating a delicious scent into the air. Finally, she turned to face me.

'How was the event at the school?'

'It was fantastic, I was impressed by how many activities they offered and the kids were so enthusiastic. It's a great school.'

Helena smiled tightly and turned away to retrieve my coffee from the machine.

'Especially since they've had a tragedy recently with Grace,' I added, watching Helena's shoulders stiffen.

She turned around slowly, fixing me with a steely gaze. 'That's not why you're here, is it? To drag Jack's name through the mud?' Her tone had an edge to it.

'No, no, not at all. I mean, I know that he knew her, but...' I stopped, watching Helena's chin wobble. Her demeanour changed, she seemed to shrivel as she handed me my coffee and pulled a tissue from her pocket to dab her eyes.

'He was having an affair, he thought I didn't know but I did.'

Shocked at her admission, I grabbed the bull by the horns and went with it. 'I'm so sorry, does he do that... a lot?' I lowered my voice, made it soft, and she nodded, turning away, not wanting me to see her cry. More than anything, I wanted to give her a hug, she looked so small and fragile, my blood boiled with what he'd reduced her to. Here he had this beautiful family and he was throwing it away with women almost young enough to be his daughters.

'Leave him, take Nathan and go,' I said firmly, hoping it sounded like an instruction as opposed to womanly advice.

'How do you know my son's name? Who are you? Are you one of his conquests too? I know you had dinner together.' Her eyes darkened, face suddenly twisted with rage.

I automatically stepped back, raising my palms. 'No, no, I'm not. *We* didn't have dinner, I had dinner, I was doing a review and he wanted to talk about Grace.'

Helena's mouth dropped open to speak, but the sound of a car engine stopped the pair of us in our tracks. She swiftly composed herself and I reached out to grab her wrist.

'I know you can't trust him, Helena. I think he might be dangerous.'

She snorted, as if the idea was ludicrous and tried to pull her wrist out of my grasp.

I held on tight, needing to get my point across.

'I think he killed Grace, I have some evidence. I've given it to the police. He's upped your life insurance, Helena; you need to take Nathan and leave,' I hissed, my words rushing out, knowing I had seconds before Jack walked in the door.

Helena wrenched her arm from my grip, rubbing at the red blotches I'd left, her cheeks almost the same colour.

'I'm worried about you, about your son. I don't want him to hurt you?'

Helena's face creased, brows nearly meeting, and her next words came out in a low murmur as the front door opened. 'Who are you?'

I stepped back, steeling myself for Jack's arrival because there was no way I was getting out of here without a confrontation, sure Helena would tell him everything. I locked eyes with her, coiled like a spring, ready to run at the first sign of a threat. To appear like everything was normal, I lifted the steaming hot coffee and took a sip.

'The delivery man has arrived!' Jack hollered from the hallway, his voice jovial, as though him and Helena were fine. Had they made up, had she forgiven him again despite the evidence mounting against him, not only for his indiscretions but for Grace's death too?

Helena jolted into action, pulling plates and tomato ketchup from the cupboards and putting them on the table with some pretty napkins. The smell of McMuffins and hash browns wafted through with Nathan as he bounded over to his mum.

'I've got a juice!' he said, giving the Fruit Shoot a long slurp before realising I was in the room. His eyes widened when he saw me and he clamped his lips shut. Jack was a few steps behind, carrying brown paper bags, dark at the bottom with grease. My stomach lurched, but when Jack found me in his kitchen, he quickly hid his bewildered expression and set the bags down on the table.

'Molly, this is a surprise.' Jack brushed his hands on his jeans and held out one for me to shake. It was too formal, too forced, and Helena raised an eyebrow in my peripheral vision, watching our awkward exchange. 'How did you know where I lived?'

I almost choked on my own spit – why hadn't I thought of that? I opened my mouth to speak, but Jack began to laugh.

'I remember, you *always* do your research, right?' He winked and my throat closed, I had to get out.

'Sorry, I didn't mean to interrupt your breakfast,' I said weakly, putting my cup down and slowly retreating out of the kitchen.

'Nonsense, there's plenty if you want some. I promised Nathan here a Saturday morning treat.' He rested his hands on Nathan's shoulders, using him as shield between us. His son stared at me, eyes like giant watery orbs, mouth gaping. If I didn't know any better, I'd say he looked terrified.

'No, it's fine, I was just writing a follow-up on World Book Day and I...' I struggled to finish my sentence, glaringly obvious to everyone in the room I was talking rubbish. 'I wondered if you had Claire's contact details, but I'm sorry, I don't know what I was thinking. It's early on a weekend and rude of me to stop by unannounced.'

I exited the kitchen, eager to run from the house and the tension in the air. Desperate to get away before Helena could tell Jack why I'd come and what I'd told her, but she was yet to expose me.

'Oh, Nathan, what have you done?' Helena's voice carried through to the hallway, where I struggled to put my trainers on, having left the laces tied when I'd slipped them off. 'Come on, I'll get you cleaned up. No more juice for you,' she scolded, but her tone was light-hearted.

She brought him out, steering him up the stairs, the front of his grey cotton joggers stained dark with urine.

'He does this sometimes.' She grimaced apologetically as the pair of them climbed up to the bathroom. My muscles slackened, she wasn't going to tell Jack, not while I was here. She was letting me leave.

I bent over, still battling with my trainers.

'I know why you've come.' Jack's voice came from behind me, whispered into my ear.

I finally got my foot in my trainer and whirled around, but he pinned me against the front door, glancing back over his shoulder to check the coast was clear.

39

I could hear the beat of my own heart thrum in my ears as Jack pressed himself against me, head lowered with his mouth at my ear. He breathed in my hair, sending tremors down to my toes. I froze, as his fingers lightly grazed my thigh, stroking upwards. Beneath the denim, my skin crawled at his touch, but I was paralysed, powerless to stop him.

'You're here for me, aren't you?' He drawled the words in a low, smooth tone, a similar display to the one he'd put on in his office, but this time darker, more dangerous. His face was so close to mine, I could smell his aftershave and the saltiness of his skin, shameless in his own home with his wife upstairs.

I sucked in air, recoiling as sensation flooded back to my limbs. Rage boiled in the pit of my stomach; Jack was trying to intimidate me. It wasn't a seduction, it was harassment. His groin pulsed with desire as he pressed it harder against the soft flesh of my stomach, hand moving around to cup my behind, his knuckles grazing the door. It was the final straw and I'd reached my limit.

Palms flat on his chest, I shoved him away. 'Get away from me,' I hissed, as his eyes widened at my rebuttal. 'I know what you did to Grace, I know you're fucking Ivy and you upped Helena's life insurance. Are you planning to get rid of her too?'

Jack's jaw slackened, creases deepened on his forehead and at the corners of his eyes, a bewildered smirk formed on his lips. 'What are you talking about, Molly?'

'I know, Jack.' I pointed at him, all my nerves pulsing. 'I know everything.'

'What do you know?' he spat, cocky now. He took a step towards me and I flinched. That made him laugh and his stupid, smug expression made me want to throttle him.

'You killed her, I know you did. You were seen, pictured even, with her, on the night she died,' I said triumphantly. 'I found it. I gave it to the police.'

His lips parted, allowing air to escape, yet he continued to frown at me.

'I know you broke into Grace's annexe, that you ripped your inscription from the book of poems you bought for her. It's over, Jack, I know everything and the police do too.'

In the space of a heartbeat, he pinned me against the door again, my head banging on the wood. His hand was around my throat before I could blink, using the weight of his body to hold me still. 'You know fuck all, Molly, because I didn't harm a hair on her head.' Spittle flew from his mouth, hitting my cheek. 'Who the hell do you think you are, coming in here, talking to my wife.'

'Your wife,' I choked, letting out a feeble laugh, carried by the anger which fired my veins. 'The wife you cheated on and humiliated, you're worried about your wife now, are you? The only thing you're worried about is the money you'll get from ending her life.'

'I have no idea what you're talking about. I don't know where you're getting your information from, but you're wrong,' Jack snarled, his fingers tightening around my throat, nails digging into my flesh. I tried to cough, spluttering for air.

'What the hell is going on? Jack, get off her!' Helena, roused by our argument which had grown in volume, flew down the stairs, a towel draped over her shoulder.

Jack let go of me immediately, springing back, and I rubbed at my neck, the skin tender. Helena's eyes were huge and unblinking as though she couldn't process what she'd witnessed her husband do. Before I could speak, there was a hammering on the door behind me, it shuddered in its frame, making me jump. Jack wouldn't shift his eyes from mine, the cogs ticking in his brain like he was trying to take in everything I'd accused him of, or perhaps he was wondering how I knew it all. How a low-fry reporter from a local newspaper had put all the pieces together.

'Mr Reilly, it's the police.' A gruff voice came through the door as it was banged again.

Colour drained from Jack's face and he took a step backwards towards Helena as if she could pro- tect him from what was coming.

'You brought the police here, to our home?' He- lena snapped, her eyes held me in a vice-like grip before she barged past me, exasperated by my lack of movement, but I was too busy glaring at Jack to be victorious. The feel of his hands on my body lin- gered, repulsing me. How dare he touch me like that, but Jack was looking through me as though I was invisible when Helena pulled open the door.

'Mrs Reilly, I'm Detective Russell, please can you open the gates.'

I baulked, like a rabbit caught in headlights, my reaction initially delayed, but now I stood face to face with the man who'd dismissed me yesterday. Helena reached for the button on the wall without question and I heard engines fire up and proceed onto the driveway.

'Is your husband home?'

Thankfully, despite his initial accusatory glare, Detective Russell ignored my presence and directed his attention at Jack. Stepping over the threshold, he took hold of Jack's arm, who looked down at his hand with something that resembled contempt.

'Mr Reilly, I'm arresting you for the murder of Grace Stewart. You do not have to say anything, but it may harm your defence if you do not mention, when questioned, something which you later rely on in court. Anything you do say may be given in evidence.'

My eyes shot to the detective like he'd thrown a grenade, but he didn't even glance at me. Triumph ballooned in my chest, he'd listened after all, I hadn't been fobbed off. My information had finally

reached the right hands and I'd been taken seriously.

'I... I don't understand, I've already answered
your questions. I didn't hurt Grace.' Jack's face paled,
the morning light glinting off his grey-speckled
stubble where he hadn't yet shaved. I feared he
might bolt for the door, but Detective Russell already had his handcuffs at the ready.

'Is this really necessary?' Helena's shrill voice cut
through the moment of silence as uniformed officers
piled into the house.

'We have a warrant to search this address, Mrs
Reilly. Please stand back and let the officers do their
job.'

'Daddy?' Nathan stood at the top of the stairs in a
small blue bathrobe, tears streaming down his
cheeks. Helena took one look at him and rushed up,
wrapping her arms around him.

'It's okay, sweetie, the policemen need Daddy's
help, they're looking for something. Let's go find
your iPad.' He clung to her and she disappeared towards his bedroom.

Suddenly, nausea struck, the smell of uneaten
McDonald's and stale breath filled the hallway despite the door being wide open. The noise of people
opening cupboard doors and drawers, searching

under beds and in wardrobes echoed all around. The officers scurried from room to room like ants, rifling through everything as though they were on the clock, and relief washed over me that I'd left nothing of mine behind.

Detective Russell directed an officer to take Jack to the waiting response car. He was in shock, not even lifting his head as he was led over the threshold.

'You've got this all wrong,' he muttered from the driveway. I dreaded to think of all the curtains twitching in Church Road at the police cars outside.

'Mrs Reilly, could you bring your son downstairs please,' Detective Russell called up the stairs, his raised voice making me flinch. Was he worried she was trying to hide evidence?

'Go easy, she's had quite a shock and Nathan is really upset.'

He turned to me and I shrunk back. He was big and imposing, filling the hallway with his presence. 'I don't know why you're here, Miss Hudson; this isn't something you should be involved in.'

'I came to warn Helena because I thought you weren't interested,' I retorted, pulling myself up to my full height, adrenaline coursing around my body, making me emboldened.

He sighed, his jaw tightening. 'After our meeting I got the team to double-check camera footage from the nearby residents' houses along Church Road, it was most enlightening.'

Whatever he'd seen had to be enough to push for a warrant, video evidence captured the night Grace went missing combined with it now being apparent Jack lied during questioning. At least now it would be under caution and they'd have evidence to put to him. Maybe he'd fold and admit what he did, but either way Helena and Nathan were safe. A murder charge, if he was charged, would mean being remanded in custody so he couldn't hurt anyone else.

'You need to go now, Miss Hudson.' Detective Russell was polite but firm, gesturing to the open door, where I could see neighbours in their gardens, watching the show, which was far more entertaining than Saturday morning television.

'Can't she stay?' Helena appeared, treading slowly down the stairs, her face streaked with mascara clad tears. Nathan clung to her; his face buried in her shoulder as his mother stroked his head.

'I don't think that's appropriate, Mrs Reilly. You are aware she's a reporter? We have some officers on the way to support you and your son, they'll be here soon.'

She nodded complicitly and turned to carry Nathan into the study.

'I'm so sorry, Helena, but you'll be safe now, both of you.'

She didn't respond but nodded, tears falling from her eyes before she left the hallway. I could sense she wasn't sure where to go, every room besieged by people searching through her things. It was awful.

I turned to leave when a young officer wearing latex gloves bolted into the hallway, electrified.

'Found this, sir.' He held up a clear polythene bag, inside was a rolled-up green coat, still with its creases after going through the washing machine.

I gasped, my hand flying to my mouth.

'There's a phone in the pocket too,' he added, handing another bag to Detective Russell, who took both before turning to me.

'Time to go, Hudson, and if I see any of this' – he shook the bags in my face – 'in print, I'll make sure the *Crawley News* is shut down quicker than you can say "exclusive".'

40

I walked from the property in a daze with no idea where I was going, no real sensation in my limbs that were moving without instruction. They'd found the coat and a phone. I had to assume it was Grace's, because it was bigger than Jack's burner. Once they'd got into it, I was sure they'd find messages between him and her. He wouldn't be able to deny their affair or if he tried because he'd not used his real phone, maybe during their search they'd find the burner too. Either way, the coat, which was bound to have Grace's DNA on it, needed some explaining as to how it came to be in the Reilly residence.

Poor Helena was shell-shocked and Nathan was terrified. I couldn't imagine how it must feel to have strangers pouring through your home, going through your most intimate things. She loved Jack, there was no doubt about that, yet now he'd been arrested, her world was falling apart.

I walked for fifteen minutes, down the hill and back towards town before ducking into a small café on a parade of local shops. There were a few people at tables, munching croissants and bacon rolls, but I ordered a cappuccino and found a corner at the back to sit with my thoughts.

Despite what Detective Russell had said, I knew I needed to report on the arrest. I wouldn't mention the coat or that anything of Grace's had been found. After all, it hadn't been confirmed, but surely I could write what was fact. A thirty-eight-year-old man had been arrested in connection to Grace's murder.

I picked up my phone and called Des, who answered with a groggy voice, like I'd pulled him from his slumber despite it being nearly half past nine.

'This better be good, Mol,' he grumbled.

'It is. I have an update on the Grace Stewart case, wasn't sure if you wanted me to call Neil,' I offered to show I was a team player, although I hoped he wouldn't take me up on it.

'What is it?'

'Jack Reilly has been arrested. He's a teacher at St Wilfrid's, happened around twenty minutes ago.'

'The guy from the World Book Day thing?' Des's voice sharpened immediately.

'Yep, shall I get something written up so we can get it live asap?'

'Sure, I'll try to get hold of Neil, see if he has anything further to add, but put something together, just the facts okay, no conjecture, we don't want to get sued.'

'I'm on it,' I said.

Before I hung up, I heard Des say, 'Good work, Mol.'

I grinned; I'd earnt that fifty-pound note Des had given me.

Pulling my laptop from my rucksack, I set about writing a short piece, only what was known and would be available in the public domain before long, no names or identifiers. As I typed, my mind turned to Sally and Roy. When would they find out there had been an arrest? Hopefully that awful family liaison officer would tell them before the article was published.

When I'd finished, I hit send, knowing with my scoop I'd be ruining Neil's weekend. Perhaps now he'd give me the respect in the office I deserved and treat me as an equal, although I doubted it.

I ordered another coffee, craving the caffeine because the adrenaline had receded and I needed a boost. While I should have used my time to work on the Town Hall demolition story, I couldn't ignore the niggling in my gut about the phone the police had found with Grace's coat. I knew it wasn't there when I'd pulled it out of the washing machine and it also wasn't in the pocket when I found it rolled up under the stairs. That coat had been washed and moved on multiple occasions, yet on searching the house when the Reillys were out I'd not found it. I wasn't sure why it bugged me so much, but my gut told me something was off.

My musings were interrupted by a call from Megan.

'Hey, you disappeared, I thought we'd go for breakfast,' she moaned.

'Sorry, I had to get back to the Reillys' fast. Good job I did too as they just arrested him.'

'Really?'

'Yep, I'm in that café, Ridley's, right now, had to write up a piece for work so we could be the first to go live with the story.'

'Well, I guess you won't be sleeping there tonight.'

'The police are all over it, searching the house, but I might try to go back, I need to know Helena is all right.'

'Absolutely not. Are you mad? You're way too close to this, Mol. I'm worried about you.'

'You don't need to worry, Jack's been taken into custody, he won't be there.'

I had no idea how I'd get back into the house, or even if I could. What if some of the footage the police had seized from neighbouring properties had me lurking about or even going into the side gate or, worse, the front door? I shook the thoughts from my head, they were searching for that specific day. The fences still hadn't been erected then, so I was coming and going via the back garden. I wouldn't have been seen.

'Can I get you anything?' the café owner called from behind the counter. The tables had emptied out, I'd been so lost in work and Jack's arrest I hadn't even noticed. My stomach rumbled on cue.

'Actually, could I get a sausage roll please.'

She nodded and it was delivered a few minutes later.

'You working on the weekend, honey?' The

woman gestured to my laptop and I suddenly re-membered I hadn't told Harry about the develop-ment. He'd likely still be on the train.

'Um yeah, always working. News to report.' I smiled politely and took a bite out of my sausage roll, turning my attention to my phone. Harry wouldn't be able to talk on the train, but a text should be good enough.

I got to the house to warn Helena, the police arrived and arrested Jack. They had a search warrant and before I was kicked out, they found the green coat... and a phone in the pocket!

The owner came back to my table with another coffee as I took the last bite of the sausage roll. I was going to be bouncing off the wall with all the caffeine.

'On the house. Are you a reporter?'

I nodded, wiping pastry flakes from my chin, my mouth too full to respond.

'Know anything about those police cars this morning, three of them drove past and someone mentioned they were outside a property up the road?' She was fishing and I couldn't blame her.

Drama always got people talking, anything to get them out of their mundane lives for a moment.

'Oh no, I didn't see them. I'm writing an article on the town hall being demolished to make way for social housing.' I swivelled my laptop around and showed her the two sentences I'd managed to write. She scanned them and shrugged. It wasn't half as entertaining as three police cars travelling in convoy up the road and her interest in me was immediately lost.

The woman left me to return to the counter as another customer came in and I shut down my laptop, leaving a ten-pound note on the table and the free coffee untouched. Outside, the air was damp and dark clouds rolled ominously overhead. My phone rang again, this time an unknown number. I answered as I thought it might be Harry, but a soft female voice was on the other end.

'Is that Molly?'

'Yes.'

'My name is Jackie, I'm Howard's niece, from number seven Church Road. I got your note and if you're still interested in looking after Buster, I could do with the help.'

For a moment, with my mind so focused on the

Reillys, I didn't understand until the old man and his dog popped into my head.

'I'm not far from number seven now, shall I pop in and we can have a chat?'

Jackie agreed and I headed back towards Church Road. It had been a couple of hours since I'd left and I was surprised to find no police presence there. The gates were closed at the Reillys' and the Mercedes was also gone from the driveway. Had the police impounded it, or had Helena taken Nathan and left the madness behind? I walked past, looking in the windows to see any sign of life, but there were no lights on.

Jackie opened the door to number seven almost as soon as I knocked. It was a stark contrast to the Reillys' modern home, with faded floral wallpaper and dark wood stain everywhere. It smelt musty, of wet dog and rolled-up cigarettes. She welcomed me inside and made me milky tea that turned my stomach. Howard was still in the hospital, due to have an operation to fit some stents in an artery any day now. Jackie lived in a flat in Kent and didn't have space to house ten-year-old Buster.

'I'd love to help, but my place is tiny,' I lied. 'There's no space there either, but I could have him here until Howard comes back.' At that perfect moment, the black Labrador slunk over and rested his head on my knee. I scratched the top of his head and he licked a stray pastry crumb from my jeans. Jackie looked relieved rather than suspicious, her mouth curling upwards.

'I guess that's okay. I mean, I work so I can't move in here right now and' – she looked around – 'there's nothing to steal. Not saying you would, of course, but I can't see what harm it could do.'

'I'm a reporter for a local paper,' I dug in my rucksack for a business card and handed one over, 'so I'm mobile. I don't need to go into the office, all I need is a Wi-Fi connection.' I smiled and watched as she examined the card.

'Well, Howard has that, I set it up for him when we got him the Sky box. I don't think he knows how to use it though.' She chuckled, rolling her eyes.

'It's okay, Buster and I will figure it out. I've got a couple of things to do today, but I can come back later?'

'It's fine, I'm not working, so I'll stay tonight, give the place a tidy-up. Tomorrow would be good though, any time before lunch.'

'Sure. Can you write down what Buster eats and how much, how many walks he needs, that kind of thing. I'm happy to help until Howard is back on his feet.' I rubbed Buster behind the ear, narrowly missing a string of drool that plopped onto the floor.

We chatted for a while longer and I left Jackie with her mammoth cleaning task, feeling secure I'd have a roof over my head for a few nights at least. It would be nice to have some company too, even of the four-legged variety, but for now I wanted to get back to the Reillys' and see what kind of state Helena, and the house, was in.

41

Outside, thunder rolled and a crack of lightning followed. Rain was soon to fall and after I climbed over the gate and knocked at the Reillys' front door, I surmised Helena was out. I wanted to get over the back fence before it began to pour, so I walked around the row of houses and towards the disused railway line, figuring I could make it over the fence this once.

When I checked my phone, I had a text from Des announcing the article I'd written about Jack's arrest was live. I quickly found it; a couple of amendments had been made, but nothing new from Neil. I bet he was furious at being scooped.

I switched to Instagram to find a photo of Nathan

watching *The Incredibles* and eating ice cream on a sofa I didn't recognise. Helena had captioned the shot with 'Impromptu trip to the grandparents'. It was obvious she'd gone there for a safe haven, to cry on their shoulders in her time of need and I didn't blame her, perhaps the police had advised she stay somewhere else. Either way, it meant she wasn't home, so I could spend the night here before moving next door tomorrow.

The fence at the back was high but solid. Stupidly I chucked my rucksack over first, then panicked I wouldn't be able to make it over into the garden to retrieve it. I didn't want to use the front door in case the neighbours' curtains were still twitching after this morning's show, but even standing on the slanted support post, I found it almost impossible to heave myself up and over the wood. After the fifth attempt, with splinters wedged in my palms, I managed to get purchase, dropping like a stone into their new flower bed ungracefully. Brushing myself off, I felt the first drops of rain and hurried to let myself in the bifold doors.

The sight that met me was awful. It looked as though the house had been ransacked. Every shelf was bare, cupboards had been emptied and some of their contents thrown back haphazardly. Drawers left open like a poltergeist had visited in the night. It was an eerie scene. I edged around the detritus on the floor, careful not to tread on anything. No wonder Helena had taken Nathan and left, clearing up would be an insurmountable task and one she likely couldn't face right now.

I felt more like a trespasser at the house than ever but began my own search, convinced there was something I was missing, something the police might not have discovered. I knew more about the case than anyone and they might have bypassed a clue I would know was critical to their investigation on what happened to Grace.

I moved through the house, not knowing what I was looking for, my mind a jumble of questions. Was Jack being interviewed right now? Was Detective Russell building his case against him, helped by the information I'd supplied? He had the photo of him with Grace, the inscription in the book of poems and now what I believed was Grace's coat and phone too. I was sure it would have messages on it, otherwise why would Jack not have disposed of it before now? In fact why hadn't he got rid of it if it implicated him? If they couldn't prove he killed her with DNA evidence recovered from Grace's body, they had to make sure the circumstantial evidence was airtight.

He had motive, he was in a relationship with her and she'd wanted him to leave Helena. I'd heard Grace say as much and I was here when she showed up at the house, ready to confront Helena. Maybe he hadn't meant to kill her, it could have been an accident. I had no idea what had happened between them, but the evidence pointed to him. I was so caught up with the Reillys, I was compelled to stay, at least until I knew Helena and Nathan were all right. I couldn't help but feel partly responsible for dropping a bomb on their lives.

Upstairs in the master suite, it looked relatively neat. Some of the boxes had already been emptied or removed and there was no other furniture to claw through. The wardrobe doors were open, Helena's shoes were still in their boxes, haphazardly stacked in there. The other side was empty and in the en suite I lifted the porcelain lid of the cistern, but nothing was inside.

My phone rang from my pocket. Des was calling.

'Hey, Mol, just checking in. You okay?'

'Yeah I'm fine. Any news?'

'Other than Neil being pissed at you, no.' He laughed and I rolled my eyes, I'd been expecting it.

'He'll get over it. So no charge as of yet?'

'Not yet, although I've been assured we'll be the

first to know,' he scoffed. I knew that was Neil's way of trying to claw his way back into favour. 'You did a really good job on this one, you're an asset to this team.'

'Thanks, Des.' My face flooded with colour.

'Anyway, I'll let you know when I hear anything, I know you're invested in this one. Have the weekend off yeah, the town hall story can wait.'

'Thanks.'

'Pop into the office Monday and say hi.'

'Will do.'

When I got off the phone with Des, I saw Harry had messaged, having arrived in Brighton, congratulating me on my 'win' with Jack being arrested. He also hinted at meeting up at some point over the weekend, but I couldn't think about that right now because below me the front door opened. Looking out of the window onto the driveway, I saw the Mercedes was back, although I couldn't hear Nathan's heavy patter on the parquet floor downstairs. Instead, I heard a sigh and the soft thump of footsteps.

For the next two hours, I listened to Helena put the house back together, room by room while I hid in the wardrobe. When she came upstairs, she blasted music at top volume so I had no idea where she was at any one time. I folded myself as far back in the wardrobe as I could, beneath a blanket, terrified she'd come up and decide now was the time to fill the space, seeing as the police had reorganised her home for her. As the light faded she retreated back downstairs and turned the music off. My stomach growled, I'd not eaten since the sausage roll in the café and was desperate for a shower, I should have stayed at Megan's.

At around six, there was a knock at the door and from the smell of freshly baked dough, tomato and oregano, it appeared Helena had ordered herself a pizza. Nathan must still have been at his grandparents, perhaps he was staying the night. I knew Helena was drinking, the pop songs were turned back on and she sang at the top of her voice, gradually sounding more and more slurred until finally the music ceased and the house fell silent again. I crept out when Helena's snoring echoed around the floor below and when I passed her room, she was splayed out on the bed, still dressed in loungewear, her lips tinged with red wine.

Downstairs was spotless once more, a near empty bottle of wine sat on the worktop beside a recently collected prescription of sleeping pills in their pharmacy bag and half the pizza had been shoved in the bin, still in the Domino's box. I wasn't proud of myself, but hunger won out and I retrieved it, stuffing the slices into my mouth until I was satisfied, washing it down with the last of the red wine. The house felt strange without Jack or Nathan's presence, but I hoped Helena would feel a little better tomorrow knowing at least her house was back in order.

As I sat with only the glow of the under-cabinet lights illuminating the space, I looked around the kitchen. Number six Church Road had come to feel like my own home, but it wasn't. I wasn't invited to stay; I was nothing but an intruder who'd witnessed a family imploding. It was time for me to move on and try next door on for size.

Perhaps the grumpy neighbour at number seven would be in the hospital for a couple of weeks, or maybe once he was back I'd be able to stay on without him knowing. It broke the no pets rule but was worth considering.

I switched off the lights and crept upstairs to spend my last night in the wardrobe. The bed with its new mattress seemed to look at me smugly when my bones creaked as I unrolled my sleeping bag on the floor one last time. I yawned but pulled out my laptop. It was time for my final blog post, from this property anyway. I owed the followers an update and

even if I gave my location away. I'd be gone tomorrow, having left no trace I was ever here.

* * *

Blog Post #9
www.phrogging.com

Hi Phroggers. I know I've said this before, but
this is definitely my last night here. I have so
much to tell you, but first, the positives. My
third phrogging expedition has been full of
drama, but I've not been caught or seen. I've
managed to live alongside this family in their
upstairs room for almost two weeks undetected. While I've been here, I've eaten some
of their food, used their electricity and hot
water but always enough to stay under the
radar. Whenever I've used anything, I've
cleaned up after myself and left no hint of my
presence. Sticking by my self-imposed rules
has worked for me.

There's been a couple of near misses, but
thankfully, come tomorrow, I'll say goodbye to
this house, the shelter it's been, and farewell
to the family that live here. I wish I could thank

them for their hospitality, but I don't think it would be appropriate. I've begun to care for these people, especially with the tumultuous time they've had since I've arrived. Some of that being down to me, I know.

So here's what you're waiting for, an update on the case of the deceased mistress. As you know from my last post, I took the evidence I'd gathered to the police, believing they'd not taken me seriously, but I was wrong. The husband was arrested today and the house searched, thankfully while I was out, otherwise I could be writing a wholly different post – one from a prison cell of my own. From what they found, it appears he's responsible for her death and now it's a matter of time until he's charged. I just hope his wife and child can recover and eventually move on, leaving that monster behind. I know it'll take me a while to process the events of the past couple of weeks.

So, phroggers, be careful, you never know what goes on behind closed doors or what sort of environment you're walking into. Always have an escape plan, know your exits and spots to hide, figure that out on day one, and if nothing else, come up with an excuse as to why you're there if you're discovered. Whatever it is, it'll be feeble, but it saves you from thinking on your feet.

Thank you for all your support and your comments. I'm moving onto a new property tomorrow and you never know, you may see a blog pop up from me while I'm there. You're a great community I'm proud to be a part of. Oh and @HomeSweetHome, I couldn't have done this without you.

42

On Sunday morning, Helena woke early and left the house at nine. I guessed she was going to get Nathan from her parents', but I had no idea how long she'd be gone, an hour and a half at least. The pub they'd had the roast in was near Sevenoaks, so I assumed they lived somewhere around there. While I had the house to myself, I took the opportunity to have a shower and put my clothes through a quick wash and dry cycle, because even though I'd be going next door later, at least I knew it was clean here.

Making the most of my final few hours in the property, I helped myself to one last bowl of Helena's home-made granola, drank the last cup I'd have of her posh coffee, then packed my rucksack. Checking the house to make sure I hadn't left anything behind and satisfied it appeared as though I'd never been there, I put the extra keys back on the keyring and crept out of the front door with a strangely hollow feeling.

I didn't have far to go, but before I took responsibility for Buster, I walked to the nearest café and got a takeaway coffee, stopping at a newsagent to buy a couple of chocolate bars and a sympathy card for Sally. I had the urge to visit her despite having no words of comfort to offer and the last thing I wanted was to cause her any more pain. Surely by now she'd know a man had been taken into custody, especially as I'd made it public, but she wouldn't know who. Even if I told her, the name Jack Reilly likely wouldn't mean anything to Sally. Grace had met him at work and that was that. If she'd had another job at a different school, she might have lived, but it was pointless to dwell on it.

I wrote the card and took a slow walk to their bungalow, posting it through the letter box and retreating quickly before the Rottweiler family liaison officer spotted me. I had to hope getting justice for Grace would give Sally and Roy some peace, although it would never bring back their daughter.

Retracing my steps, daydreaming about

heading to Gatwick and jumping on a plane to see my parents, I came back to Church Road, intending to visit Jackie and secure my new lodgings. This time when I passed number six, the Mercedes was back.

Although Jack was gone, sitting in a cell in Crawley police station, I worried about Helena and Nathan, and the temptation to check they were okay after yesterday's trauma was too great to ignore. Before I could stop myself, I was knocking at their door. When Helena answered, she looked tired, her eyes were bloodshot and she wasn't as well-groomed as usual. Her loungewear had a brown smudge on the trousers and her usually sleek hair was scraped back into a messy ponytail.

'I'm sorry to turn up like this, I just wanted to check you and Nathan are okay.'

'Come in.' Her lip twitched and she glanced over my shoulder as if she expected the paparazzi to be outside, waiting to take her picture. 'It's been quite the couple of days,' she gave me a tight smile, 'but I wanted to thank you for coming yesterday, for warning me. It was very brave of you.' Relief washed over me at the warm welcome, I'd been expecting the opposite.

'I'm not sure Jack would have hurt you,' I wrung

my hands together, 'but if he had, I would never have forgiven myself.'

She led me through to the kitchen and set the coffee machine whirring, pulling two mugs from the cupboard without asking if I wanted one.

'How did you know the things you knew? The life insurance and about Grace?'

I squirmed and chewed the inside of my cheek; glad she had her back to me.

'I'm a reporter,' I shrugged, 'I was investigating Grace's disappearance initially, which led me to Jack and... I had some help.'

Helena placed her hands on the counter, as though it was holding her up. Eventually, she turned to face me.

'That's how you found out about his affair?'

I nodded. Would she believe my bullshit? I guessed she didn't have any choice. I was hardly about to tell her I'd witnessed the pair of them because I'd been secretly living upstairs.

'Nathan,' she hollered, 'snack time.'

I shrank back at the shrill voice summoning her son before she stirred and handed me the coffee.

'What else did you find out?'

I'd leave the rest of the details to the police, no good would come from telling her about Ivy. 'That's about it, I was worried about your safety and I wanted to tell you how sorry I am, about all of this.'

'The police want to interview me later today,' she sighed, rubbing the back of her neck, shoulders tight with tension, 'but I don't know anything. I'd guessed he was having another affair, we'd survived one and moved to start afresh. I never found out who she was, perhaps it was Grace all along and he never ended it. I'd decided to leave him.'

Nathan crept around the corner, almost making me jump. He moved uncharacteristically quietly, whereas normally he stomped everywhere at a hundred miles an hour. Perhaps it was because he'd heard Helena had a guest.

'You're the chocolate fairy,' he blurted, a huge grin across his face.

I swallowed, panic solidifying my insides. How did he know?

'Oh, Nathan, don't be silly. I told you, fairies don't exist.' Helena laughed, almost embarrassed.

'They do!' he said belligerently. 'Yesterday I thought you were the other woman, the sleeping one, but you're not, you're the chocolate fairy. I saw you, outside my bedroom door.'

'Nathan!' Helena snapped, her tone razor-sharp.

She looked at me, shaking her head and smiling weakly.

I swallowed the lump growing in my throat. I had been seen after all, but when? Either the time I'd stubbed my toe on his iPad in the night or before Sam had arrived to babysit when he was lying on his bed with the door open. *Shit!*

I morphed my expression into one of amused perplexity, hoping Helena would put it down to childish fantasies.

'Out of the mouths of babes, right,' she said, passing him a packet of fruit strings and waving a hand to dismiss her son.

Cold unease edged its way around my body, my nerves tingling as Nathan's words echoed around my head. Who was the other woman he spoke of?

I rummaged in my pocket and crouched down. 'Here you go, buddy, maybe I am the chocolate fairy after all,' I winked and placed a small bar of chocolate in his hand.

He took it, eyes widening, and flashed me teeth of varying sizes.

'See, I told you Mummy!'

I knew it wasn't right to give him chocolate without asking permission, especially when Helena was so particular about what Nathan ate, but I needed to get him on side.

Over my shoulder, Helena had returned to the sink, her back to me, running the tap.

'What sleeping woman?' I whispered as Nathan tore through the chocolate bar, fruit strings forgotten.

'She fell asleep on the floor; she made Mummy cry and—'

'Nathan, that's enough.' Helena spun around, and I froze when I saw the kitchen knife gripped in her hand. 'Go to your room.' Her voice was a low, dangerous whisper.

I stood up, facing Helena and using my body to shield her son.

'Helena, put the knife down.'

A solitary tear rolled down her cheek and she snorted.

'Whatever it is, we can work it out.'

'You'd think I'd hurt my son? I'd die for him; I'd go to the ends of the earth to protect him.'

I raised my palms, submitting, keeping my voice soft and low. 'I know you would, any mother would.'

She stepped towards me.

Nathan began to cry and I moved back, taking

him with me, his chocolatey hands clinging to my thighs.

'Come here, Nathan,' she demanded, still wielding the knife, which glinted in the cabinet lights.

'No!' he screamed, hiccupping, residue from the bar smeared around his mouth.

'Helena, you're scaring him. Put the knife down and we can talk about this.'

'You have to leave. Go, Molly, forget what he said and don't come back.' She pointed towards the door, but I remained rooted to the spot.

'I can't do that, not with you like this.' There was no way I was leaving Helena with Nathan, she was unhinged, eyes wild, darting around as steady tears dripped down her cheeks. She moved slowly towards us and I mirrored her every step forward with one backwards, guiding Nathan behind me towards the hallway. He cried, big wracking sobs.

'It's because it's my fault, I yelled at her and she fell,' he blurted and Helena let out a guttural howl, dropping to her knees on the parquet floor, the knife clattering away from her. Bent over, she dragged her fingers through her hair, ponytail coming loose, pulling at the roots as her shoulders shook and heaved.

'Noooooooo,' she wailed.

'I'm sorry, Mummy.' I turned around and lifted Nathan onto my hip, surprised at how heavy he was. His fingers and face were coated in chocolate and so was I when he buried his tear-streaked face into my neck.

'It's okay, it's okay,' I soothed, bumping him up and down like a baby, my eyes never leaving Helena, who remained crouched and inconsolable on the floor. I wanted to leave, take Nathan and run, but he wasn't my child and I had no doubt Helena would use any means to stop me.

It was only then Nathan's words landed. I lowered Nathan to the ground and fished for my phone, bringing up the screenshot I'd taken of Grace's missing post on Facebook.

'Is this the sleeping woman?' I whispered.

His big brown watery eyes looked first at the screen, then up at me. His chin wobbled and he bit his lip, giving me a solitary nod.

43

'She was making Mummy cry and I yelled at her.'

Helena gasped, raising her head, staring at me through sodden lashes with her palms flat on the floor. I recoiled. Jack hadn't killed Grace; he hadn't broken her neck in some kind of momentary loss of control. It had been an accident all along. I'd been looking for a conspiracy where there had been none.

'Please don't tell them. I can't let them take my boy away.'

I sat Nathan down at the table, furthest away from Helena, and went to her, kicking the knife behind her into the kitchen, out of reach. Clutching her around the shoulders, I gently helped her up and into a seat at the other end of the table where she slumped as though she was a rag doll.

'Tell me what happened,' I implored, sitting beside her, my forearms resting on my knees, trying to get her to look at me, but she only had eyes for her son.

'Nathan, sweetheart, Mummy's sorry. I'm okay now. I'm just a bit sad, that's all.' She sniffed, wiping her nose with her sleeve. 'Why don't you go and play Nintendo, take some crisps from your snack drawer and go up to your room so I can talk to Molly.'

Nathan did as he was asked, seemingly happy to escape the misery, and the two of us remained. The silence was oppressive and I feared I wouldn't be able to get her to open up, to tell me what I desperately needed to know. Did Jack have any idea his son had been involved in Grace's death, was he covering for him?

'I need a cigarette,' Helena eventually said, sounding defeated, as though she'd been carrying the weight of the world on her shoulders and could bear no more.

'Shall we go outside?' I suggested.

Helena walked calmly into the kitchen, crouching to pick up the knife, and I held my breath, ready to run, but I watched her put it back in the block. She was no longer a threat; the cat was out of the bag now and no matter how hard she tried, she wouldn't be able to stuff it back in. The only thing that mattered now was the truth.

I watched as Helena took two glasses out of the cupboard and reached for a bottle of red wine, unscrewing the cap.

'If I'm going to tell you what happened, then I'm going to need a glass.' She looked around at me, her expression sheepish. 'I know it's early.'

I nodded as she poured. I'd never been a lover of red wine, to me it always tasted of vinegar, but if it got her talking I'd suffer it.

My phone rang loudly from my pocket, making me start and distracted I dug it out. Neil was calling, likely to give me shit about the article and muscling in on his patch, but I couldn't talk to him now. I fumbled with the phone, tapping the screen to send it to voicemail.

Helena retrieved her cigarettes from a high cupboard and both of us stepped out onto the patio, still damp from the rain overnight. I took the glass and a cigarette when she offered them to me, I had no idea why, it seemed like the right thing to do and I needed something to calm my nerves as much as she did. My head was reeling from Nathan's revelation.

We sat on the rattan furniture, the dew seeping into my jeans. Taking a drag reminded me of my youth, Megan and I smoking at the local park as dusk settled, waiting for the boys from school to join us. Now, the taste was foul, the smoke acrid in my mouth, but it gave Helena comfort and I waited for her to speak. All the poise and grace I had come to expect from her had diminished, she looked a shell of the professional woman I'd watched and admired from afar.

'That night Jack went out, saying he had some work thing, I was running late and he'd called Sam, a babysitter we'd used a few times. When I got home, Sam had only been here half an hour, but I gave him ten pounds and sent him on his way. We'd just finished eating and Nathan was upstairs getting ready for his bath when she knocked on the door.'

'Grace?' I interrupted, working out the time frame in my head when Jack was captured in the Instagram post with her. It had to have been after, when Jack was on his way to meet Ivy at the Golden Lotus.

Helena gave me a piercing glare but nodded. 'Yes, Grace. She barged her way in, told me who she was, declared her and Jack were in love and she was having his child...' Helena choked, wiping her nose again with her sleeve. 'That he was going to leave me.' She flicked her ash and I watched it roll away onto the damp patio.

'Grace wasn't pregnant,' I said, eager to slip it in, to relieve Helena of that lie. It would have come up in the autopsy report. She paused, her eyes filling again, but nodded, blowing her nose with a tissue before continuing.

'I thought as much. I told her to get out; I said, not in front of my son. I practically pushed her out of the door, but then Nathan screamed from the bathroom and I ran up to see if he was all right.' Helena smiled then. 'He was running the bath and saw a spider.' She gave a half-hearted laugh.

'But Grace hadn't left?' I asked.

Helena shook her head, jaw clenching. 'She'd followed me upstairs, as I'd not closed the front door. I should have shut it, locked her out because she was angry, vicious even, getting in my face and Nathan was frightened at the commotion. She was shouting, prodding my chest, saying Jack loved her, not me.' Helena sobbed, closing her eyes and lifting her head skyward.

She took a moment to gulp her wine. I followed suit, the bitter taste making me wince.

'I just wanted to protect him, I didn't want him to

listen to her venom, all the stuff she was saying
about his dad, but she kept going. It all became too
much and I broke down, begging her to leave,
then...'

She paused, swallowing, and looked at me, eyes
red-rimmed as though she could barely bring herself to finish.

'Nathan rushed into the hallway and screamed at
her, "Leave my mummy alone, you're making her
sad." She stumbled backwards, tripping over one of
his toy cars and fell down the stairs.'

My lips parted, heart breaking for her, for
Nathan, even for Jack who was currently being held
under suspicion of Grace's murder. I'd got it so
wrong. It had been nothing more than a tragic accident; no wonder Jack had been shocked when I told
him I knew he'd killed Grace.

Helena had some more wine and I did the same,
grimacing and pushing the glass away. Patiently
waiting for what was to come next, for Helena to explain how Grace had ended up on the disused
railway and why everyone, including me, believed
she'd been murdered.

44

'I thought she was unconscious, that she'd banged her head, but there was no blood. Then I saw the unnatural position of her neck. Grace had no pulse, there was no saving her.'

Helena took another drag, in full flow now, as though she had a need to unburden herself.

'I told Nathan she was sleeping and he should have a bath while I woke her up, that I'd be up in a minute. I panicked, I didn't know what to do.' Helena paused to look down towards the end of the garden. 'I should have called the police; I know that now, but I was terrified they'd take Nathan away. It was an accident, he didn't mean to hurt her.'

'Of course it was,' I soothed. It was easy to think

GEMMA ROGERS

we'd know how to act, what to do in such a situation, but I hadn't walked in Helena's shoes. I'd not been the one fearing someone would wrench my son from me and take him away.

'The only thing I could think of was getting rid of her. If someone else found her, they'd think she'd slipped, had an accident. The fence at the back was still down, so I got some tarpaulin, rolled her onto it and dragged her into the garden. It was exhausting, but I pushed her down the bank and took her as far as I could away from the house.'

I swallowed, my gut churning with every word of her cover-up. I drank some more wine if only to remove the acid from my mouth.

'I came back and checked on Nathan. He'd bathed and was playing Nintendo in his room, blissfully unaware I'd even left the house. I got him some sweets, told him the woman had woken up and gone home and he shouldn't tell anyone she was there...' she let out a sob and covered her hand with her mouth, 'otherwise the chocolate fairy wouldn't come back.' Helena shook her head, her face a mask of self-loathing. 'I panicked about DNA, what if mine or somehow Nathan's DNA had found its way onto Grace. I knew we weren't in the system, but what about the future, what if the police did a random testing. So I went back, took her coat and phone, threw her keys into a bush and covered her in bleach in the hopes it would destroy any evidence. When I returned, I cleaned most of the mud off my trainers and hosed down the tarpaulin. It wasn't long after that Jack came home and I had to pretend everything was fine. I'd put my work clothes back on and gave him the impression I'd not long been home.'

I remembered that night, hiding around by the water butt while Helena smoked on the patio, the only time I'd seen her smoke before now. She'd been sniping at Jack and said she was exhausted. I imagined she was.

'Ever since, I've been terrified, always on edge, searching the web for news in secret when Jack was asleep. When they found her body, I thought that was it.'

'How can you let Jack take the fall?' I blurted out. 'He's your husband, Nathan's father.'

'He's a lying, cheating bastard,' she shot back. 'I was going to leave him. You know as well as I do Grace wasn't the first and she wouldn't have been the last. He's got a problem, an addiction, he can't control himself!'

'But, Helena, he's going to go to prison.' It wasn't lost on me that I was the one who'd put him there.

'He'd do it for Nathan, if he knew. Despite everything, he may not be a good husband, but he's a good
father.'

'The police won't take Nathan away, not for an
accident.' I didn't want to add I knew full well they'd
charge Helena for her part in it. For removing
Grace's body, covering up the accident and for
dousing her in bleach. It was something I couldn't
get over, it seemed so callous and heartless, but in
Helena's desperate and misguided attempt to protect
her son, I could see she'd have done anything. If
only she'd called an ambulance, explained what had
happened, with Nathan as her witness, all of this
could have been prevented, but she'd inexplicably
made it worse.

Helena crossed her legs, flicking ash onto the
patio and drawing on the last of her cigarette to the
butt. After a minute, she seemed to regain her com-
posure, pulling her shoulders back and straight-
ening her spine. She wiped away her tears,
unflinching eyes locking on mine, and her voice took
on a cooler tone.

'I won't let you take my son away, Molly, I can't, I
hope you understand that.' It slowly dawned on me
it was a threat and despite the warmth from the

emerging sun, an icy finger traced its way down my back.

I took a second to have another mouthful of wine while she watched me like a hawk. I wanted to choose my next words carefully, knowing I was on precarious ground. Helena wasn't thinking clearly, she was a lioness protecting her cub and I was now the perceived threat.

We stared at each other, waiting, I didn't dare to breathe. Should I make a dash for the door or side gate? Could I overpower Helena? She was taller than me and had more to lose letting me walk away. I didn't try to convince her I'd keep quiet; it would be pointless; she'd see straight through me. It dawned on me Helena had no intention of letting me leave Church Road. I had no hope of anyone visiting, stopping by for a distraction, and Nathan was upstairs, shut away from what was happening, shielded once again.

My head grew fuzzy and I found myself blinking more often, eyelids heavy as Helena's mouth twisted into a grimace.

'It's okay, Molly. I promise it will be quick.'

Her voice faded away as my head dipped, lolling on my shoulders. It was so heavy I struggled to hold it up. I lifted my arm, which weighed a ton and didn't feel like it was connected to my body, plus there was a funny aftertaste on my tongue, something chemical. Reaching across the table, I nudged the wine glass, tipping it over. Red ran over the edges of the table like blood.

'Tsk, tsk.' Helena leaned back in her chair. 'You've made quite a mess.'

I vaguely remembered being moved, pulled along the floor by my wrists, T-shirt riding up at the back and being bumped over a ridge. Beneath me, the floor was cold, seeping through my clothes onto my skin, but I could barely keep my eyes open for more than a few seconds. Another cold surface, this one smelt of bleach, and it crinkled noisily as I was turned over and over, smothered into the dark. I heard footsteps and a door close before drifting away without a single thought in my head.

Time seemed to fast forward and when I blinked, peeling my eyes open, it was dark, no natural light crept in. My head was woozy and I wriggled against the constraints of the plastic, worried the noise was going to bring Helena because she'd clearly put me here. I had to get out, but as I used my feet to pushed upwards on my back to the top of the covering, the realisation hit me. I was in the garage, wrapped in tarpaulin and the smell of bleach was so strong it turned my stomach. I shuffled like a caterpillar, rolling from side to side to loosen how tightly I was rolled. Going one way, then another, but it wouldn't unravel.

My arms were by my side and I patted my pockets for my phone, but it was gone. I was lying in Grace's death sheet; the mode of transport Helena had used to drag her body down the bank. Every inch of exposed skin itched and burned and my clothes were a little damp. Was it sweat or the remnants of the bleach Helena had poured over Grace's lifeless body?

From somewhere in the house I heard shouting, which made me push harder to escape my constraints. Was Nathan in danger? Had Helena lost her mind? No, she wouldn't hurt her son, it was why I was here, she believed I'd use what she told me to separate them.

That wasn't my intention, not at all, but the truth had to come out. I couldn't let an innocent man go to prison for something he didn't do. It didn't matter that Jack had lied and cheated; he hadn't murdered Grace. Right now he was sitting in a cell, wondering why on earth he was there. I imagined his solicitor telling him it didn't look good. There was so much circumstantial evidence against him and if I didn't tell the police what part Helena had in it all, I had no doubt a jury would convict him and it would be all my fault.

Eventually, I managed to get my face out of the tarpaulin, pushing like I was a butterfly emerging from a cocoon. Finally free of the stench of bleach which had taken up residence in my nostrils, the air was fresher. The reprieve was short-lived as a crash came from inside the house. Panic bubbled up in my chest, not only was I fighting to save myself from whatever Helena had planned but Nathan was in the crossfire.

Sweat beaded at my brow and beneath my armpits, soaking into my T-shirt as I strained against the plastic, seeing now it had been tied to keep from unravelling. Had Helena believed she'd drugged me enough to kill me? My mind cast back to the new prescription of Heminevrin on the kitchen side, had she put those in my drink, emptied the capsules and dissolved the liquid in my wine?

Finally, I wrenched my arms free, scooting backwards until I was out. Limbs uncoordinated, I staggered backwards, light-headed. The door from the house flung open, blinding me with light.

'Oh, you're awake.' Helena's icy voice broke through my fog.

45

I rushed at her, head down as though I was a rugby player trying to tackle an opponent. She hadn't been ready and I headbutted her torso, wrapping my arms around her hips and throwing her onto the parquet floor. Winded, she gasped but clung onto me. We rolled around and a flash of silver caught my eye before pain bloomed in my thigh. Sticky wet blood dripped onto the floor, smearing on the parquet as we wrestled, each of us trying to get the better of the other, but Helena was strong, powered by fear and motherly instincts. Nathan screamed from the top of the stairs, begging his mum to stop, pleading with her to drop the knife.

'Nathan, run,' I wheezed when Helena, with a

crazed look in her dark eyes, climbed atop my chest. Arms flailing, I pushed at her face and neck as she waved the knife around like a madwoman, scratching my flesh.

'I won't let you tell them,' she screeched, 'he's my son.'

There was no point trying to reason with her, she was beyond pacifying. Adrenaline was powering the both of us on as I tried to defend myself against the frenzied attack. The knife swished through the air; the noise so terrifying, in other circumstances it would have incapacitated me. My arms were a bloody mess, covered in nicks and scratches, my thigh a dull throb where the cut had been deeper.

I could no longer see Nathan, he'd vanished, but I wasn't sure if he'd come past us or not. I prayed he'd gone to get help because my energy was fading. I took my eyes off Helena for a second and she plunged the knife into my shoulder. I screamed out as pain rocketed around my body and Helena scrambled off me, her face white as a sheet framed by bloody smears. She staggered back as though she couldn't believe what she'd done, unable to comprehend she'd driven her knife through flesh and muscle. I could no longer move, blood seeped from beneath my wound, melting into my hair on the floor, turning it pink as I blinked at the lights above.

'Oh God, oh God,' Helena wailed, her expression a mass of utter panic. She looked at her hands, which were empty yet covered in blood. The blade was still in me all the way to the hilt, pinning me to the floor. I panted, waiting for the excruciating pain to subside before I tried to move, knowing there was no way I could defend myself any longer. Hoping Helena would either see sense or at least make it quick, I closed my eyes and waited, but banging came from the front door, blasting my ears.

Suddenly, the hallway was filled with people rushing in, yelling at Helena to get down on the ground. As my eyes floated in and out of focus out, I saw a hazy Nathan peak out from behind the banister at the top of the stairs, his small frame hidden behind the wooden pillar. No one had noticed him yet, too busy trying to stem the bleeding from my wound, the others restraining Helena.

'Nathan,' I whispered, my eyelids heavy.

'Don't try to talk, it's okay, the ambulance is on its way.'

'My son, my son,' Helena screamed as she was forced onto her front, her hands behind her back, all the time kicking her legs and trying to resist.

Nathan slowly descended the stairs, his eyes like saucers and brimming with tears. I watched his every step, determined to stay awake long enough so someone realised he was here. It was irrational, but I had a responsibility for the little boy with the wonky smile, who loved his iPad and Pixar movies and chocolate.

'Nathan,' I said again.

The police officer, blocking my view of him as she leaned down, held her ear above my lips, trying to understand what I was attempting to communicate. Finally, her head lifted and turned towards Nathan, who'd reached the bottom of the stairs, staring first at me and then at his mum, clutching his muslin which was covered in red lorries.

I sighed, pain radiating through my shoulder as my lungs deflated. He'd be safe now and I let my eyelids close, a wave of exhaustion crashing over me. I no longer had to fight to stay conscious. I was safe, Nathan would be taken care of and Helena was detained.

Nathan's wobbly voice burst through my drifting thoughts as I wavered between consciousness, making me smile.

'Did Mummy kill the chocolate fairy?'

EPILOGUE

ONE MONTH LATER

I let the sand weave its way between my toes on the La Mata beach, my parents a few metres behind. The sun warmed my skin and I'd put extra sunblock on my scars, which were still pronounced, ugly raised bumps, but had healed. I'd been told it would take a while for my skin to regenerate and they would soften and fade. It didn't matter; I wore them with pride. The cut on my thigh hadn't been much more than a scratch, only needing a couple of stitches, but my shoulder was a whole different story. Some of my nerves had been damaged and I still couldn't move it like I used to, although my physio said with time I would.

My parents were furious when they'd found out

I'd stayed in hospital for a week after Helena's attack. I knew they'd fly over if I'd called them, and I wanted them to save their money to send me a ticket. Now, basking in the glorious Torrevieja sun after what had been a rainy start to April back in the UK, I didn't regret my decision one bit. I did feel bad about letting Jackie down at number seven, she had to find someone else to look after Buster, but Howard was out of hospital within a week and the pair were re-united. Before I flew out to Spain, I took him round a fruit basket and Buster some treats, leaving a still grumbling Howard my number in case he needed any help when I got back.

Mum had done nothing but fuss over me since I'd arrived a few days ago and I couldn't deny I was enjoying the parental care. After the initial shock and once Des realised I was going to be okay, he was thrilled about the in-depth article he knew would be coming – something he'd said would put *Crawley News* on the map. I'd laughed, knowing it would be a while until I could report on what I'd learnt that day at the Reillys'. Not until the court case began and evidence had been heard. Plus, I was going to be a witness, something I wasn't looking forward to. Nathan was a witness too, I'd been told, by video-link and under strict safe-

guarding guidelines. He was undergoing coun-
selling for the trauma of what he'd witnessed, with
me and with Grace, but I'd heard he was responding well.

Helena had been immediately arrested and
charged soon after with attempted murder for the
injuries she inflicted on me. In the past week, I'd
heard from Detective Russell she'd pled guilty to the
lesser charge of grievous bodily harm, alongside pre-
vention of the lawful and decent burial of a dead
body. It had all come out in the police interviews.
Nathan had admitted Grace's accident and Helena
had stuck to the same version of events she'd told
me. Terrified at being separated from her son, she'd
covered up what had happened. Traces of Grace's
DNA were found on the tarpaulin and four large
empty bottles of bleach in the recycling bin.

Des seemed to think she'd go down the mental
health route, driven to it by Jack's affairs, but, to be
fair to her, she admitted her culpability. When she'd
thought the police were closing in, she'd decided to
keep Grace's coat and phone in case she needed evidence to frame Jack. In a rash decision, she'd forged
his signature to increase her own life insurance so as
to lead the police away from her and to him. She
wanted them to think Jack was getting rid of the

problematic women in his life, offering him up to take the fall so she could remain with Nathan.

Her confession meant Jack was released, so after Nathan spent a couple of days with his grandparents, he was reunited with his father. I hadn't seen either of them, but Jack sent me a self-flagellating letter, taking responsibility for the destruction of his family due to his selfish actions. He wrote that he'd learnt his lesson and would remain celibate until Helena was released and they could be together again. In the meantime, he would concentrate on being the best father he could to Nathan. At the end, he thanked me for helping to procure his freedom, although I hadn't done it alone.

Detective Russell had found Jack's burner phone during the house search and once analysed he'd immediately interviewed Ivy to see when Jack had switched the contact known as Ian from Grace's number to Ivy's. The last known text from Grace's phone to Jack's burner was a simple message *I'm going to tell Helena everything.* They'd argued on Church Road that night, forever immortalised on Instagram. Jack wanted to call the whole thing off between them. Despite caring for Grace, she was becoming too needy and he'd already had his head turned by Ivy.

Thankfully, once Jack had confirmed whose messages belonged to whom, Detective Russell sent some officers to pick up Helena for an urgent interview. They'd arrived at the house at the right time, breaking down the door when they'd heard Nathan screaming. Any later and I could have died. As angry and determined as Helena was to not let the truth come out, I didn't believe for a second she would have harmed a hair on Nathan's head. I intended to tell the court as much when it was my time on the stand.

Jack had his suspicions about his wife although he never voiced them, but Helena had done what she'd done to protect her son, plain and simple, to stop him being taken away. Grace had knocked on her door that fateful day, enraged and aggressive. Who knew what would have happened if she hadn't fallen down the stairs?

It was why Helena had attacked me. She'd believed I posed a threat and in her eyes she'd had no choice but to eliminate it. I had no animosity for her, although whenever my shoulder ached, I'd be lying if I said I didn't curse her name.

Despite Jack fishing in his letter to me, he never asked outright how I knew so much about his affairs. I managed to keep the phrogging at number six

Church Road a secret from everyone. He even said he forgave me for the accusations of murder, admitting he broke into Grace's annexe to steal the inscription in the book of poems, desperately trying to sever their connection, knowing how her death made him look. Luckily, he'd been given a suspended sentence but was asked to leave St Wilfrid's. Number six Church Road was already up for sale and Jack was looking at moving closer to his in-laws in Kent while he waited for Helena to complete her upcoming sentence.

Grace's body was released so Sally and Roy could lay her to rest. A service attended by over a hundred people in the community was held at Worth Church. Roy was still going through his chemotherapy and I visited Sally as much as I could. Although still beside themselves with grief, they took comfort in the knowledge that Grace's death was a tragic accident and that it was near instantaneous with minimal suffering. They knew nothing of her affair with a married man and were relieved to learn she wasn't pregnant when she died, despite what she had purported to Helena. Dawn's crowdfunding campaign paid for a beautiful headstone, where Sally laid flowers every week.

My trip to Spain was just the rest I needed, but I

was heading back home in a few days. This time, Dad was returning with me, driving in my recently purchased 1973 VW camper van. It was majestic, baby blue with a tiny stove and countertop, still with its retro brown cushioned seats. It needed some work, which we'd already started, but the engine was sound. Dad had found it for sale by a local artist who was emigrating to Australia. It had some rust due to its age and needed new brakes, but I was in love. Dad had haggled and I had money left over to make the improvements which he began straight away. As long as it got the green light to run safely by the local mechanic, he'd bring me back home in it – our own little road trip.

The van would give me the freedom I craved, the ability to go wherever I wanted as long as I had petrol. I could follow the news stories up and down the country when I was lucky enough to bag myself a job at one of the nationals, but in the meantime, Des had promoted me and I'd lost the 'junior' part of my job title. I'd got a nice raise too, so I wasn't in a rush to look for something new. Neil had handed his notice in and with the relationship I was forging with Detective Russell, Des was letting me trial being the local crime correspondent. I had no reason to move on yet, plus

Harry and I were overdue for a catch-up, this one in person.

As soon as the van was up and running, I was going to spend a weekend in Plymouth, where we'd be going on our first date. I wanted to thank him for his help in getting the truth out there and we'd barely spent a day where we'd not been in contact since the incident. He'd been too quick off the mark about Jack's girlfriend in the nineties. Tanya Bishop had run away but, when eventually found months later, she was taken into care and moved to the Midlands. She'd ended up being adopted by her foster family, taking their last name, which was why she wasn't easy to trace. Jack had dropped the 'O' in his name due to the backlash about his missing girlfriend. He'd struggled to find work locally, which had prompted the move to Crawley. It seemed the cards were stacked against Jack from the outset.

Megan's whirlwind romance with Adam had resulted in them moving in together, which opened up a room for me in the flat above the betting shop. With the camper van now purchased, I decided to take Cassie and Louise up on their offer, giving me a base until it was fully roadworthy or I intended to travel. It made Mum happy if nothing else that I'd entered the world of adult living, paying for rent and bills, no longer trying to live for free. As for phrogging, I'd enjoyed the experiences and my stay with the Reillys hadn't put me off trying again, but for now I'd be happy to go between living at the flat and in my camper, where both entire spaces, although tiny, would be mine.

I did write one last blog post from my hospital bed which amassed more likes and comments than any of the nine posts before it. I tried to sum up my phrogging experience but I couldn't really find the words. Because what started as an experiment of free living ended with a woman who was going to prison. All because of a rash decision to protect her child after her husband had set in motion a series of self-gratifying events that would blow their family apart. All in all, I couldn't work out who was the real villain of the story, but I knew none of them would ever be the same again.

* * *

MORE FROM GEMMA ROGERS

The next pulse-pounding psychological thriller from Gemma Rogers is available to order now here:
https://mybook.to/GRogers2026BackAd

ACKNOWLEDGEMENTS

Firstly, I'd like to thank the entire Boldwood team for their unwavering support. They really are a force to be reckoned with and I'm so grateful for their ongoing belief in me. Who'd have thought I'd sell half a million copies! Caroline Ridding, thanks for being editor supreme and guiding me to be the best storyteller I can be. Thank you to Jade Craddock, my excellent copy editor, who has been with me since the start, you're amazing at what you do; and the lovely Shirley, my proofreader, who catches more than she should have to.

Thanks to my wonderful husband who takes on so much, giving me time to write; it doesn't go unnoticed. My two daughters, Bethany and Lucy, who are growing up so fast before my eyes, I love you more than words. One day, when you're old enough, I hope you'll read all my books and think maybe your mum is pretty cool.

Lastly, and never forgetting, a huge thank you to

my readers. To those who pre-order the books and read everything I write, recommending to friends and posting on social media. I couldn't do any of this without you and when your messages come through, they always brighten my day. Another thank you for all those readers who write reviews and leave ratings, it makes such a massive difference.

ABOUT THE AUTHOR

Gemma Rogers was inspired to write gritty thrillers by a traumatic event in her past. Her debut novel *Stalker*, released in 2019, marked the beginning of her writing career. Gemma lives in West Sussex with her husband and two daughters.

Sign up to Gemma Rogers's newsletter to read the first chapter of her upcoming thriller!

Follow Gemma on social media:

ALSO BY GEMMA ROGERS

Stalker

The Secret

The Teacher

The Mistake

The Babysitter

The Feud

The Neighbour

The Flatmate

The Good Wife

The Honeymoon

The Night Shift

The Stranger at No.6

THE *Murder* LIST

THE MURDER LIST IS A NEWSLETTER DEDICATED TO SPINE-CHILLING FICTION AND GRIPPING PAGE-TURNERS!

SIGN UP TO MAKE SURE YOU'RE ON OUR HIT LIST FOR EXCLUSIVE DEALS, AUTHOR CONTENT, AND COMPETITIONS.

SIGN UP TO OUR NEWSLETTER

BIT.LY/THEMURDERLISTNEWS

Boldwood

Boldwood Books is an award-winning fiction publishing company seeking out the best stories from around the world.

Find out more at www.boldwoodbooks.com

Join our reader community for brilliant books, competitions and offers!

Follow us
@BoldwoodBooks
@TheBoldBookClub

Sign up to our weekly deals newsletter

https://bit.ly/BoldwoodBNewsletter

www.ingramcontent.com/pod-product-compliance
Lightning Source LLC
Chambersburg PA
CBHW010658100726
47900CB00010B/2714